THE BITING COLD

By MATTHEW HELLMAN

For information, or to order additional copies, please
contact:

Beacon Publishing Group
P.O. Box 41573 Charleston, S.C. 29423
800.817.8480| beaconpublishinggroup.com

Publisher's catalog available by request.

ISBN-13: 978-1-949472-46-2

ISBN-10: 1-949472-46-2

Cover photograph by Daniel Bennett.

Published in 2022. New York, NY 10001.

First Edition. Printed in the USA.

Dedicated to my friend Daniel Bennett and others who fight monsters to protect others from harm.

TABLE OF CONTENTS

THE BITING COLD

PROLOGUE
December 31, 1842

Sven's legs plowed out a relentless rhythm as he drove each snowshoe clad foot forward. The crescent moon cast just enough light that he could see the well-packed trail that faded into the darkness leading out onto the ice. His breath formed ice crystals as it steamed out through the wool scarf tied tightly around his face. Without the garment, the light but frigid breeze would frostbite his cheeks in minutes. The hood of his heavy, animal-skin parka was pulled tightly over his head, holding on the wool cap and helping to shield him from the sub-zero temperatures. Never in his thirty-three years had Sven experienced such extreme cold. Despite the bite in the air, he could feel rivulets of sweat tracing down his back. A deadly problem in these weather conditions. But not as deadly as what pursued him.

He hoped the rest of the villagers were miles out in front of him, but he had no way of knowing. The big lumberjack, Henrik, would be breaking the trail through the deep, early winter snow, followed by his equally imposing brother, Jarkko. The rest of the village would plod behind, the strongest in front to pack the trail. At the back of the procession would be Christophe and

Hans, pulling the supply sled loaded with tents and firewood. Packs of food were carried by every one of the fleeing villagers, each according to his or her ability.

The young Swede didn't relish spending a night in a tent out in the middle of a frozen Lake Superior. But it beat the alternative.

From behind him, a crescendo of barking carried to his ears across the flat, snow-covered ice before coming to a violent, staccato silence. His team.

He started to run.

After the grueling cat-and-mouse chase, he'd had to leave the spent dogs. They were work dogs, used to long slow treks, not all-out, pell-mell running. He had planned on bringing the team all the way to the rendezvous at Isle Royal, but his role in this desperate gambit had proved too taxing for the animals. They'd led the creature to the south, away from Copper Harbor, drawing it farther from the terrified village by sledding along the network of trails through the woods.

At one point, Sven thought he may be able to escape down the Keweenaw Peninsula to bring back help. But somehow the monster had managed to circle out in front of him, cutting off any escape. More importantly, his young wife and the rest of the townsfolk would need every able-bodied man if they were going to successfully traverse the fifty-five miles across Lake Superior to Isle Royal and then survive once they got there. And everything depended on whether the lake was frozen all the way across. This early in the winter, it was a mad gamble. But the water was freezing quickly in the thirty-below temperatures. If they were lucky enough to get across, they would weaken the ice to ensure the heavy monster didn't. A job for which they would need Sven and the axe strapped to his back.

In the darkness behind him, Sven heard harsh breaths and soft footfalls on the packed snow. He risked a glance behind him and saw two shapes in the dim light of the moon. They were closing fast. The two youngest and strongest dogs on his team, Tree and Bull, caught Sven in seconds, their eyes were wild with fear, urging the man to run faster as they passed.

A second later, he felt the ice tremble, sending foreboding vibrations up his legs. Over and over the ice shook, a silent messenger telling of the horrible creature's pursuit. As the shock-waves grew stronger, the young miner realized he would not escape.

"Run!" he screamed into the darkness before him.

He stopped then and pulled the axe from his back, determined to waylay the blood-thirsty monster as long as he could. He turned around and watched as a huge, dark form blocked out the moon's glow. The sound of heavy breathing and smacking chops drew his attention to Tree and Bull who now stood next to him, one on either side. Together they would take their stand.

"Tonight, we feast in Valhalla," he said, a sad smile pulling at his lips. The dogs' tails wagged once and then ceased as their lips pulled back in fear and anger, deep, bass growls issuing through bared teeth.

They watched the beast approach, the ice shuddering under its weight. The cold seemed to penetrate Sven's heavy clothing as the creature came fully into view in the wan light. "Tyr!" Sven yelled. He charged forward, axe held high, a dog on each side.

A few minutes later, Sven, Tree and Bull sat down to a feast in Valhalla.

CHAPTER ONE

"The whole damned town disappeared." Ernest Kearse gazed down with his blue eyes on a skeptical, young, Brandon Hitze. Seated next to him at the bar counter, Bill watched his fifteen-year-old son take in the old tavern-keeper's tale. Bill was starting to see tidbits of himself in his son's unfamiliar face. The boy had changed a lot since he'd last seen him.

"What do you mean, 'disappeared'?" Brandon asked.

And Ernest had hooked another one. Bill grinned. The tavern-owner certainly knew how to draw them in.

Ernest gave Bill the stink-eye. "Bill, haven't you told him about it?" Bill gestured for him to continue, and the old man smiled. "It was 1842, the copper rush was just starting. Copper Harbor here was one of the best places for ships to take port and load up. Couple of mines nearby, a logging camp, and everyone was happy. Thing is, there were not many roads up here. Only travel was by dog sled in the winter, and ship in the warmer months."

When Bill was just a boy, he'd thought Ernie was old as dirt. Now that he was a grown man with his own son, he realized that Ernie was probably some sort of immortal old fart created to hook kids and tourists in with his creepy tales and outrageous stories. Bill had been frequenting Jotnar's Tavern and Brewery since his father had brought him in here when he was only ten. And in the little town at the northern-most tip of Michigan's Keweenaw peninsula, it was still one of the best, and only, eateries to be found.

"Things were going along fine, prob'ly around two-hundred or so folks living here. Then, late in the winter of 1842 - I guess it would have been early 1843- folks down in Houghton noticed no sled teams had come down for supplies. They didn't really concern themselves too much except it was a really hard, cold winter. Guess they figured the Copper Harbor folks didn't want to venture out in that kinda cold if they didn't need to."

Brandon hung on every word the old man said until he seemed to realize what he was doing and tried to put on a more nonchalant air. Bill couldn't help but smirk.

"When the end of February came, and they still hadn't seen hide nor hair of anyone from up here, they sent up a sled with some supplies. But the guy returned to Houghton, still with all his supplies, and said there wasn't anyone up here. And there were other things..." The old barkeep's brow furrowed and his mouth tightened in a serious frown.

Brandon's face scrunched up. "Other things?"

Ernest nodded. "The weather warmed up, got up to in the high twenties, and Houghton sends up a couple of teams, armed and what-not, to look for the villagers. They found out the first guy wasn't lying. No one here. But there were plates on tables, chimney flues open like fires had been burning. It was like people just vanished into thin air. Snow all in the streets like no one had been there in months. But that wasn't all."

Brandon stared at Ernest, waiting for him to continue.

Ernest looked up and down the bar as if what he was about to say shouldn't be heard by anyone but Brandon and his dad. "Couple of the cabins had been smashed to bits. Like a bear going after a honeycomb. There was blood all inside, but no bodies. They never found a single person."

Brandon squinted in disbelief. "They ever figure out what smashed the cabins?"

Ernest shook his head. "Nope. But now here are some other interesting points. Just before that happened, in the fall of 1842, the Chippewa ceded their claims to the lands up here in the upper peninsula." The old man's eyes narrowed. "Think maybe they knew something the white man didn't?"

"I dunno," Brandon answered. "Maybe."

Bill smiled as he watched his son. Brandon wasn't buying everything Ernest was selling.

"Well that ain't all," Ernest continued. "By 1844, the government had built up Fort Wilkins. Why did they build a fort way up here? Not much risk of invasion at the tip of the Keweenaw in 1844." The old man threw a glance at Bill, apparently sharing in his anticipation of Brandon's answer.

Brandon thought for a minute. "Probably just to keep the peace. They were mining, right?"

Ernest suppressed a smile and shook his head. "You keep believing that young man. But I tell ya, something happened up here that they needed a fort to protect folks. That park ranger fella, Sam, he'll give you some standard government reason, but now you know the truth."

"How do you know all this?" Brandon asked.

"I know. My great-grandmother was a girl down in Eagle Harbor, fifteen miles away, and they heard terrible things. Something smashed those cabins and it got the whole town. Never found a one of 'em." Ernest waved at some tourists who'd just sat down at the bar then returned his attention to Brandon. "They say we're gonna have a hard winter this year, just like back then." Giving Brandon a final ominous wink he went to service the newcomers.

"What do you think of that?" Bill asked.

"Is it true?"

Bill shrugged. "I guess it is. At least the part about the people disappearing. But I imagine Ernest adds a bit of embellishment."

"I'll say."

"Hear that kind of cool tale in Minneapolis?" Bill asked.

"No. But then there was actually stuff to do in Minneapolis. And they have reliable cell service," Brandon answered. To emphasize his point, he held up his cell phone, moved it around in the air and said, "Ooh. One bar. Oops, no, it's gone."

Bill's good humor sizzled and blinked out like a television taken out by lightning. He knew he should be more sympathetic, that he should try extra hard to build this relationship, but he couldn't help himself. "Why do you have to be on that damned phone all the time?" Bill hated the out of control reliance on social networking.

"So I can see what my friends are doing."

"Maybe you should do something yourself, instead of worrying about what everyone else is doing. Which, apparently, is just staring at their phones."

Brandon put the device away. "Do something? Like what? There's nothing to do up here!"

The gauntlet was thrown. His son thought he'd been banished to the last corner of the Earth where no teen-age kid could grow up properly because they'd be disconnected from reality. "You've just become unaccustomed to doing things. But you're going to re-learn it. Believe me, now that you're up here, you're going to see some cool stuff."

"Is that someone's thumb?" Brandon asked.

"Yeah," Bill Hitze answered with a sigh. He examined the white, swollen digit impaled on the hook of his son's fishing lure. He turned the lure around looking at the appendage from all angles. "Great." He let go of the line and the meaty hook swung like a morbid pendulum from the end of Brandon's pole. Brandon cringed, holding the tip as far away from his body as he could, lest the gooey finger bounce into him.

Bill turned to his boat radio, grabbing the microphone with one hand and his GPS unit with the other. He tuned to channel sixteen and contacted the local Coast Guard, reporting what he'd found and where. He was told to take the recovered body part to the local sheriff's office and the State Police would take care of the search for the rest of the body, most likely tomorrow since they'd have to get a Lake Superior dive team together and deployed.

Bill fired up the twin inboard motors on his twenty-seven-foot fishing yacht and guided it around to head for the dock near the sheriff's office. He had hoped that Brandon would learn to love fishing, as he did, and that they might begin to repair their fractured relationship. He had never been able to get much in the way of visitation rights since Brandon was five years old. For some selfish reason Bill could not comprehend, Renee had prevented it. But now she was gone and Bill had brought Brandon back only two weeks ago, the memory of his mom's death still painfully fresh.

Bill had ten years to make up. Now, with such a perfect July day, and no charter fares on the calendar, he'd wanted to have a good time. Just he and Brandon.

They'd fished for hours with nothing to show for it. Finally, Brandon reeled in his first catch: a thumb. Now the trip was ruined. Things weren't nearly as bad as it must have been for whoever was in the deep, cold Lake Superior water. Bill felt a tinge of guilt for selfishly putting his own troubles over some drowning victim's. But he couldn't help the dead guy now, so...

He looked back at his son who sat looking out the back of the boat, occasionally throwing a glance in the direction of the gruesome catch, resting on the floor just two feet away. Brandon pulled his cell phone out of his pocket and snapped a quick picture. Then with a grim smile, he typed away at the phone, only to groan when he realized there was no service. He let the phone rest on his thigh, screen side up. On it, Bill saw the photo of the white, bloated digit with the caption, "Great day fishing! Thanks Dad!"

It was a gut punch.

"What are you doing there?" Bill asked.

Brandon looked over his shoulder, "Was sending a picture of this to my friends. But of course, there's no service."

"Isn't very respectful to be sending that," Bill said.

Brandon turned back to the waves splaying out in a white-capped "V" behind the boat and stuffed his phone into his pocket.

It took about a half-hour to get to the dock. Neither of them had said anything else during the ride. Bill had quit worrying about his son's spoiled tendencies and started thinking about the situation at hand. He could see the sheriff and one of his deputies waiting at the dock, no doubt having heard over the radio. Good. He could get rid of the stupid thumb and try again tomorrow.

"Hey Bill," Sheriff James Miller said. He and most of the local law enforcement officers had been out on one of Bill's charters at one time or another, "Got something for us?"

"Right over here," he said nodding at the floor of his boat.

Brandon got up and stepped gingerly over the thumb and clambered out of the boat to wait on the dock. The Sheriff and Deputy Bruce Stance peered over the gunwale of the fishing yacht.

"Yep. Look at that," Stance said. He pulled on a pair of latex gloves and pulled a small plastic bag from his pocket. From a rear pocket, he drew out a pair of wire shears and carefully snipped the barbed end off the hook and slipped the gelatinous thumb off and into the bag, grimacing every step of the way. He sealed the bag with some tape marked "evidence" and labeled it with a Sharpie. He held it up to eye-level and shook his head. "I dunno if we're going to get any prints off of this thumb. Have to send it for DNA analysis."

Sheriff Miller nodded his consent.

"Any idea who's it is?" Bill asked.

"None. Haven't had anyone go missing up this way for years. Maybe it's from an old wreck."

Brandon's head snapped around at the sheriff's words. "An old wreck?" he asked.

"Lake's too cold for most bodies to surface. They sink down and stay down. Don't really decompose and emit gases that'll raise them up. Probably a lot of sunken old ships out there with bodies still in 'em."

"Do you think we found a wreck, dad?"

Bill saw an opportunity. "We can come out tomorrow and find out when the divers look around."

Brandon nodded.

"Sheriff, can you give us a call when they get here tomorrow?"

"Will do."

The ride back to the marina was filled with questions from Brandon. How many ships have sunk in Lake Superior? When was the last one that sank? Where do they usually sink or is it all over? Why do they sink?

And on and on. At least they were talking, despite it being a rather morbid subject.

Bill detoured slightly so they would pass over another productive area of the lake. He told Brandon to toss out his line and they'd troll a bit. It paid off and Brandon caught his first fish on Lake Superior, a decent seven-pound Steelhead. Brandon's smile split his face. What kid wouldn't beam after catching their first fish? Brandon's first fish, at fifteen. The thought hit Bill like a wrecking ball blasting into the side of a car. He'd learned to fish when he was about five. He'd missed so much time with his son. Renee left when Brandon was five years old, having been enticed away by a rich customer of Bill's. She and Brandon moved to Minneapolis where she could get her fix of fancy things, and she and her rich new boyfriend hired an expensive lawyer to make sure Bill didn't get visitation without a legal fight that he couldn't afford. So here they were now, catching his first fish at the ripe age of fifteen. There was nothing he could do about it, so he decided to keep moving forward. He tossed the fish in the live well, hoping that Brandon would enjoy it for dinner.

CHAPTER TWO

Brandon was up early the next morning. At least for Brandon. Eight-thirty. He helped himself to some breakfast and was showered and dressed without being told. Bill's son was anxious to see what the state police discovered. If there was a sunken ship there, it was not one anyone knew about, but Brandon would be excited that they had found it. Bill wasn't holding his breath, but he secretly hoped they'd stumbled across something too.

Around ten-o'clock, Bill got a call from Sheriff Miller saying the state guys had arrived and were launching their boat. Brandon had come running as soon as the phone rang and stared at Bill during the brief conversation.

"They're here?"

"Yep. Let's go."

At that moment Bill felt kind of like a dad. He and his son were sharing in an adventure, grisly as it was. He hoped that Brandon felt a connection too, though he still seemed distant. Still in mourning, Bill supposed. Trying to share in his son's need to escape, he made sure they didn't waste time getting down to the marina.

After arriving, Bill spoke briefly with the officer in charge, verifying the GPS coordinates, and asked if he and Brandon could trail along. The police were okay with it, but they'd have to take their own boat and stay out of the direct search area, something Bill was planning to do anyway.

A couple of the officers were looking at the gray clouds that spotted the sky, their faces none too happy. Bill looked up and then down at the western horizon, where blue and gray were mixed in a stuttered pattern. The weather would require constant monitoring. If a solid wall of dark clouds developed, they were heading back to the marina. Getting caught on Lake Superior in a storm, even a weak one, could mean death. Capsizing and going into the forty to fifty-five-degree water meant hypothermia in minutes. And no one would get you out and warm before it was too late. But watching the sky was part of his job.

The ride out was uneventful, with Brandon not saying much other than to raise the question, yet again, if they would find a sunken ship out there. When Bill saw the police boat settle in the water and stop, he throttled down and started to cruise in a slow circle around it. He maintained a distance of a couple-hundred yards, watching the crew prepare two divers. When he saw the first man drop over the side of the vessel, Bill shut down his motor.

After only about twenty minutes the divers surfaced and were pulled on-board by other officers. Bill heard snippets of the men talking as they gesticulated and motioned about their heads.

"Did they just say 'gone'?" Brandon asked.

"Think so."

"Maybe they mean his boat is gone, like disintegrated. Wow."

Bill hoped that was the case because the way he was reading the body language, his interpretation was much darker.

They watched as a large basket was lowered over the side and the two divers reluctantly splashed back into the frigid water. After a few minutes, Bill could see the wheel of the mini-crane start spinning as the body was retrieved. The grim cargo was hauled aboard, followed by the divers. Bill started his engine and slowly started toward the recovery vessel. When they got next to the police boat the officer in charge waved him away.

"No. You don't want to see this,"

It was too late for Bill. He could see the body lying in the basket, its head and neck, from down between its shoulders, was missing. He quickly turned around and dragged Brandon into a seat, hoping he wouldn't see the mess.

"Was there a wreck down there?" Brandon asked, raising his voice to carry the fifteen feet to the police boat. He strained to stand again and threw an annoyed look at his father who held a firm hand on his shoulder.

The officer shook his head. "No. Looks more likely we're dealing with a homicide and body dump."

Bill and Brandon exchanged a glance. "Homicide?"

"Yeah. But I'm thinking the culprit is probably dead too."

"Why?" Brandon said.

"'Cause this guy looks like he's right out of the eighteen-hundreds."

"Really?" Bill said.

"How do you know it's a murder?" Brandon asked.

"His head is gone."

CHAPTER THREE

"Oh good. God's gift to the universe," Ernest Kearse said as he glared at the man walking into Jotnar's Tavern. Bill turned to see Jeff Jansen, self-made millionaire and self-anointed genius, strut into the tavern, smiling and glad-handing anyone within reach.

"No, Jeff. I won't sell it to you, so don't ask," Ernest said. Jeff had been trying to purchase the quietly thriving establishment since he'd come into his fortune. Unsuccessfully. Kearse swore he'd take Jotnar's with him to the grave before he sold to Jansen, whom he, not so secretly, despised.

Jeff Jansen, early thirties, blond hair, blue-eyed, today dressed like a Wall Street thief posing as a philanthropist. All in an attempt to buy good will. He'd financed the construction of a new pier in the harbor. He'd even paid for the expansion of the natural gas lines in the immediate area. Of course, he had needed to run the lines to his not so modest home up the hill too, so why not make it look like you're taking care of others in the process by paying a little extra to run the supply to a couple of streets that were on the way. Jansen was still single despite being handsome and aware of it. Perhaps *because* he was aware of it. When it came to Jeff Jansen, people in town fell into one of two camps, those who were glad Jansen was here to take care of the community, and those who didn't buy his bullshit, seeing him as a narcissistic prick who thought he could pay for whatever he wants. A lot like the boyfriend of Bill's ex-wife.

Bill and Jeff disagreed on what could be bought.

Jansen's eyes settled on Bill and then bounced to Brandon, a cold light sparkling from the blue orbs.

"Well, Bill. Who's this?" Jansen asked as he extended one hand to Brandon while his other patted the young man on the shoulder.

Doing his best to be polite Bill said, "This is my son, Brandon."

Jansen shook Brandon's hand enthusiastically before he let go, leaving his left hand on Brandon's shoulders. "Nice to meet you. How is it Bill has a son so obviously big and strong and I haven't ever met you? He keep you tied up in the basement?" A sarcastic smile played across his lips. Brandon huffed out a laugh.

"No. I just moved up here from Minneapolis."

"His mother recently passed away," Bill said. He locked eyes with Jansen.

Jansen ignored the silent message. "I'm sorry to hear that," he said. He gave Brandon's shoulder a squeeze and let his hand drop. "So you'll be living up here then?"

Brandon nodded, his gaze falling.

"Well, if there's anything I can do to help you make the adjustment, let me know. Or if you're looking for a job, you could come give me a hand."

"I don't think-" Bill started.

"Have you ever heard of 'Rabid Turtles'?" Jansen asked.

Brandon's head came up. "Of course. Got it on my phone. It's awesome."

With the smarmiest smile Bill had ever seen, Jansen said, "I designed it."

"You designed 'Rabid Turtles'?" Brandon asked, eyes widening. "Get out!"

"That's how I make my money. I design apps and games for phones."

"What else have you done?"

Jansen blanched. "Nothing else that you'd have heard of. But I'm working on some new stuff."

Yeah, right, Bill thought. *You had one hit and haven't done anything since.*

"You know, I could use the help of a guy your age. I'd like to get your opinion on some ideas for new apps."

"Oh yeah," Brandon blurted.

Jansen scribbled on the back of a business card he'd pulled out of his breast pocket. "Here's my home address. Come on by this evening and we can get started."

"We've got plans tonight, Jeff. Maybe some other time," Bill said.

"Dad? What?"

"Some other time," Bill repeated.

"The offer is open. Come by whenever you can," Jansen said. He shook Brandon's hand. "I'll see you later." Then he walked to a booth by the wall and picked up a menu.

"Prick," Ernest said. "Can't believe that shit he pulled."

"Huh?" Brandon asked. "He seems like a great guy."

"Stay away from him," Bill said.

"Why?"

"Just stay away from him."

"Dad. That'd be so cool! I could maybe help design-"

"No."

Brandon scowled and pulled out his phone and started playing 'Rabid Turtles' with the sound up so it was easy for Bill to hear. Ernest just looked at Bill and shook his head and shrugged. Glancing in Jansen's direction he mouthed, "Prick."

Jansen sat at the table, menu held in front of his face, smiling at the sound of his one and only game being played at the bar. Brandon seemed like a nice kid. And being from Minneapolis, he'd be up on the recent trends among teens and others whose lives were dominated by the almighty smart-phone. Jansen was sure that he and Brandon would become fast friends, though Bill would hate that. Actually, they'd become friends *because* Bill would hate it.

Truth was, Jansen needed a magic bullet. The last couple of phone games that he'd published fizzled. Between the two of them, he'd made only about twenty-thousand dollars. Some people would be very happy with that. But 'Rabid Turtles' had rocketed to the forefront of popularity, selling well over three-million copies at ninety-nine cents each. And then the advertising piled on when it was clear how popular the game had become.

Thinking he was on his way, Jansen started blowing through the money, wasting some of it on community projects. He'd paid for a nice outdoor hockey rink for the kids and the renovation of the main pier in town. One would think his philanthropic acts would garner more power and good-will in town. But most of the ingrates simply said, "thank you," and went on as if nothing else had changed. Now he was at serious risk of running out of money within the next five years if things didn't turn around quickly.

If he hired Brandon to help him develop a game, he could pay the kid an hourly sum and then reap the profits when they started rolling in. No doubt a fifteen-year-old would be naive enough to jump at a job making games without worrying about who got the profits.

Jansen could then invest this load of money and live frugally until he got the next hit. He just had to get his mojo back.

The waitress interrupted his thoughts to take his order. She was semi-decent to look at, but nothing to write home about. At least he didn't have to put up with Ernest's bitch of a wife, Suzy. To this day Jansen didn't know why she hated him, but she did. She didn't even try to hide it. Bitch.

He stared at Bill's back as he sat hunched at the bar next to Brandon. And what was that guy's problem? Shit. Jansen had tried to hire him to take himself and some friends out fishing and the guy lost his nut. He didn't care how much money Jansen was offering, he was already taking some guy and his two kids out. Blah, blah, blah. He had hoped Bill's charter business would sink. Literally. He had even created a bunch of fake online accounts to give him bad reviews. It had worked initially, but eventually, Bill had managed to get the reviews removed. But over the last two years, his business continued to thrive. Asshole.

Jansen smiled and nodded when Brandon glanced in his direction. Oh yeah. They'd become good friends. And Bill Hitze could just suck it.

Bill sipped at a beer trying to ignore the idiotic sounds emanating from his son's cell phone. How could one man be such a worm? Jeff Jansen just thought he could have whatever he wanted, no matter how it might hurt someone else. He'd had it in for Bill ever since Bill told him there was no way he was canceling a scheduled customer just because Jansen was throwing money at him. There was a reason people reserved fishing trips with him and he would honor that. Especially when it was a family.

Huh. He thought about that. He'd lost his family and now, suddenly, his son had been thrust upon him once again. He was very glad for it, not having had the opportunity to be a dad when Brandon was little. But now he had to jump into the role when Brandon had been poisoned to him and was on the verge of becoming an adult. Bill knew he was in over his head. He took a slug of beer, hoping it might quell the fire that was igniting in his stomach.

He threw a covert glance at the blond turd in the corner booth. Maybe, if Jansen hadn't been such a jerk, he and Jeff would actually have become friends. Maybe he'd be happy to let Brandon go over to the man's house and help him work on whatever dumb phone app he was developing. Brandon was obviously interested. And Bill wanted his son to find an interest here in his new home.

But Jansen was just trying to piss him off, offering Brandon a dream he knew Bill would crush out of hand. He *could* let Brandon go work with Jansen...

Adjusting to being a full-time dad was going to be hard enough without some a-hole purposely creating rifts. Jansen was such a dick-head.

"Whoa! That guy's huge," Brandon exclaimed. He was looking at the 6'10", 290-pound mountain who had just walked out of Jotnar's brewing room, a towering can of energy-drink in a fist the size of a bowling ball. Matti Tervonen was Ernest's head, and only, brewer of craft beers. With light brown, close-cropped hair and a thick beard that dropped a neat two inches from his chin, Bill wondered if Matti had some of the fabled Finnish-giant gene in him. There had been a Finnish guy, "Big Louie", just 30 miles away in Calumet who died in 1913 that was claimed to have been 8'1" and over 400 pounds. Though "Big Louie" would make Matti look small, the man still evoked images of mythical lumberjack Paul Bunyan.

Matti saw Bill and gave him a smile. When he noticed Brandon sitting there, he downed a swig from his can of liquid power and approached, extending a hand to the boy.

"You must be Brandon," Matti said. "Your dad said you'd be moving up here. I'm Matti. Glad to meet you." His eyes were wide and alert, darting around the room before bouncing across the boy's face.

"You too," Brandon said. His head tilted back as he stared up at the smiling giant.

"Got a good dad here," he said. Then he took Bill's hand in a hearty shake before pulling him in for a one-armed man-hug. "Billay!"

"Matti is the brewer here," Bill said, trying to stay on his feet. "He makes a great Pale Ale, but his Milk Stout is the best in the state."

Matti smiled and huffed out a laugh. "Gotta wait a couple of months for the stout. Still doing the lighter beers." Words spilled out of him like water from a fire hose. "Though I'll be doing an Oktoberfest soon. You might like that. Should be ready about the end of September."

"I look forward to it," Bill said.

"You strong, like your old man?" Matti asked. Brandon looked at him, a quizzical expression on his face. Matti looked down at Bill. "Didn't you tell him?" Bill shook his head sheepishly. The huge brew-master leaned down to get closer to Brandon's ear, then said quietly, "Your dad is stronger than I am. Like, freakishly strong."

Brandon looked at his father, the unspoken question in his eyes.

"Lifted a fallen maple tree off of Butch Malmstrom. What was that two years ago?"

"Sounds right," Bill said.

"Thing must have weighed seven-hundred pounds. I couldn't lift it the way your dad did."

"Was it adrenaline?" Brandon asked his father.

"Naw!" Matti said. He took another drink from his can. "He does shit like that all the time. You should work out with him, you'll be monster-strong too."

Matti stopped talking when he noticed Jansen. When he looked back at Bill he asked, "Everything good?"

"Yeah."

Matti was also the unofficial bouncer at Jotnar's, though his services in that regard were rarely needed. He knew Jansen and Bill could get heated at times, though they'd never come to blows, in large part because Matti would show up and tower over both men.

"Brandon, I'll see you around. You're going to love it up here. It's fucking awesome." With another smile, Matti sped away into the kitchen.

Brandon watched him leave. "Wow. Why isn't he playing basketball or football or something?"

Bill shrugged. "He doesn't want to. Likes what he's doing and where he's living."

Brandon looked at his dad like he had two heads but didn't say anything. Finally, he said, "I'm glad he's friendly. I'd hate to be on the wrong side of someone that big."

CHAPTER FOUR

When they got home, Brandon said, "Why can't I go to work for that Jansen guy?"

"You have no idea. Trust me, you don't want to work for him."

"There's nothing else to do here," Brandon yelled. He'd sounded more like a little kid having a tantrum than he would have liked, but he was exasperated. What the hell else was he supposed to do, collect leaves?

His father looked like a balloon before it bursts. A red balloon. "He's not the quality of person you should learn from. Just stay away from him."

Brandon stormed out of the little house, not sure where he was going. He wasn't even sure what he wanted to do, other than to get away from his dad. Here was a fantastic opportunity to do something cool and his dad dismissed it with no explanation. And he forbade Brandon from even talking to Jansen. He was going to have a miserable fucking life.

He started walking and passed through the shadows of the big white pines, oaks and maples and stepped onto the cramped road that ran two directions into nowhere. To his right, the crumbling pavement declined toward the harbor and what people around here called "town". To his left, it rose toward the peaks that overlooked the entire tip of the Keweenaw peninsula, the trees giving way to tall golden grass and flowering weeds. Maybe he'd get cell reception up there?

A call to his old friends down in Minneapolis might be cathartic. No doubt they would be able to sympathize with his plight. He pulled out his phone and checked for a signal. Nothing.

Now with a clear purpose in mind, he struck a pace up the hill hoping to put distance between him and his dad and discover a link to civilization.

The sky was unbelievably blue and clear, the sun a comfortably glowing orb still two or three hours from sinking below the horizon. He looked at the clock on his phone; seven-fifteen. Geez! It stayed light a long time around here. Back home in the city, any time it was this clear and sunny, he'd be complaining about the unbearable heat. For some reason he didn't quite understand, he wasn't sweating. Nor did he feel like he was in a steam bath where the air is moist and thick and hard to breathe. Comfortable warmth radiated up from the gray black-top and a mild breeze drifted through the tall grass that lined both sides of the road. Grudgingly he had to admit, it felt very nice outside.

But that didn't change the fact that he was stuck with the man who'd never been there for him the last ten years. The man who'd apparently felt that his job was more important than his wife and son. The man who, according to his mother, didn't even fight for visitation rights.

The sudden thought of his dead mother triggered a hitch in his step and he stopped. He turned around and gazed down at the lakeshore and the elongated bay they called Copper Harbor. Sapphire water reached out as far as Brandon's young eyes could see, the sunlight twinkling back at him off of the gently undulating surface. All he could hear was the shushing of the wind as it played through the bushes and grass around him. His mother was gone. And this was his consolation prize.

For just a minute, his eyes became glassy. He longed for the scent of his mother's skin, clothes, perfume, whatever it was that he could smell on her every day. And for just a minute, he thought he actually smelled it.

Then he caught a whiff of the unique scent again. And it didn't go away.

He turned and looked up the road, the slight breeze hitting him full in the face, and drew in a deep breath. It was as though his mother was right in front of him, her brown eyes shining as her narrow lips split into a warm smile.

But his mother was dead, and Nick had never adopted him. That left him here.

Continuing up the hill, his mother's perfume drifted to him with increasing regularity.

Where the road made a gentle curve to the left, Brandon saw movement. Not someone walking. Not an animal foraging, but something low to the ground.

A long weed, dirt-ball clinging to dangling roots, made an arc through the air and landed on the side of the black-top, a dusty cloud trailing in its wake. Not quite sure what he was seeing, Brandon closed the distance.

Finally, he saw a girl, about his own age, leather-gloved hands wrapped around the stalk of another weed, tugging upward until the plant tore free of the dry ground. Without looking, she tossed this one behind her as well. She was dressed like no other girl Brandon had ever laid eyes on. She wore brown pants that appeared to be made of canvass or very course denim. Her beige shirt looked to be home-made, sleeveless, revealing toned arms that were used to hard work. She didn't have on dainty designer shoes, or sparkling jewelry, or have intricately primped hair. Instead, she wore work boots, her sandy hair was pulled back in a semblance of a pony-tail, and something made of green leafy bulbs hung around her neck. And she definitely smelled like mom.

Brandon cleared his throat and she turned to face him. He immediately noticed her pale blue eyes. Not sky blue, lighter, almost like ice, though they radiated more warmth than the sun.

"Hello," she said.

"Hi." He pointed at the weeds. "What are you doing?"

"Pulling weeds," she answered, then smiled.

Brandon looked around at the grassy hillside, heavily populated with what Brandon considered weeds, dotted here and there with a crabapple tree or scrappy Jack Pine, no residence evident. "Out in the middle of no-where?"

"It's garlic mustard."

Brandon shrugged.

She regarded him as though she were looking at someone who didn't speak English. "It's invasive. I'm pulling it out. Trying to keep it from taking over."

"Oh," Brandon said. He bobbed his head as though he knew what she was talking about. "Good idea. I'm Brandon, by the way." He extended his hand.

She took off her gloves and reached out with a hand that made Brandon think there was more dirt inside those gloves than was on the ground. Her nails were not manicured and shiny. No. They were short, with dirt crammed beneath them. Despite her rough callouses, Brandon liked the touch of her hand. "I'm Tril Post."

Brandon tilted his head. "Tril?"

"It's short for Trillium Joy. My parents are kind of hippies at heart."

Brandon stared at her.

"Trillium. Like the wild-flower?" Tril prodded.

Brandon shrugged, still not sure what she was talking about. "Nice name. Never heard it before."

"So are you here visiting?"

"No. I moved up here two weeks ago to live with my dad." Then after a pause, he added, "My mom died."

"I'm so sorry," Tril exclaimed. She took his hand and patted it, genuine concern in her eye. How could she seem so sad for him when she had just met him? "Who's your dad?"

"Bill Hitze." Brandon produced a wan smile, noticing Tril's grip did not lessen.

"Mr. Hitze. I run into him once in a while. Does fish charters and studies the environment, right?" She released his hand with a gentle pat.

Brandon nodded. "I guess." He wondered about the 'environment' comment.

"What grade are you in?"

"Going into tenth. You?"

"I'm going to be a junior. We'll ride the bus together."

"I haven't even seen the school yet," Brandon said.

"It's down in Calumet. About twenty miles away. Little kids have a school here."

Twenty miles to school? He'd have driven through fifteen different districts down in Minneapolis in that distance. They really were way out in the sticks.

"The ride goes fast. Not a lot of stops," Tril said.

"Hope so." He shrugged. "So what do you do for fun up here?"

Tril's face lit up. "Oh boy. There is so much to do. I hunt. I go hiking and fishing and biking. I usually keep an eye out for garlic mustard when I do. At night the stars are so bright and clear, they are amazing to just stare at. Of course, in summer it doesn't get dark until about 11:30. One o'clock is better."

She may as well have said she rolls a hoop down the road with a stick. Brandon felt his stomach tighten. "Don't you have a movie theater or mall or something fun?"

Tril stepped back and a flash of annoyance shot across her face, her posture stiffened. "No. We don't have any of those 'fun' things." She started pulling weeds again.

"I just moved up from Minneapolis, so that's kind of what we did." Oh crap.

"Ah." She did not look up.

"Do you know where a good place to get cell reception is?"

She looked at him, squinting her eyes. "Do I look like I have a cell phone?"

"I just thought..."

Tril shook her head. "Keep walking up the hill. Maybe you'll get reception so you can play your video games, or whatever."

With a sigh, Brandon resumed his trek, Tril's scent still lingering in his nostrils.

CHAPTER FIVE

Bill sharpened his eyes as he looked at the number displayed on his buzzing cell phone. He didn't recognize it, though it was local. At least in the 906 area code, which narrowed it down to the entire upper peninsula which was only about 320 miles east to west and 125 north to south, making it bigger than Massachusetts and New Jersey combined, though the population was less than half that of Boston. He almost let the call go, but curiosity got the best of him.

"Hello."

"Mr. Hitze? This is Stephanie Crowe. I'm an archaeology professor at MTU. Do you have a minute to talk?"

A professor from the university? What the hell?

"Archaeology?"

"I understand you found that body out in Lake Superior a few days back?"

"Yes..."

"I've had a chance to examine it and from what I've seen, I believe it dates back to the mid-eighteen-hundreds."

"Wow." Bill didn't know why he should care. This was all so out of the blue.

"Do you happen to remember exactly where you found it?"

"I think the coordinates are still tagged in my GPS. What is this about?"

He heard her exhale. "I know I'm not explaining myself very well. Let me get to the point. Can you take me back out to where you found the body? I can pay you."

That's the first thing he had heard that made sense. "I think Tuesday is available. 8:00 AM. That work?"

"Yes! Yes. That would be perfect."

"Four hours or eight?" Bill asked. His charters were always 'half-day' or 'full-day' outings.

"I'd like the full day, please. I can pay you overtime if we go over."

"I take it we aren't going to be fishing," Bill said.

"Research," Dr. Crowe answered.

"Not sure what we'll do for eight hours, but OK."

Bill concluded the call by giving Stephanie directions on where to meet him and that he'd have gear and food for her. She said she'd have her own gear. He didn't know what she meant by that.

"Huh. Archaeologist," Bill said to himself. He stared at the screen showing Dr. Stephanie Crowe's image and research interests on the university's website. She looked to be around Bill's age, but that was wishful thinking as she was probably closer to thirty-five than his well-established forty-three. With very dark hair, brown eyes and a warm smile, she was nice to look at. Great. He hoped she didn't look as good in person. The last thing he wanted was to spend the day sounding like a bumbling idiot.

He hadn't realized that there were any archaeologists at the school. Its main emphasis was engineering with alternative offerings in engineering and some electives in math and engineering. But archaeology was a science, so he figured she had her place.

One last glance at her photo kicked his heart into gear and ignited a fire in his gut. She was attractive alright. Of course, if she was anything like the toad, Jansen, who'd also been a professor, she'd become a lot less attractive and he'd be comfortable being himself. But if she was as sweet as she looked, he'd become an awkward, anti-social weirdo. At least in her opinion. He was not smooth with the fairer sex.

It had been ten years since Renee and Brandon left him, seeking material wonders being offered by some smarmy, rich asshole from Minneapolis. Nick, the a-hole in question, had been generous enough to pay for the divorce and for the high-priced, scum-bag custody attorney that Bill couldn't afford to fight. So Bill got screwed out of visitation with his son. But now Renee was dead, and Nick hadn't bothered adopting Brandon.

And in those ten years, Renee had done a lot to make Brandon believe his biological father hadn't wanted him. Bitch.

He disconnected from the Internet and got up from his desk, needing to focus on something, anything else. That was in the past. Grabbing the truck keys from the table he looked around for Brandon. Oh, right. He'd left in a huff, still pissed about not being able to chum around with Jansen. He didn't have the energy to think about that.

The drive down to the marina was a short one, too short to reset his brain. He walked out to his boat and climbed aboard. Hopefully, he had tagged the GPS coordinates on his unit to guide him and Dr. Crowe out to where they'd found the body. He powered it up and walked through the menu system to check. Finally, he found the new set of coordinates, the last in a list of good fishing holes. Using the on-board electronic navigational map, he entered the numbers and looked at the inverted tear-drop shape that popped up at the destination. There was nothing about it that gave him a clue as to why a body would be there unless he had been murdered and dumped. He supposed it was a possibility, particularly since the guy's head was gone. Bill remembered with grisly vividness the arc that bit between the shoulders where the neck would have been. The poor man's head hadn't been cut off with a sword or anything like that. If anything, Bill would have guessed that maybe he'd had his head chopped off by a bear trap.

Wondering if the body could have been transported from any other nearby town, Bill zoomed the map image out to show him relative distances to possible ports. Copper Harbor seemed the nearest. Wondering about shipping lanes, he zoomed out a bit more and a small land-mass appeared at the north edge of the map. He stared at the image and noticed something interesting, but probably nothing. A thought skittered through his brain, like a butterfly in a high wind, trying unsuccessfully to find purchase. Then it was gone. Maybe he'd mention the image to Dr. Crowe and see if she could come up with the notion that eluded him.

CHAPTER SIX

"Is this real?" Brandon asked.

"Yep. One estimate dates it back to around 1000 A.D., toward the end of the Viking era." Bill and Brandon gazed down at the image of a Viking long-ship carved onto a stone. Most of the locals knew of the petroglyph, though no one really knew if it was real. Archaeologists had examined it and were left puzzled by its apparent age. The scientists couldn't say it was a hoax which translated to a green light for the locals to mention the ship carving to tourists. It just provided an added level of uniqueness to the community.

"What's it doing here?"

"Good question," Bill said. "Whoever carved it was obviously familiar with the long-ships. But why they carved it here is a mystery."

Brandon lifted his eyes to the waters of Lake Superior that stretched to the horizon. From this high vantage point, easily eighty feet above the lake, the curvature of the earth was clearly evident where the waters met the sky. He could see the tip of the peninsula to the east and layers of green, dense forests to the south and west. "You suppose the Vikings actually sailed around up here?"

"Maybe. Anything is possible."

"Why didn't they stay?"

Bill considered the question. "You're assuming this petroglyph is authentic, and that whoever carved it saw one of the ships up here. If those assumptions hold, then who knows why they didn't hang around?"

Brandon laughed. "Maybe they disappeared like the whole town did."

"That's it. You're on to something."

"Okay. So that is pretty neat," Brandon conceded. "And the view from here is awesome."

Together they looked out at the massive lake and enjoyed the cool air that blew in from its surface. In these dog-days of summer, the Lake Superior air-conditioning felt nice. In a few months, not so much. Having had only a half-day charter earlier that morning, Bill decided to use the afternoon and bring his son up here to give him a dose of clean air and awesome views. He was glad he did.

Brandon pulled out his phone and held it up to take a picture.

"Hey! Three bars," Brandon said. "Can we stay here for a couple of minutes while I..."

"Yeah. Go ahead," Bill sighed. He found a comfortable looking rock and sat down to enjoy the scenery while his son re-established his lifeline with civilization.

"I wonder if I can get four," Brandon said. He walked around, looking down at his phone, trying to find the signal-strength sweet-spot.

Bill knew the adjustment to the Upper Peninsula, or U.P., was going to be difficult for Brandon. It may not have been so hard if Renee had allowed Bill to take Brandon for visitation, the way normal people did. Bill took a deep breath and cleansed his mind. That bullshit was over.

"Dad!"

The cry shook Bill from his thoughts. He jumped up and saw Brandon on his stomach, clawing frantically at the rocky ground and sliding backward, disappearing into the earth. Bill sprang forward, desperate to reach his son. Brandon grabbed hold of a small bush and he jerked to a stop. Bill was there a second later, seizing the boy's wrist.

"I got ya!" Bill yelled. Then he heaved, pulling Brandon up. They moved well away from the hole, a feature that hadn't been there only moments before. "Are you okay? What happened?"

Brandon brushed himself off, wincing at the abrasions on his arms. "I'm okay. I don't know. It was like the ground got pulled out from under me." He looked at the crevice that had almost swallowed him up. It was only about three feet by two feet.

Bill sidled closer and looked at the hole's edge. He noticed that the stone featuring the petroglyph was gone. Below the surface, he could see shattered timbers that had been covered by layer upon layer of dirt and stone. The petroglyph had been sitting right on them. "Someone covered this with logs or something a long time ago." Leaning over, he peered into the blackness. "Wow. That looks deep." He tossed a stone in and waited a full two seconds before hearing it clack against a surface, only to bounce several more times on the way to the bottom. His stomach dropped with that stone. If Brandon had fallen in...

Brandon wrinkled up his face. "Yuck. What is that smell?"

A rancid odor assailed Bill even as Brandon was speaking. He sniffed in the direction of the sinkhole. "Whoa. That's nasty. Smells kinda like rotten fish." He could hear the whoosh of air as it slid through the opening into the void below, pushing the stench upward and out.

Brandon held his nose and looked around. "Was the carving thing sitting on top of the hole?"

"Kind of looks like it," Bill answered.

"Oh, no," Brandon said.

"What? What is it?"

Brandon retrieved his fallen phone and held it up to show Bill the spiderweb of cracks that radiated out from the corner of the screen. Bill sighed.

"Nice. Yeah, this was totally worth it," Brandon said. Then he turned and trudged down the trail toward town.

High atmospheric pressure coaxed the gentle summer breeze through the hole in the dirt and timbers, flowing out of the confines of the dark cavern through various cracks and fissures far below. Down the air washed. Ten feet. Twenty. Fifty. Eighty. Down into near-total darkness where the light filtered down in narrow, dust-filled beams from the sky far above, shining through the hole that had nearly been Brandon's death-trap.

At the bottom of the forgotten chamber the temperature held at a consistent fifty degrees, unaffected by the outside air that, until now, had no way to enter in any quantity. Now the fresh air mingled with the stench of death and rot, swirling together in a macabre embrace that fouled the sweet breath dropping in from outside.

No wildlife scurried. No bats took refuge. Even insects seemed non-existent here.

And still, the warm summer breeze blew down through the hole.

But it wouldn't always be warm.

Not able to find anything worth watching on the one-hundred or so channels of shit on T.V., Bill turned off the television and pulled out a book. He settled in to read for a while and just plain relax. The accident this afternoon had taken something out of him. No doubt it had taken something out of Brandon too. They'd gone to the one local doctor who gave Brandon a cursory exam and cleaned up his scraped arms and belly with some painful antiseptic. But it didn't seem that he'd suffered any major damage, just cuts and some developing bruising around his ribcage a bit.

Bill didn't know what he would have done if he'd lost Brandon like that. The thought chilled him more than he could imagine, perhaps because he had been there and seen the look of terror in his son's eyes.

He was finally getting into his reading groove when Brandon emerged from his bedroom, having just awakened from the last of his, apparently normal, three daily naps. Disheveled and bored, the boy plopped down in an easy chair and cast a mournful eye on the blank television screen.

"You have Netflix?"

Bill looked up and shook his head.

"Amazon?"

Another shake.

"Do you have anything for streaming?"

"The only streaming I do is with a fly rod."

Brandon huffed. Then he looked Bill in the eye, growing more serious than Bill had ever seen.

"Dad, can I hook up my Playstation to the TV? I can hardly use my phone."

Crap. He knew that request would come out eventually, but he'd hoped to forestall it longer than this. He didn't want to lose his son to a virtual world of death and mayhem. Not when there was so much fun to be had outside. But right now they weren't doing anything, and the kid had had a rough day.

"Yeah, I suppose."

Brandon jumped up and turned to grab his machine, but Bill stopped him.

"But listen, I don't want you on that thing all day long. Four hours at most." Brandon's shoulders slumped. "You can divide up the time however you want. Two hours in the morning, two in the evening, whatever. But, and this is a big but, if I say to turn it off, you turn it off now. Got it?"

Brandon nodded and darted into his bedroom, returning a second later with a box that had cords dangling from it. It didn't take him long to connect the infernal brain killer.

And in even less time, Bill decided that the boy needed some headphones so he didn't have to listen to an endless supply of fifty-caliber machine gun rounds firing for hours on end while he tried to read. Yahoo.

CHAPTER SEVEN

The following morning, Bill was pleasantly surprised to see Dr. Stephanie Crowe come striding down the dock to his boat a full half-hour before their planned departure time of 8:00 AM. Though, in light of how frantic she'd been to get out on the lake, he shouldn't be surprised. He couldn't imagine why she had been instantly amenable to paying the minimum fee for three people when she was the only passenger, but he wasn't going to look a gift-horse in the mouth.

He was already there, of course, loading food and fueling up for a full day on the lake. The weather was clear and warm, promising that it would be a nice, perhaps perfect, day out on the water. He knew this was not going to be a fishing trip, though its full nature was still a bit of a mystery.

Brandon was at home, in bed, having semi-consciously declined Bill's offer to bring him along today. He supposed his son would spend all day playing his video-games. Not what he was supposed to do, but he was a teen-aged kid whose dad wouldn't be around to pull the plug. Game-city. Bill didn't worry about it too much. At least it didn't seem his son was into drugs or doing stupid stunts to post on the Internet. Yet.

Dr. Crowe came down the pier, hefting a big black duffel-bag with both hands. It was impossible for Bill to not appreciate the raven-dark hair that reached just below her shoulders. She approached the side of Bill's boat, a broad, sweet smile on her face. "Hello! Mr. Hitze?"

Oh shit. She was prettier than her picture. "Yep. But...Bill, just call... Bill's fine. You're here nice. Ah, nice and early. Clearly, you're Dr. Crowe." *Nice going Don Juan*. He reached for the black canvass bag that she extended out to him, avoiding her eyes.

"I was hoping you could help me with some of my gear," she said, handing her burden over.

"There's more?"

"Not a lot, but I will need help with the next thing." Her warm, dark eyes shined as she looked at him.

He swallowed. Damn near swallowed his tongue. "All right." Bill clambered over the gunwale and grasped Dr. Crowe's extended hand. It was so soft and smooth, but still strong.

"Call me Steph. Only my students call me Dr. Crowe." She turned and led him back to a small pickup truck. She opened the tailgate and Bill stared at the device that sat there, large foam collars at each end of it to cushion it in a suspended state off of the truck's bed.

"Is that-"

"A remote-operated submersible," Steph finished. She flashed another smile at him. "It isn't very heavy, but it's nearly impossible to carry by yourself. She grabbed the end closest to the front of the truck bed and swung it down toward the tailgate so that the sub was within easy reach for Bill and waited. Bill grabbed his end and lifted. She was right, it was pretty light. It was about five feet long, a foot in diameter, with wings that stuck out six inches on both sides, presumably to direct its attitude in the water. A small propeller was at the back, a thin guard encircling the blades to prevent damage. The end Bill held was the nose, clear plastic molded into a half-sphere shape through which he could see a camera. An insulated wire was wrapped countless times around the center of the sub. Attached to the wire was a bright orange ball that reminded Bill of a giant bobber.

They started down the pier, Bill shuffling backward. "What in the world are we going to be doing?" he asked.

"I thought you'd never ask." Her eyes flashed with excitement. "I told you that I examined that body you found. Well, more accurately, the attire he was wearing. I'm not a forensic pathologist, I'm more of an archaeologist. And a historian."

Bill watched her expectantly, waiting for her to continue.

She giggled. "Not like Indiana Jones, of course. I focus on the history of the upper peninsula, in particular the Keweenaw region, before and during the mining boom and even before white man made it here."

They set the submersible on the gunwale of Bill's boat, Steph holding it as he climbed in, then vice versa. They set it on the only open area of the boat's deck.

"Right. Why the urgency to go out on the lake?" Bill asked.

"I'll get there," she said. Then with a smile, she asked, "Did you know that copper, native to this area, was found in the Mediterranean that dates back to about 1200 B.C.?"

"That's weird."

"Isn't it? There is so much we don't know about the area and the mining that occurred long before recorded history. But wait," she said, waving a hand. "That isn't relevant to what has me here. Like I said, I examined the attire of the body you found and it is consistent with clothing from the mid to late eighteen-hundreds." Her words were starting to fly out of her.

"You said that on the phone. So the guy is really old. Lake Superior 'doesn't give up her dead'. It's too cold, everyone knows that. Probably a lot of old bodies out there." *Yes. Please keep the talk technical and businesslike. That works.*

She nodded emphatically and rubbed her hands together. "I know, but with his proximity to Copper Harbor and the clothes he was- Oh, he was wearing winter clothes."

"Maybe he got caught on an ice floe when he was fishing?" Bill interjected.

Stephanie froze, her eyes scanning across the top of her sockets, then started nodding in short jerky motions. "Yeah, maybe, OK. But no." She shook her head with certainty. "There was definitely something about him that makes that unlikely."

Bill recoiled. "Oh, right. His head." An image of the headless body flashed through his mind like a gruesome, private, slide-show.

Steph scrunched up her nose and face. "You saw that, huh?"

"Unfortunately."

"I'm looking into whether he could have been someone from the missing Copper Harbor settlement of eighteen-forty-two." She clipped off the 'two' like a lawyer that had just delivered the most compelling closing statements in a high-profile murder trial. And followed it up with a close-mouthed grin.

Bill stared at the smiling woman in front of him. "The missing... I thought that was just an exaggeration."

She stepped forward and grasped both of his shoulders and looked him dead in the eye. "Oh no. The town really disappeared in the winter of eighteen-forty-two and forty-three. The tales are all the weird ghost and monster stories people tell to explain it."

"You think he's from the missing settlement?"

"He's from the right time-frame. Even the right season."

"So what's the rush?" Bill asked.

"All those tales, about the vanishing? Some may be closer to the truth than you might think."

Bill scoffed. "Okay." *And here's where she will tell me how dumb I am.*

Steph's cheery face darkened. "I'm serious. Turns out, several Native American settlements disappeared from this area before Europeans ever arrived."

"Again. Why the rush?"

"From the records I've examined and interviews I've done, the Native Americans disappeared about one-hundred-seventy-seven years before the Copper Harbor vanishing. And though I couldn't find adequate records, it seems that roughly two-hundred years before that, something similar happened up here."

Bill dropped his head, still unable to unravel why he was taking this woman, this doctor of archeology, out on some weird treasure hunt.

"It's 2019," Steph said. "One-hundred-seventy-seven years after the residents of Copper Harbor disappeared without a trace."

The fisherman stared at the emphatic professor and saw the earnest sincerity on her face. Her implication wasn't lost on him, but he was more than skeptical about the possibility of history repeating itself. "OK. It's your money," Bill said. "You have anything else to load up?"

She tightened her lips, leaving something unsaid, and shook her head. "Thank you for taking me out. This could really be helpful." She gave his shoulder a friendly rub.

Bill just smiled and started the motor, getting ready to cast off.

Brandon's eyes burned and blurred. *Damn! I gotta blink more,* he thought as he frantically mowed down another wave of Nazi zombies with a machine gun. Then the screen turned red and he turned his virtual character around to see countless zombies fall on him followed by the words, "You died!".

"Dammit!" He dropped the PlayStation controller on the couch next to him and flopped back into a reclined position. His stomach rumbled. Time to eat. Again.

He walked to the kitchen, his bare feet scuffing across the dusty wood floor, and opened the refrigerator, one arm hanging onto the top of the door while he examined every item contained therein. He opened a couple of Tupperware containers, sniffing their contents, before dropping each on the counter. After selecting what looked like an ample supply of food, he went about heating and then devouring all of it. He left the empty containers and dirty dishes in the sink.

Satisfied, at least for now, Brandon sauntered back to the couch, retrieved his shattered cell phone off the coffee table and stared at it. He could still use it, kind of, but playing games on it was not going to work unless he didn't mind shredding the ends of his fingertips.

"Shit." He tossed the phone back on the table and looked out the window. The sun was shining and he could catch a glimpse of Lake Superior in the distance, its water a deep blue that met the sky miles in the distance.

Already clad in shorts and a t-shirt, he slipped on his sneakers and headed outside. He was met by the most refreshing air he had ever breathed. It was a comfortable seventy-four degrees, low humidity, and there was a barely perceptible breeze coming in off the lake. He stood for a moment and looked at the startlingly clear sky and wondered if his mother could see him.

"Whatever," he said to himself. It was no use thinking about her. It was no use trying to ignore her either. The pain was there and would be for some time. He tried to numb himself against it, took a deep breath as he looked out at the lake. The lake where his dad was. At least the guy wasn't a drunkard or abusive, but he was more like a burdened uncle than a dad. Why hadn't his biological father wanted to visit, just visit, with Brandon when Brandon was growing up? His shoulders slumped. One more thing that didn't matter. Just three more years...

Not sure what to do, he decided to head up the road to where he'd run into that girl, Trillium. It'd be nice talk to her and maybe un-ruffle her feathers. She hadn't seemed too impressed last time they talked.

He trudged a long way up the road with neither car traffic nor Tril anywhere to be seen. He was about to turn around when he saw a small cloud of dust floating across the crumbling pavement. A few more steps and he could see Tril, on her knees, a pile of weeds laying next to her, wiping sweat from her grimy forehead.

"Hey, Tril!"

She turned and regarded him briefly before allowing a small grin to pull at the corners of her mouth. "Brandon, right?" she asked. She stood up and took off her gloves.

"Still after those weeds, huh?"

She turned and surveyed her progress, scanning farther up the ditch. "Yeah. Luckily there aren't a lot of them. Finding them is half the battle." Her gaze returned to Brandon. "Find anything 'fun' to do?"

Brandon felt the blood rise in his cheeks. "Uh, yeah. I just gotta get used to the area, that's all."

Tril grunted.

"So, I almost died yesterday," Brandon blurted as though he was talking about getting a flat tire.

"Oh. How?" Tril asked, just as conversationally.

"You know that...uh... boat carving?"

"The petroglyph? Yeah."

"Well, my dad took me up there to show it to me and a big hole opened up and I nearly fell down it. My dad had to grab my arms 'cause my legs were dangling in the hole."

Tril perked up at this. "A hole? How big? How deep?"

Brandon made a portion of a circle with his arms. "About like this. And it was *deep.* Couldn't see the bottom."

She frowned, looking matronly. "Sounds dangerous. We should go check it out."

Brandon nodded. He was glad she seemed to be giving him another chance. "Okay."

Trillium stuck her gloves in a back pocket of the short-legged bib overalls she was wearing and brushed past Brandon. He caught a brief but pleasant whiff of her perfume again. The one that reminded him of his mom. It sent him into a moment of paralysis as memories and feelings swirled around in his head.

"You coming?" Tril asked.

Brandon blinked off the fog in his brain and stepped lively to catch up with the dirt-covered girl that was nothing like any of the girls he'd known in Minneapolis. Any of those would have died if a boy had seen them dirty and ratty. Tril seemed indifferent to his opinion on how she looked. But he had to admit, he kind of liked her appearance. Somehow, he could see through the mud and dust to the pleasing girl beneath it all.

At least this boring town, north of nowhere, had Tril. He'd better not muck this up.

It took them a full hour to hike up to the hole from where Tril had been weeding. Brandon walked her over to where the dark void opened in the middle of the ground. Tril would have strode right to the edge of it had Brandon not grabbed her arm.

"Wait. Don't get too close. There were timbers underneath that broke."

Tril looked at him with a strange expression. It reminded Brandon of a dog tilting its head and perking up its ears at an unfamiliar sound. "Where's the petroglyph?"

"I guess it fell in the hole."

Tril eyeballed the area around the sinkhole. "Hmm. Gotta be careful. Hold my feet." She knelt down and started crawling toward the edge to where she could peer down into the blackness.

"What?" Brandon nearly dove to grab the crazy girl's ankles. "Geez! Be careful."

"I will," she said without looking back. When she was nearly there, she laid herself out flat so that her face peeked over the edge of the hole. "Whew," she said. "Boy, does that stink."

"Can you see anything?" Brandon asked.

"No. It's just dark. But I can see the timbers. Looks like someone covered the hole with them, then covered it with dirt."

"Yeah. Any idea who did it?"

She shook her head. Tril picked up a stone from the rocky ground, held it over the hole like a primitive getting ready to sacrifice a virgin into a volcano, and dropped it. She turned her head sideways to let one ear focus on sounds coming up from below.

"I didn't hear it hit anything." She grabbed a bigger stone and repeated her experiment. Brandon saw her eyebrows arch. "I heard that hit something. But it took a while. That's one deep hole."

She pushed back and raised up on her hands and knees again, crawling back to Brandon and away from the hole.

"You almost fell in that?" Brandon nodded. "You're right. You almost died." Then, with a warm smile, she added, "I'm glad you didn't."

"Me too." Not wanting to let the positive vibes die, he asked, "What's the story with the Viking ship carving?"

"Didn't your dad tell you about it?" Tril asked.

Brandon would have helped her to her feet but she bounded up like a jack-in-the-box. He gained his own feet instead. "He did, kinda. But I want to hear what you think."

The look of delight that lit up her face did not go unnoticed by Brandon. "Well, let me tell you. There's been a lot of argument about whether it's genuine or not. But an archaeologist or something came out and said he thought it was real."

"Really? Wow."

Tril nodded. "The question is: why did they put it up here? Most people think it's because whoever did it was up here when they saw the ship. You can see a lot of the shoreline from here."

"I can see that," Brandon said.

"But," Tril said, a conspiratorial tone flavoring her voice, "I think it may actually be a marker."

Brandon frowned. "A marker for what?"

Tril shook her head. "I don't really know. Maybe this hole! Viking treasure maybe? But think of it; this point would be easily recognized from out on the lake, so they could come to shore and hike up here. They look around for their mark and-" She looked at the hole, her eyebrows creasing. Brandon followed her gaze, his own mind now whirring.

"You suppose there's something in there?" he asked.

Tril's head moved back and forth as she considered the question. "I can't imagine the stone being on top of this hole was an accident."

"It is a weird coincidence," Brandon agreed. "But it's so deep. How would they ever get their treasure out of there?"

Tril's face scrunched up. "There is that problem." Then her eyes lightened, sparkling at Brandon. "I'm sure they had ropes. And they were fit. They probably just planned to climb down, tie the treasure to the end of the rope, climb up, pull up the loot!"

"I suppose," Brandon said. "Still..."

Tril raised her eyebrows and displayed a wicked grin. "You know-"

"Oh no. You're kidding, right? We can't go down there."

"How much rope do you think we'll need?" Tril asked.

"What if we fall? Geez!"

"We both won't go down. You can stay up here and hold onto a safety rope tied around my waist."

Brandon's eyes flew wide. "Wait. *You* want to go down there while I wait up here?"

"Sure. I can climb ropes really good." She stared at him, daring him to object.

He grunted with frustration. "I dunno. You're the only one I know here. I'd hate to do something that gets you killed."

She patted his shoulder like a mother soothing a child who'd just awakened from a nightmare. "Tomorrow. I'll get the ropes. Come over to my house at ten-"

"In the morning?" Brandon blurted.

"No. At night. Of course in the morning. We may have a long day of hauling up treasure."

"Or a long day of trying to get rescued."

"Here we are," Bill said as he killed the motor. "What's the plan?"

"This is it?" Steph asked. She looked south-east, toward where they came from and saw nothing but water. "How far from shore are we?"

"About fourteen miles."

"Can we anchor here so I can look around?"

Bill laughed. "Not with this boat. We're in about 150 feet of water and I don't have the rope or patience to do that."

Steph snickered. "I guess that'd be a bit impractical. How hard will it be for us to stay in this spot?"

"Wind is weak right now, so shouldn't be too hard. Twenty, thirty yards close enough?"

"That's perfect," Steph said happily. She dug out a controller for her submersible, checked the power and then unwrapped the lengthy antenna from around the tube of the miniature submarine. She threw the end of the antenna that was affixed with the orange float into the water and laid the craft across the rear corner of the boat. The propeller whirred to life when she flipped a couple of levers and the short wings pivoted in response to her commands to dive or surface. Apparently satisfied, she lowered the yellow sub into the water, nose-first. Flipping another switch brought a color display to life on her controller.

Bill checked the GPS. Seeing that they had not yet started to drift significantly he peered over Steph's shoulder.

She smiled at him. "Here we go."

The propeller spun up and the "Lakefly", the name painted on its side, started its spiraling descent into the depths of Lake Superior. Steph watched as it slowly became first a distorted yellow shaft, then a small yellow blob, and finally disappeared from sight. She turned her attention to the small display on her controller, a screen into the deepest blue depths, the camera on the front of the Lakefly transmitting its view to her.

"There is another monitor in my bag," she said.

Bill reached into the black canvass sack and found the monitor, about fourteen inches wide, and pulled it out. He unwrapped the cord that was wound around its body and handed the end to Steph. She plugged the end into the bottom of her controller.

"Power switch is on the left side, bottom," she instructed.

Bill flipped it on and the screen fluttered to life. He held it so both he and Steph could see the image which continued to darken as they watched. Suddenly a beam of light shown forth, lightening the view somewhat.

"That'd be better if there was something to see besides empty water," Steph said around a smile.

They watched for several more minutes before the bottom of the great lake came into view. When it did, Bill could see the sand, littered here and there with large stones, some very large, perhaps even car-sized.

"Time to look around," Steph said. Expertly she piloted the Lakefly around the bottom, its light illuminating the essentially boring lake floor. She set out a search pattern that spiraled outward from where she started.

"What exactly are you looking for?" Bill asked.

"Anything. Anything that might be a clue as to what happened to that guy you found. Or how he got all the way out here. Or why."

Bill nodded. "Yeah, I wouldn't want to be fourteen miles from shore on the ice, even with a snowmobile." He thought a minute. "Of course, he could have been in a boat out here in November or something. He would have needed the warm clothes."

"Absolutely," Steph replied. "So we might find remains of his boat or fishing gear. But none of that answers how his head got..."

"Gone," Bill finished. "Right."

"So we're looking for pretty much anything that might be attributed to his presence out here."

Bill spent the next two hours either watching the monitor or maneuvering the boat to be close to the Lakefly. At the end of that time, Steph brought the little craft up to swap out batteries. She set the old battery to charging, asked Bill to move them about one hundred yards farther out, and launched the sub again.

Bill was looking around at the lake fantasizing about dropping in a fishing line. To the west, a thin gray line appeared on the horizon. His patience for not fishing had expired an hour ago, and now it surfaced. "I can't imagine you're going to find anything, if you haven't already. We should have easily seen some sort of boat."

"Maybe," Steph answered. She remained surprisingly cheerful. "If he had a boat."

Bill rolled his eyes. She might be pretty, and cheerful, and sweet, but dammit, she thought she was better than him. She was a professor, she must think it. "Fourteen miles from shore, mid-eighteen-hundreds... he had a boat. Or whoever dumped him here did."

"You think that's what happened?" Steph asked.

"Disposing of a body has been around as long as murder," Bill replied.

"Uh-huh," Steph grunted. Her attention was on the monitor that sat propped up on one of the boat's seats. "What have we here?"

Bill stepped over to look for himself. The light shone on the sand bottom where something protruded at an unusual angle. "Looks like the branch of a buried tree."

"A branch? That looks way too straight. And the end looks like it's been sawed flat."

They watched as the Lakefly circled the protrusion, displaying it from different angles.

"Hmm," Bill exhaled. "Maybe you're right."

Steph brought the Lakefly in closer and stopped it, changing the focus of the camera to the sand where the piece of wood penetrated the lake floor. "And that is what, exactly?"

Bill looked at the dark metallic shape that was partially buried but still covered with silt. "Looks like metal."

"Let me try something." Steph powered the Lakefly forward until it was most likely positioned over the object and then jammed her throttle control forward. She smiled mischievously at Bill. "Prop wash."

The way her face glowed when she said that made Bill's tongue suddenly swell, so he nodded.

She backed off on the throttle and turned the sub around to close on the object again. The view was partially obscured by the cloud of dust she'd turned up with the burst from the propeller. She stopped where they'd be able to see once the water cleared.

As they were waiting, Bill cast a wary glance westward. The line of gray on the horizon had darkened and moved higher in the sky. "Ah crap," he said. "We gotta go."

Steph looked at him, alarmed. "What? Why?"

"Storm's coming. Damned Lake Superior weather."

The scientist turned her attention to the monitor. "Look. What's that look like to you?"

Bill risked a quick peek at the image and furrowed his brow, confused. "Looks like an axe-head."

"That's what I thought."

"That's nice and all, but we gotta go. Now." The thin line of gray had become a roiling wall of black, towering up from the horizon.

Steph looked at the looming storm. "That's still miles away."

"And it will be on us long before we get to shore. Now get your little sub up here or we are leaving it behind."

Steph flipped a lever bringing the Lakefly into an upward trajectory and jammed the throttle forward. "Can you take a quick reading on the GPS?" she asked over her shoulder.

"Yes, yes! Hurry it up." Bill was losing his patience. He had been fishing Lake Superior long enough to know that clouds that climbed the sky from the horizon so quickly meant the storm was closing at high speed. And being caught on the massive lake during a storm, in a fishing boat, no matter how big, was the kind of excitement he could live without.

"Going as fast as I can," Steph answered. Her voice was gaining an uneasy edge, perhaps picking up on Bill's frazzling nerves.

Bill jotted down the GPS coordinates and stuffed them into his pocket for safekeeping. Then he cranked up the engines and left them idling, the boat sounding impatient in its own right. "Can I help?" he asked after moving to stand behind Steph.

She moved away from the side of the boat, making room for him to stand near the gunwale. "Grab it when it comes up."

"I don't see it." Bill snapped.

"Sixty feet down. Almost here."

Bill stared into the water and could see the darkness permeating the depths as the sun was slowly choked from the sky. After seconds that seemed like hours, he finally saw a splash of yellow. The Lakefly. Then the orange float on the submersible's antenna broke the surface.

"Oh," Steph uttered. "Oh, nuts."

"What?" Bill asked, spinning to face her. "What's wrong?"

"Battery died. It's dead in the water."

"So are we if we don't get the hell out of here. Shit." He looked down into the water and without hesitation reached down and grabbed the light wire antenna and started yanking.

"Ahh," Steph screamed. "Careful with that!"

Bill ignored her and quickly pulled fifty feet of long, flexible wire into the boat, letting it fall in a heap on the deck. The Lakefly resisted the pull, traveling in big, slow arcs as it fought being tugged to the surface by the antenna attached to the middle of its cylindrical body. Finally, the little vessel broke the surface and Bill scooped it up and stuffed it into Steph's arms.

The boat was already rocking as it rolled over the increasingly large swells. Bill grabbed onto seat-backs as he staggered to the helm. "Put that down and grab a seat. We're in for a rough ride. And put on a life-jacket." The charter captain thrust his arms through a bright orange vest of his own, fastened the three clasps across the front and started the boat forward slowly, pulling hard on the wheel to bring it around to face shore which lay some fourteen miles south-east.

"How did this storm come up so fast?" Steph asked.

"Lake Superior," is all Bill said. He increased throttle and the boat surged ahead, sliding down the backside of a four-foot swell where the bow crashed into the water, abruptly slowing their forward momentum before rising again as the big motors thrust the boat up the next wave. If they were unlucky, and he was pretty sure they were, they would be riding six to eight-foot swells before they made the breakwater.

Fifteen minutes later they were in the middle of a white-crested roller-coaster, the bow digging deeply into walls of water as Bill expertly piloted his boat through the treacherous waves. The wind came at them diagonally from the rear which made traversing the waves slightly less hammering but required intense concentration on Bill's part as he worked the steering wheel back and forth in an effort to prevent the boat from turning completely sideways in the troughs or stuffing the bow straight down into the water where they would stop and get hit by the trailing wave. More than once the front of Bill's boat broke deep, the very tip of the boat driving down like a spade in the dirt before its buoyancy lifted it through several feet of ice-cold water that rushed over the top of the windshield and cascaded into the cabin where it soaked and chilled Bill and Steph. On one such occasion, the water nearly swept the Lakefly straight out the back but Steph managed to grab one of its wings before it toppled into the churning lake. It was fortunate for her because Bill would not have turned back for it if she'd lost it now.

Bill flipped on the pump, knowing that if he kept taking on that kind of water, they'd become swamped and then, most likely, die. A stream of water issued from the starboard stern, the pump doing its job.

The canvas bimini top overhead snapped and thundered as it caught the wind and then slackened, providing a wild and random percussion section to the symphony of the big inboard engines that chugged relentlessly below them. With the wind and rain increasing in intensity, visibility dropped to less than a quarter-mile. Bill now looked at his GPS map display for navigation. The shoreline at this area of the Keeweenaw peninsula was very rocky and perilous, with small, rocky islands jutting up from the waters at various spots closer to shore. Only the islands showed on his GPS mapping software. As for the unmapped rocks, Bill knew where the larger ones were, but there were plenty of smaller ones that he had to see to avoid. And those could destroy his boat in a heart-beat if they met one sliding down the backside of a wave.

A glance at the monitor told him what he didn't want to know; he was coming in too far west. This meant that he would have to turn such that the waves would be almost hitting them broadside if he was going to make it to the large gap that opened into Copper Harbor on the east side of Porter's Island, an island that served as part of a natural breakwater sheltering the harbor. But these massive waves could throw his boat ten to twenty feet sideways if things went poorly and that could crash them onto any number of rocky projections.

"Rocks ahead!" Steph's voice rang through the pounding of the rain on the canvas roof and the roar of the surf and thunder.

Bill's eyes had seen them the same moment Stephanie gave a warning. The combination of wind and waves meant the likelihood of his being able to go around the stony islet on the lake-side without them being smashed to bits was extremely small. That meant he'd have to go between the dangerous protuberance and the natural breakwater, a thin strip of land the locals called "Hunter's Point".

"Hang on," Bill shouted as he spun the wheel to the right. The boat rolled towards its left side before the bow dropped heavily into a trough. Bill struggled to stay upright, both hands locked onto the wheel. Steph was propelled out of her seat and flung forward into the passenger side dashboard, grasping futilely for a handhold. With one hand, Bill tried to steady the flailing archaeologist, the other trying to control the pitching boat. In a fleeting moment of stability, Bill saw the gap that lay between Porter's Island and Hunter's Point. In this kind of surf, it was too small to be a comfortable access point to the harbor. But if he fought the waves to try to get east around Porter's Island to the larger entrance, he was all but certain they'd be thrown onto the rocks. If they made it through the gap, the waters of the bay would be tranquil by comparison. His decision made, he released Steph and grabbed the wheel with both hands and steered toward the gap. The bow of the battered fishing boat suddenly lurched skyward as it climbed the next swell. He felt Steph's hand smack into his arm as she toppled backward over her seat, still unable to get a grip on any fixtures. She did a backward roll over the seat, landed on her feet and fixed him with wide eyes as she struggled to get her footing, stumbling toward the stern with every out-of-control step.

"Bill," she screamed, reaching out with both of her hands, fingers splayed.

He let go of the wheel and thrust out a hand, trying desperately to grab her before-

Too late. Her legs hit the transom and she flipped over it, into the raging Lake Superior water.

CHAPTER EIGHT

At Tril's urging, Brandon and she had high-tailed it home, not wanting to be caught on the high peak during a lightning storm. They stood in the living room of Bill's little house, dripping on the floor. They hadn't been fast enough to beat the rain. Brandon couldn't believe it. He'd never seen a storm close in so quickly before in his life. It had raced up to them and then parked overhead, dumping buckets of cool water down, soaking their clothes, their hair, their skin, everything. Brandon even had water in his ear. He jumped up and down, shaking his head to that side as he tried to break the suction holding the deafening fluid in his ear canal.

"This is awesome," Tril said. Perfect, white teeth showed through her smile as she watched the lightning and churning clouds with the wide eyes of a toddler seeing a lion at the zoo for the first time.

"It is a pretty good view," Brandon said. The big window looked out toward the lake through a sparse frame of tree branches.

Then he turned his head, looking at the empty driveway. He faced the hallway to the bedrooms and called, "Dad!" There was no response.

"I didn't see his truck in the driveway," Tril said. "Where is he?"

"He was supposed to be going out on the lake today."

Tril's smile faltered and she turned to look at Brandon. Then the smile returned, though it wobbled. "Your dad has been around the lake a long time. I'm sure he got off of it before the storm hit. He'll probably be home in a few minutes. Or maybe he went to Jotnar's."

Brandon cast worried eyes to the now demonic-looking storm. "Yeah. You're probably right."

"Stephanie!" Bill grabbed the throttle lever and yanked it to 'stop'. They hadn't made it into the gap yet and the boat started to roll and bounce like a cork in a hot-tub. Bill grabbed one of the stern lines, wrapped the end around his left wrist and looked out into the frothing water. He heard a short scream that ended in a gurgled hack and saw the bright orange of Steph's life-jacket, already about twenty-five feet behind the boat. He launched himself as far as he could into the lake and immediately started swimming to her. Steph was fighting to close the distance, one-minute high above him on the crest of a wave, the next minute disappearing down the backside.

He had to reach her and get both of them back on the boat before it hit the rocks. Without the boat, their bodies would be smashed mercilessly against Hunter's

Point. The next wave lifted Steph above the trough from where Bill looked up at her terrified face. As the water shifted, Bill thrust forward, reaching out with his right hand and roughly took hold of Steph's life-jacket and yanked her to him. Her arms wrapped him up in a death-grip.

"Thank you! Oh, thank you!"

"Stop," Bill yelled. "Grab the rope. Go hand over hand. I'm right behind you. Fast, now!"

Her panicked eyes glanced at him for just a minute before she seemed to understand his urgency. Then she took the rope and started pulling herself through the roiling water. Bill was right behind her, the icy lake sapping the strength from his limbs. She had to be weakening faster, having been in the water longer, but she was gliding up the rope like she had a motor pulling her. Several times waves broke over their heads, causing them to choke and sputter. At last, they were at the boat which was still bouncing around at the mercy of nature.

Steph flipped down the ladder that was attached to the stern and tried to mount it. She got her hands on it, then finally one of her feet reached the bottom rung, but she just clung there like a bull-rider trying to make eight seconds. Bill could see she was too weakened to climb up. He pulled up tight behind her, holding onto the ladder with his left hand he planted his right squarely in the middle of Steph's ass, instantly appreciating its firmness, and shoved. The poor woman all but flew over the transom onto the deck of the pitching boat where she landed with a grunt.

Bill tried to get his foot on the bottom rung, but his leg slipped between two steps when the boat buoyed up suddenly. Cursing he tried to pull his hips back enough to get his foot out, a task made incredibly daunting by the turbulent water. His fingers were starting to stiffen, unable to work in the cold water. He didn't even know if his hands now gripped the sides of the ladder, the feeling all but gone. Finally, he got his footing and raised himself over the transom and into the boat. He immediately started flexing his hands in an effort to feel them again as he stumbled to the helm.

Steph tottered up next to him and sank shivering into the passenger seat, taking hold of the chrome 'grab bar' next to her with both hands. The waves were now nearly hitting them broadside on the port side and their world rolled wildly from side to side. Bill cranked the wheel to the right and jammed the throttle forward, piloting them toward the gap that would dump them into Copper Harbor. With some swearing and a lot of spinning of the steering-wheel, Bill successfully slipped between Porter's Island and Hunter's Point, dumping them into the small, choppy surf of the harbor.

Bill met Steph's eyes. "Whew."

She looked forward. "Thank you. God, that water's cold." She held herself in a hug, her long black hair clinging to her head and neck.

Bill felt his face flush. He should have got them in long before that storm hit. He had just let his attention wane a bit too long. And now she was thanking him?

"Don't thank me," he said with a shake of his head. "It was my fault we got caught in that mess."

To his surprise, she smiled at him. "No. I asked to stay longer. It was as much my fault as yours. And you didn't have to jump in to get me."

He scoffed. "If I hadn't, you wouldn't have made it. I couldn't throw the rope that far in the wind."

"I had my vest on."

"You would have gone hypothermic and been smashed on the rocks." Bill shook his head and shivered.

After several moments of silence, she said, "You really launched me." Her pursed-lips grin said much more.

Heat burned Bill's cheeks. "Sorry. I didn't hurt you, did I?"

"Just my pride." The smile she gifted him made him forget how cold he was.

CHAPTER NINE

Bill brought the boat to a stop next to the pier, grabbed the bow-line and jumped out to tie it to the mooring pole. As he hurried to get the stern line before the boat drifted too far from the dock, he said, "We should go get something to eat." Bill's eyes widened before he forced them to what he hoped looked like a normal aperture. Had he just said that out loud? His mind must be numb from the cold, basically asking this pretty woman out to dinner, both of them soaking wet. He wouldn't normally do something like that when he was at his best, and right now, he certainly wasn't.

"That sounds nice," Steph said. She smiled at him as she wrung the water from her long hair. It was the smile of someone who'd just been handed a charming gift, not someone who'd just survived a near-death experience.

"After all, it's all I can... could. I should do this." And he was back. To his horror and delight, her smile grew even larger and she patted him on the shoulder. Turning away, he tied the rope to the cleat on the dock and jumped back into the boat, flipping bumpers over the gunwale to prevent the wooden dock from damaging his craft.

After securing the boat and moving all the equipment back to her truck, they climbed into Bill's vehicle and rode over to Jotnar's Tavern. Thankfully, it was a quiet ride. He held the door for her as they went inside and immediately regretted his choice of establishments. Seated in the corner was Jeff Jansen, whose eyes tracked directly to the soaked, disheveled, yet still comely, Professor Stephanie Crowe. Bill cringed when he saw the corners of the slime's mouth turn up in a sleazy grin. He escorted her to the other side of the tavern where they sat in a booth.

"This is a neat little place," Steph said.

"Jotnar's Tavern," Bill answered. "I think it's the first building ever in Copper Harbor. And the food's great."

"Bill! What in seven-hells happened to you two?" Ernest called from behind the bar. "Ya look like a couple of drowned rats."

"It's really raining," Bill yelled back over the din. He didn't want to go into their mishap just now, especially with Jansen here. Ernest waved them off.

"Interesting guy," Steph said, smiling at the old inn-keeper. Then her face took on an analytical shadow and she folded her hands in front of herself on the table. "We need to discuss that axe-head we saw. We actually have a lot to discuss."

Discuss. Great. At least if they were talking about something like business, maybe he could hold his own. He waded in. "Assuming it was an axe-head."

"Do you usually take one with you when you go fishing or boating?"

"No."

"Right. So what about back in the eighteen-hundreds? Can you think of any reason why someone would have an axe on a boat?"

Bill thought. "If it was a big enough boat, could have been a fire axe."

"Yeah, but we didn't see any signs of a boat. One that big should have left us something."

The waitress interrupted with two glasses of water and a pair of menus, followed by the night's specials. She took their drink order: a beer for Bill and a White-Russian for Steph.

Bill looked at Steph who was staring at him with intent, brown eyes that gleamed with a touch of mischief. Then he said, "Seems you have a theory already?"

"Yep." She didn't try very hard to conceal the pleasure she took from his acknowledgment, her teeth showing easily through that delightful smile. "Here's what I think, he was out on the ice, in December 1841, and had the axe as a weapon."

"A weapon for what?" Bill asked.

"To defend himself from whatever was chasing him."

"You mean 'whoever'?"

Steph shook her head. "You know what happened to the town back then? The people totally disappeared, like they were sucked into space."

"You think they were abducted by aliens?" Bill asked, his eyebrows arching.

"No... well, I dunno. Maybe. But the thing is, some of the buildings in town had been ripped open or smashed in. In short, the buildings had been attacked."

Bill relaxed a little, just a little. "People will tear down structures to get at someone if they need to." The conversation was getting outside Bill's comfort domain.

Steph nodded. "But, how many people would it take to destroy a log cabin if someone inside was bent on defending it, with a whole town bent on defending it. That isn't what happened, which is why it's still a mystery. Several buildings were torn apart, not a soul left in town, and no sign of any army coming in and scooping them up."

The waitress delivered the drinks to the table and Bill drained half his mug in one tilt of the glass. They placed their orders and then Steph took a polite sip of her White-Russian.

Steph continued. "My people have passed legends down many generations, speaking of an evil too big to defeat."

Bill cocked his head. My people? Then he examined her dark, straight hair, the brown eyes and high

Hellman

cheekbones, the smooth skin, just slightly darker than his own. Now he saw it clearly. "You're native American."

She nodded, took a sip of her drink, then moved it aside so there was nothing on the table between them except the beer Bill clasped firmly between both hands.

"All right. You have me on the edge of my seat. What do you think happened?" he asked.

Steph peered at him with her dark, intelligent eyes, never blinking, never looking away. "I think the entire village fled out onto the ice, trying to escape something."

Bill wrinkled his brow. "Like what?"

She shook her head, looking pensive. "I don't know. A massive black bear, a Dire-wolf. Maybe a grizzly or polar bear made it here somehow."

"Polar bear?" Bill asked thoughtfully.

"They've been known to break into dwellings to get to the people inside."

The fisherman and the archaeology professor sat in silence, contemplating the possibilities.

"They had guns. They'd just shoot it." Bill said.

Steph shrugged. "If it was huge, maybe they couldn't chance it."

Bill thought for a moment. "I guess that's possible. But why flee onto the ice? A friggin' polar bear is at home out there. Seems like you'd have a better chance going through the forest."

"I can see you're not a stupid man." Bill frowned. Steph pinched her lips together. "Or maybe it's something we've never seen before."

Bill squinted at her. "What do you mean? Bigfoot?"

Steph shrugged and shook her head weakly. "The theory isn't perfect. But you get my point."

Bill was silent for half a minute before saying, "All that stuff is true, huh? About Copper Harbor?"

She nodded.

"I thought ole' Ernie was just a good story-teller." He gestured to the bar where the old man was walking back and forth, serving up drinks and chatting up a storm.

"Doesn't mean it isn't true," Steph said. Looking around she asked, "Where are the restrooms?"

Bill pointed to the opposite corner of the rectangular dining room where a dark hallway led to the back of the establishment. "Right over there."

Steph thanked him and got up, placing her napkin on the wooden bench of the booth, and disappeared into the darkness of the hall.

Bill sipped at his beer now, the multitude of theories of what could have happened to the people of Copper Harbor back in 1842 jockeying for relevance like a pack of dogs fighting to gain dominance of a soccer ball too big to get their jaws around. Nothing seemed to make any sense. A whole village could have teamed up to kill a polar bear or grizzly rather than flee out onto the ice in December when they would hit open water eventually. And, of course, he didn't know of there ever having been a sighting of either animal anywhere in Wisconsin, Minnesota, or the Upper Peninsula. If they did flee onto the ice, as Steph suspected, what were they running from? Could it have been aliens?

He scolded himself for letting his imagination run away. Whatever the case, it was old news waiting to be discovered. Nothing more would come of it in this day and age.

Then, out of the corner of his eye, he noticed Jansen perk up, looking in the direction of the hallway to the bathrooms. Suddenly he stood up and put on his best smarmy smile and walked in that direction just as Steph emerged from the dark corridor. Bill could hear the fake, overly warm greeting as Jansen reached for Steph's hand and then stepped between her and Bill, his back to the annoyed fisherman. He could see the two of them nodding and heard Steph's lilting laughter drift over to where Bill slowly took a swig of beer. Clearly, Jansen felt the need to dick around in Bill's affairs. First Brandon, now Steph. Jerk.

Finally, Steph patted Jansen on the shoulder and stepped around him. Jansen turned to watch her retreat, though his eyes sought out Bill's, not where the man's eye would normally track. Steph finally arrived back and drew Bill's attention, a wide smile still playing on her lips when she sat down at the table.

"Wow. Haven't seen Jeff in a while," she said.

"You know each other?"

"I knew him from when he was teaching at the university," Steph answered. "We went to coffee a couple of times, but we were in different departments and it just-" she shrugged.

Of course. "Huh. Didn't take him long to leave the university when he got that game to hit, did it?" Bill asked, trying to hide the edge to his voice.

"No. He took off on his own. It sounds like things are going okay for him. But enough about him," Steph said, her smile dying. "Back to business. I'm not sure what could have driven everyone from their homes back then, but if they did go out on the ice, it could explain why they were never found."

"You think they went through?" Bill asked. The thought of an entire population being so scared that they'd go out on Lake Superior, only to break through the ice, was chilling in more ways than one.

"It'd definitely explain why they were never found."

Bill nodded, then signaled the waitress that he wanted another beer. "You want another drink?" Bill asked, even though he could see Steph's glass was at least half-full.

"No thanks. One is fine. I gotta drive home tonight."

"I kind of like your theory about them going out on the ice. But I don't buy a polar bear or grizzly chasing them out there."

"There's something up here, Bill. My people don't make things up. Details may have been lost through time, but there are too many stories to ignore. So we have to get facts. Facts that will point us to what happened."

"Like..." Bill waited.

"More bodies."

Bill frowned. "We didn't see any more bodies."

Steph looked thoughtful. "What were we, fourteen miles from shore?"

"Pretty much."

"That's a long way for bodies to be strewn. What if the guy you found was way out in front, or lagged behind the others?"

Bill contemplated the task she was describing.

"Can we go out again tomorrow?" she asked suddenly.

The seasoned fisherman laughed quietly and shook his head. "Steph, it was supposed to be good weather today. The next couple of days are supposed to be stormy. Do you want to go out tomorrow?"

Steph frowned. "Not if it's *supposed* to be lousy." She looked from side to side, clearly pondering something. "Okay. Let's go out as soon as you can, I'll pay, and until then I'll look into using something that may help speed things up a bit."

Then a big man, about 6'3", who looked like he threw cinder-blocks around all day, pushed himself into the booth next to Steph, squishing her against the wall. He slapped a one-hundred-dollar bill on the table, dropped his right elbow on the table with his forearm extended upward, palm open.

"Hey," Steph protested.

"Come on, man," Bill said. "We're in the middle of something here." He scowled at the big man sitting across the table from him.

"Come on. Hundred dollars says I can take you." The brute flexed his open hand and smiled.

"Fine." Bill smacked his right elbow on the table and snagged the stranger's hand in his own. "On three."

Steph stared, incredulous, at the two men about to arm-wrestle in front of her for hundred-dollar stakes.

Bill's word "Go," was followed almost immediately by the big man's knuckles cracking against the table-top. Bill snatched the Franklin and said, "Now get out of here."

The big man's mouth dropped open and he rubbed his hand. Shaking his head, he stood and walked away.

"What was that all about?" Steph asked. Her brows were furrowed and an uncharacteristic frown tugged at the corners of her mouth.

"I've learned it's faster to not argue and just get it over with."

"You creamed him. And he looks so strong." She watched as the big man sheepishly took his place next to his friends at the bar.

"I'm stronger than I look."

"I guess."

Bill was about to ask her to tell him about her plan when the waitress approached and lowered her serving tray to the table with a thud and confirmed the meals as she handed them out, leaving steaming plates of food in front of the couple.

"Dig in," Bill said. "I'm buying." He held the cash aloft with a sour smile.

They had almost made it through the meal when jerk-face Jansen appeared at their table.

"Hey Bill," Jansen said. "Steph told me you had a frightening day on the lake today."

"We're both still here," Bill answered. He wiped the corners of his mouth with his napkin and leaned against the booth's backrest. He was now officially annoyed with the interruptions.

Jansen slid into the booth next to Steph, wrapping one arm around her shoulders. "This is one of the nicest professors at the school. I'm really quite fond of her, though we don't work together. So I must insist, please do not drown her." His narrow smile was wicked.

Bill met Jansen's icy glare with silence.

"Oh, Bill was quite the pilot out there," Steph chimed in. "Next time, I won't insist on staying when he says we have to go."

"Fair enough," Jansen said, turning to look at her. "I know he's one of the best charter guides in town. I can't imagine he'd put you in harm's way twice." He stood up. "I've got to run. It was nice seeing you again." Then he left.

Bill watched the human suck-fest leave the premises. When his gaze returned to Steph, he found her staring at him with an amused look on her face.

"Male bravado," she said around a smirk. "Clearly, you two know each other as well. And not in a good way."

Bill shook his head, tried to conceal his contempt. "It's nothing. We exist in detente."

"Doesn't look like it." She looked at him with an unspoken question on her face.

"It's a long story. Very long."

"We'll have plenty of time on your boat while we search for the bodies." She let the unspoken implication hang.

Bill just pinched out a smile.

It had quit raining by the time Bill got home, though the sky was still heavy with black clouds that served to usher in an early darkness. When he pushed his way through the door with the cooler he carried he was greeted by the unsurprising picture of Brandon flopped on the couch, feet on the coffee table, game controller in hand with his fingers frantically flashing around the buttons and joysticks. Brandon looked up and dropped the device, jumping to his feet.

"Dad!"

"Little help," Bill said, holding the cooler out.

"Where were you?" Brandon asked.

"Working. There are two more plastic tubs in the truck. Bring them in here and set em' by the hallway."

Brandon strode out into the wet night in his stocking feet to comply. Bill just shook his head and carried the cooler to the kitchen and set it on the table. He transferred the remaining soda, water and food to the refrigerator. The front door clunked open and he heard Brandon drop the two plastic storage crates on the floor, having carried them in stacked one on top of the other.

Taking a cleansing breath, Bill asked, "How was your day?" He was prepared for the teenage-typical, "it sucked" or "crappy" he'd received most every time he asked the question.

"Pretty good. How'd it go on the lake?" Brandon sat down and picked up his game controller.

Bill grabbed a beer from the fridge and walked over to the family room where Brandon was settling in to pick up where he left off in his game. "Not so good. Got caught in that storm, almost crashed into Hunter's

Point, had to jump in the lake to save my client. One of the worst times out."

Brandon paused his game and sat up straight, fixing Bill with a look as though he'd never seen his father before. The boy's chest started to heave as he stammered. His face wrinkled. "You got caught in that?"

It was Bill's turn to flop down on the couch and put his feet up. He twisted the cap off his bottle of beer and took a swig. "Unfortunately. It was kind of my fault. We got caught up in what we found just long enough that I didn't check the horizon. When I finally did, it was already tight. Then we had to get this little submarine back on board. By that time, it was too late."

Brandon swallowed hard. "What happened?"

In a few weeks, Bill would tell the tale with more swagger and saltiness. But now it was just a flat, factual story. He recounted everything for Brandon who watched with a mixture of concern and disbelief. He recounted everything except what he'd thought of Dr. Stephanie Crowe. Steph. When he finished, Brandon just sat staring at the floor.

After a few moments, Brandon said, "I'm glad you're okay. I didn't realize you were even out there when the storm hit."

Bill watched as Brandon spoke, the words coming out slowly and quietly. It very much reminded him of when Brandon had first arrived at Bill's house after they drove up from the funeral in Minneapolis.

"I try not to be out there during storms. I have no plans on repeating that adventure." He hoped the words would reassure his son, but wasn't quite sure what Brandon needed right now. He cleared his throat. "You said you had a good day. What'd you do?"

Brandon seized on the chance to go down a happier road. "I met up with Tril, this girl I met the other day, and we went hiking."

Bill tried not to appear too pleased. "Good day for it, up until the storm. Where'd you go?"

"We-", Brandon huffed a weak laugh, then continued. "We went up to the rock with the ship on it. I showed her where that hole opened up."

Now it was Bill's turn to be concerned. "Alright. Don't spend a lot of time around that hole. It isn't safe. It could open up even wider."

"No. We didn't get too close. She just wanted to see where it was. Anyway, we're going hiking again tomorrow morning."

"Weather isn't supposed to be very good."

"We'll quit if it gets too crappy."

"Hmm. You get anything to eat?"

"I had some leftover pizza."

"You get enough?" Bill asked.

"Yeah," Brandon answered. He picked up his game controller and settled back into the couch.

Bill stood up to leave when Brandon said, "You aren't going out on the lake tomorrow are you?"

"No."

"Good." Then he started blowing away bad guys.

CHAPTER TEN

Bill was surprised the next morning when Brandon came walking into the kitchen carrying his backpack at 9:30 and downed some breakfast.

"You're up early."

"Gotta go over to Tril's"

Bill smiled to himself. At least Brandon had found a friend, one whose life didn't depend on a cell phone. "Where're you hiking today?"

Brandon stiffened. "Uh, I'm not sure. I'm just kind of trailing along with Tril." He stood up from the table and dropped his dishes in the sink. Then he grabbed his backpack from the floor, went over to the refrigerator and started stuffing assorted food items into it, as well as some water bottles. From the look of it, the kids were going to be gone for a week. Bill had to remind himself that he was watching a teenage boy preparing to be away from the kitchen.

"If you see lightning, find yourselves some cover, *not* under any big trees."

"Okay," Brandon said. Bill was certain he'd have received the same response if he'd told him not to become an alien-monster-super-slug.

"What'd I just say," Bill asked.

"Trees," Brandon said. "Don't go under them."

"The really tall ones. Don't go out in the open either." Bill sighed. He knew Tril and her parents, Ken and Diane. They were kind of nutty, outdoorsy, but in a good way. She knew the Keweenaw and wouldn't do anything stupid in a lightning storm.

"When will you be home?"

Brandon hesitated, then said, "Three O'clock?"

"Okay. Have Tril tell her parents where you guys will be hiking in case we have to send the Ranger after you." He smiled at Brandon's disconcerted expression.

"Right. See you later." Brandon slung his pack over his shoulder and left.

Brandon felt kind of bad for lying to his dad about where they were going. But he was trying to make a friend and it wouldn't go well if the first thing he did was rat her out to the parents who'd just say 'no, no, no!' Besides, they were actually going down into the hole, with a rope, not just hanging around the top where they could fall in. Well, Tril was going down the hole while he manned the safety line. At least that was the plan right now.

It didn't take him long to get to Tril's house on his bike. Nothing was very far from anything else in this secluded little town. When he pulled up into Tril's front yard, the front door opened up and Tril stepped out wearing faded jeans, a brown tee-shirt, leather gloves with her hair pulled back in a pony-tail that was tied with a black cord. The big pack on her back looked as though it would crush her if she leaned forward just an inch or two farther. But none of this caught his eye as readily as the big knife that hung in a sheath from the girl's belt. From where he stood, it looked like it was adequate to protect her from a grizzly bear.

Just before she let the door slam, she turned and yelled into the house. "We will. I'll let you know what we find." She turned to face Brandon with a confident smile. When she saw the puzzled expression on his face she asked, "What?"

"You told them where we're going?"

"Of course. If something goes wrong, they need to know where we are." She bent over to pick up her bike from where it lay on the grass and nearly fell forward. Brandon jumped off his bike to assist.

"Geez! Careful. What have you got in that pack?" He lifted her bike though she had already seized the handlebars. Her eyes squinted slightly and a smile started before fading away as she spoke.

"Just the ropes. I grabbed a lot of it. And some food. And water." She climbed on her bike and kicked herself forward before dropping her feet on the pedals and started up the road. Brandon hurried to catch up.

"Do you want me to take your pack? It looks heavier than mine," he said when he got alongside.

"No," she said and stifled a laugh. "It's only about forty pounds."

About a third of your weight, he thought. "Okay. Let me know if you change your mind." This girl was tougher than he thought. Never had he met a girl like this. Or rather, never had he paid any attention to a girl like this. He glanced at her casually as they ascended the road to the trail that would take them to the hole. She looked both supremely happy and totally satisfied. It was reassuring.

When they got to the trail entrance, Tril didn't hesitate at all, driving her mountain bike off the road and onto the steeper incline of the winding path. Scrub brush and blueberry bushes were on either side with trees sparsely scattered such that, on a day that wasn't overcast like this one, they'd be in full sunlight for most of the ride. Today the clouds created a low, lumpy ceiling of bruised blues and grays.

Tril finally dropped a gear or two on her bike shifter, giving Brandon the macho-preserving permission to do the same and save his legs from the fire that had been building since leaving the road. When they arrived at the hilltop site, Brandon was breathing hard and could feel the droplets of sweat sliding down between his shoulder-blades.

Tril got off her bike and promptly dropped the huge backpack. "Whew. That was getting heavy." Brandon could see the big wet spot where the pack had rested against her back, making her perspire. She looked around and pointed to a thick-trunked tree, taking off her leather gloves. "We'll tie off on that one," she said.

"You sure you don't want me to go down there and you can wait up here?"

She dug in her bag and pulled out two hefty coils of rope, tossing one at Brandon who struggled to catch the unexpected projectile. "Hell no," Tril said with a giggle. "I wanna see what's down there." Then her smile evaporated and she fixed her eyes on Brandon. "Besides, if truth be told, you'll have an easier time hauling me up than I would have hauling you up."

"Haul you up? I thought you said you could climb a rope."

"I did. I can. But if something goes wrong, I mean." She tied one end of the rope she carried around the trunk of the tree and tossed the other end into the hole.

Brandon approached the tree and wrapped the end of his rope around the tree, trying to remember anything of what his father had shown him about tying a boat to a pier, but nothing seemed to apply here. He could sense Tril's eyes on him and he reluctantly peered at her out of the corner of his own.

"Want some help?" she asked.

"Uh, yeah. Don't want to screw this up if you're on the other end."

"I appreciate that," she said. She came over and knelt down, taking the rope from Brandon. She demonstrated how to tie a running bowline knot, then made Brandon do it. Then she tested it. "See. Pretty easy, huh?"

"Yeah, it is," Brandon answered. He smiled at Tril and was pleased to see it returned.

She popped up, trotted to her pack and pulled out a long, rectangular strip of leather with one end narrowed down to a cord and a slit in the other end. She wrapped this around the tree, pulling the cord through the slit and tying it off on itself. Brandon studied what looked like a belt wrapped around the tree, trying to figure out its purpose.

"What's that for?" he finally asked, unable to deduce why it was there.

"Watch," Tril said. She picked up Brandon's rope and walked over to the hole, draping the rope onto the ground as she moved. At the hole's edge, she turned around and came back leaving more rope lying next to the first strand. Then she reached the whole bundle around the tree and headed back to the hole where she started to tie the other end to a funny, home-made looking harness that she pulled from her supplies and donned. Brandon furrowed his brow, watching her.

"Come over here," she said. He walked over and stood staring at the industrious girl. When she was finished tying off the rope to the harness she said, "Pick up the rope and put all of the slack in a pile at your feet."

He did as she said and noticed that every so often the rope pulled little pieces of bark off the backside of the tree. Tril scurried over to the tree and lifted the rope so that it rested against the leather strap until the rope was out of slack and ran tightly between Brandon's hands, the leather-armored tree trunk, and Tril's harness. Then she walked back to the hole requiring Brandon to feed out slack to accommodate her movement.

"There," she said with a smile. "Now if I fall, you won't be pulled into the hole. You'll be pulled back toward the tree. And the friction around the trunk will help you stop me from falling."

"That's pretty smart," Brandon conceded.

"Of course. Now, if you have to pull me up, you'll want to unwrap from the tree when you pull, then wrap again to rest. The power of friction."

Brandon just chuckled and nodded. To think he'd been attracted to girls whose greatest accomplishments were properly coordinating their shoes with their outfits. Seems girls could be a whole lot more interesting.

Tril pulled a flashlight out of her bag that had a small length of twine attached to the handle. She tied this to her belt and gave Brandon another triumphant smile.

"Time to get on with it." She sat at the edge of the hole and dangled her feet inside. Then she grabbed the rope she had dropped into the hole, clenched it between her feet and swung her hips over the abyss. With an excited but nervous glance at Brandon, she dropped out of sight, Brandon letting out rope as she went.

"Oh," Brandon heard resonate up. "Yeah. No wonder you broke through. It was only a matter of time."

Brandon peeked over the edge and saw Tril suspended about eight feet down, shining her flashlight up at the rim of the opening. "What is it?"

"These timbers look really old and rotten. They're only about eight feet long, but they gave way right near one end. Where you are looks like solid ground. But don't stand on the other side of the hole, that's where the timbers still are."

Brandon looked down at his feet, then across the hole. "Yeah. Okay." He peered down at the girl staring up at him, her face still illuminated by the gray light. "Why do your parents trust you so much?" He was still amazed that Tril's parents hadn't thrown a fit like his dad would have.

Tril looked up with a thoughtful look on her face, the only thing visible over the rim of the hole. "It's because they know I won't be a dumb-ass."

Brandon grunted. He wondered if he'd ever felt that trusted by either of his parents. Then, remembering some of the stupid things he'd done, didn't really blame them for being concerned about his well-being.

Tril looked down and shined the light below her, letting the beam play around the rocky walls. "Still can't see the bottom." With that, she doused the light and started to descend once more.

Brandon continued to play out the rope little by little as Tril climbed farther down. "How's it going?" he shouted at the mouth of the hole, not wanting to stand so close to it to look below.

"Pretty cool," she answered. "But it kind of stinks down here."

"See any bats?"

"No. Definitely no guano down here. At least not yet."

In the middle of feeding out the line, Brandon felt it suddenly go slack. "Everything okay?"

"Yeah. Just looking around. Really stinks. Kinda like... I don't know. I'd say roadkill, but it's somehow different than that."

Brandon found that thought more than a little disconcerting.

Tril could feel the harness bite into her thighs and shoulders again as Brandon reeled in the slack above her. She wished he'd leave it a little looser, but he probably wanted to feel like he was helping. With the climbing rope wrapped around one leg and trapped between her feet, she could hang there for some time without getting tired. But he didn't know that.

Taking a solid grip on the rope with her left hand she flipped on the flashlight with her right. She shone the light around her and saw that the lower she went, the further away the stone walls were. They were dark gray, like most of the stone in this area. Here and there she thought she saw the green traces of oxidized copper and the striations of the rock were clear, oriented at roughly a 75-degree angle. She mentally noted all of this for the discussion she knew she'd have with her mother, an amateur geologist, when she got home.

She looked up at the gray light of the sky above her and smiled to herself. She didn't really think there was any treasure down here, but it was a good excuse to convince Brandon to come along. He was nice enough but didn't know much when it came to the real world. Though when it came to the virtual world, she was sure he was an expert. She'd have been happy to let him do this part if she thought he was capable of it, but she honestly doubted his strength and ability to keep his wits about him. He was still a bit of a mystery when it came to survivability.

She wrinkled her nose at the stench which grew stronger with every foot she descended. Her only relief came in the occasional puff of fresh air that blew down from above. She was sure that was going to cease before long. The temperature had dropped significantly already, though she thought it would probably stabilize at around 55 degrees. She cursed herself for not thinking to wear a sweatshirt for this. But with gloves on, and the strain of climbing, she wouldn't be too cold.

Shining the light below proved frustrating because all she could see was empty blackness. She left the light on and continued down, her harness at first tightening and then relaxing when Brandon realized she was moving again.

Now she thought she could hear something, something rhythmic echoing up from the depths. She stared below as she lowered herself, the light spinning as it dangled from her belt, the light playing across the walls of the chamber which seemed to be closing in again. Then she thought she noticed something about fifteen feet below her. It looked like a giant eye, with an indescribably black iris. She realized she was looking at the bottom of the chamber. At least, the bottom for her. After several more feet, she landed on solid stone. There was yet another hole in this floor that continued into the earth, partially blocked by a big stone.

"You okay?" Brandon's voice sounded muffled and distant as it bounced off the walls to reach her ears.

She turned her head upward and shouted, "Yes. On the bottom." For a split second, she thought she saw his face over the rim of the opening, at least fifty feet above, but then it disappeared.

Turning her attention to her surroundings, she picked up the flashlight and shone it around the floor of the cave. It was only about eight feet in diameter, with a two-foot diameter opening slightly off-center. She looked at the stone that covered part of the hole and realized there was writing on it. On the other side of the big rock, she saw the familiar petroglyph. But no one had ever seen writing on the boulder before. Upon looking at the orientation of the Viking longship, she realized that the side that held the writing must have been faced down as the longship had faced skyward. The fall into the hole revealed its secret.

She dug into her pocket and pulled out the cell phone she'd denied existed. With the lousy coverage, she mainly used it for photos, which is how she put it to use now. She snapped picture after picture of the cryptic symbols from both near and far. She felt herself squirm and her feet bounce as she finished and stowed the phone in her pocket. *Wait until Brandon sees this,* she thought.

Carefully, she straddled the hole and directed the flashlight beam down into the emptiness. She may as well have been shining it into murky black waters, for all she could see.

Standing above the opening she could feel air surge up in a steady cadence, each pulse throwing up a fetid odor that made her think she had been lowered into a burial ground. The sound that accompanied the blasts of air made her think of the waves that crashed against the rocky shoreline. She wondered how far away the shore was from here. There could be a cavern below that ran all the way to the lake, and the repetitive wave action would act like a bellows thrusting the air upward. One such gust came just as she inhaled. The reek nearly made her puke.

She stepped back to the wall of the cave, trying to maximize the space between her and the source of her disgust. Why hadn't she seen anything through the hole? It couldn't be that far down, could it? An idea came to her.

Looking up she yelled, "Brandon!"

"What?"

"Mark the harness rope at the edge of the hole."

"What?" he called. She repeated the command several times before Brandon understood.

Finally convinced he was taking care of her request, she moved to the hole once more and crouched down, holding her hand over it. She could feel the puffs of air with every cycle of the waves. It was almost as if the earth itself was breathing. If it hadn't been so fetid, she would have been delighted. What could smell so bad? It was possible that something had fallen into the hole and died, but it would have had to make it through the second hole too, and then start decomposing abnormally fast given the hole had been open only two days.

She shone the light through the hole to the 'next level' and thought she saw something move. Just a shadow, nothing more. But something. Then a sound, or what she thought was a sound tickled her ears. Voices? No. One voice. The world felt different, like she was in a centrifuge that was slowly starting to spin. What was the voice saying? It was so low and deep and the words unintelligible. Something about winter, something about running. Something about death.

She saw her flashlight beam start to dance on the dark, stony walls around her. Why was it moving? Wasn't she still shining it in the hole? The puffs of putrid air hit her in the face causing her to pull back and stumble against the wall. This was all wrong. Somewhere back in her mind, a frightening realization came to the forefront of her consciousness. Air. She needed air.

With her eyes fighting to stay focused on the rope dangling in front of her she began to climb. She thought of calling out to her friend above... his name was... something. Hand over hand she pulled herself up, fearing that it was already too late to reach fresh air. Her muscles burned already and she could hardly keep her feet touching the rope, much less supporting her weight. With a spark of joy, she felt the safety line tighten. What's-his-name must know she's coming up.

Another foot or two higher she rose. Then her breathing came in slow, harsh gasps and she could feel her fingers loosen their grip on the rope, her strength leaving her body like water down a drain. Then, nothing.

Brandon felt the safety line suddenly go taut and it jerked him toward the anchoring tree. In a panic, he dug his feet in and, with the help of the friction of the rope around the trunk, prevented Tril from falling.

He turned toward the hole. "Tril! Tril!" He called. No response.

"Shit," he said to himself. Hand over hand he worked his way to the tree, being careful not to let his friend fall. Something had happened to her and he had to get her out. Fast. Taking a strong grip, he slowly moved around the tree so he was facing the hole, with the tree between him and it. Placing his right foot on the trunk he leaned back, pulling Tril up a small amount, then leaned to his right effectively engaging the friction of the tree again so he could pull himself upright, hand over hand up the rope. Then he disengaged the tree, leaned back, hauling on the rope, and again wrapped it on the trunk, repeating the procedure.

He discovered that Tril was heavier than she looked. For a minute he worried about the effect the rough, rocky edge of the hole would have on the rope. But it was apparently very rugged, showing minimal signs of wear. When his arms burned to the point he could hardly use them, he wrapped the rope around the tree several times and tied it off. He jumped to his feet and ran to the hole.

"Tril!" He tried to peek down but was afraid to get too close to the edge. Suddenly the round beam of the flashlight splayed across the far wall of the chamber.

Brandon cursed again. She was still about thirty feet down.

A blinding flash followed by a tooth-jarring rumble tore Brandon's attention skyward, just in time to get a face full of the downpour that unleashed on the stricken young man. The rain came down with such intensity that Brandon thought it had to let up almost as quickly as it had begun. But it didn't.

Dashing to the tree he untied and unwrapped the rope and renewed his rescue efforts. For a full five minutes he labored, sweat being swept away by the rain that drenched his hair and clothing. His hot breath took flight as white, misty exhalations in the cool, damp air. Brandon's work ceased when the rope met with instant and infinite resistance.

"Crap," he muttered. He must have smacked her against the bottom edge of the hole. Letting the rope out slightly, he wrapped it around the tree and tied it off again.

When he got to the edge of the hole, water was running into it at various points, sending miniature waterfalls to dissipate into the blackness of its depths. Tril was hanging limply, her head, arms and legs all dangling as though pulled by some unseen force below. Except for a small trickle of blood that ran down her face, she looked intact. Just not conscious. Brandon looked at the rope that was tight against the rocky ground, going back towards the tree a full eight feet before it raised enough that it would allow him to slide his fingers under it. Scanning the area, he quickly located a length of a dead tree about six inches in diameter. He ran and grabbed it and then stuck it between the rope and ground, sat down and started jamming it towards the hole's edge. When it was mere inches from dropping into the cave, he stood up and took one deep breath. Then he squatted down, gave the rope a twist so Tril's head was away from the underside of the rock, and heaved with all his strength.

Tril's body came up nearly even with the edge of the hole when her arm got stuck. Desperate, Brandon started to shuffle backward, hoping her body would correct itself and he could drag her out. But the ground had become slick and he lost his footing, kicking the log into the void and going down hard on his right side, dropping the rope. Tril's body fell back and the rope lashed hard onto the left side of Brandon's left leg, pinning it to the ground. He cried out in pain and frustration.

He struggled to free his leg, Tril's dead-weight pulling the rope taut on the limb. He used both hands to lift the rope and slid his leg out. A searing stinging radiated out from where the rough fibers had bitten into his flesh. He jumped to his feet, and unable to find another log, grabbed a rock and managed to wedge it under the rope. Once again, he squatted down, took a tight hold, and hoisted. This time, instead of trying to walk backward, he tried to stand upright. But the wet rope slipped through his fingers and he nearly toppled into the hole trying to catch it again. He looked at Tril's limp body dangling against the black pit. Staring failure full in the face, he chose what he hoped was the lesser of two evils.

CHAPTER ELEVEN

It was just before noon when there was a knock on Bill's front door. He peered through the door's window and Dr. Stephanie Crowe looked up and flashed him a girlish grin. Smiling to himself, he opened the door.

"To what do I owe the pleasure?" Bill asked. Impressed with his own smoothness, he motioned her in and took a glance at the gray, misty sky as he did.

"I needed to talk to you about my concerns," Steph said. She turned around just inside Bill's family room and locked her gaze on his.

"Concerns?"

"I'm really going to need your help looking for more evidence out on the lake."

"Hmm. Grab a seat. Do you want anything to drink?"

"I'm good," she said, taking a spot in one of the two loungers. "We need to see if we can figure out what happened to the people of Copper Harbor back in 1842."

"What do you expect to find out there?" Bill asked, raising one finger to point to the massive lake.

"I don't know. A diary, another ravaged body we can examine, weapons with DNA on them that we can test. Something."

Bill settled into the couch. "You know that lake has about the same surface area as South Carolina, right? And what we're looking for could be 400 feet below the surface?" He shook his head, the corners of his mouth pulled down. "What you're talking about could take forever. I still have a regular business to run. I'm not sure how much time I can give you."

"I'll pay. I have a grant specifically for this research."

"It's not a matter of pay," Bill said gently. "It's a matter of time. I can't just cancel other scheduled charters. It'd be the beginning of the end of my business."

Steph squirmed in her seat and any remnants of a smile fell from her face like the dead petals falling from a rose-blossom. "There is more to the story. If a bear or some animal was responsible for Copper Harbor disappearing in 1842, it'd be long dead by now. And if a Native American settlement disappeared long before Copper Harbor did, by the same means..."

Bill interrupted her. "Yes. But that's hardly a pattern."

"It happened twice before 1842. At least, it seems to have. I admit the data is pretty sparse and vague dating that far back. I'm sorry if I was misleading when I said anything about a bear, but my real theory is... kind of out there. But if I'm right, and something is going to occur again this winter, or next, we need to prepare for whatever is coming."

Bill examined the professor sitting in front of him. "What do you think it is?"

"I don't know. Only that it is fierce and nothing we've been able to defeat." She rubbed her temples. "Something we consider mythological, I guess?"

"And you're assuming the answers are 180 feet below the surface, somewhere out there?" He pointed in the direction of Lake Superior.

"It's been the first hard evidence since the disappearance. Yes. I think there is more out there."

Bill closed his eyes and dropped his chin, shaking his head. "Maybe. But I don't understand why you are so convinced whatever happened back then is a repeating cycle."

Steph leaned forward, resting her elbows on her knees. "There are writings from some of the missionaries from the summer of 1842. They were the stories, or prophecies, told to them by some of the elders of the local Chippewa and what has been passed down orally through my people. And it's all the same. Apparently, when the Earth eats one of its young and regurgitates them, a harsh winter will follow that includes an unstoppable fury. The records indicate that the prophecy was met in 1842, along with a harsh winter, and of course, the disappearance of Copper Harbor."

Bill stared, open-mouthed, at the pretty, young professor. "And?"

Steph's eyes widened. "And... the Chippewa signed a treaty in the fall of 1842, ceding the lands up around Copper Harbor to the United States. They got out of Dodge! And that winter, a 'harsh' one by all accounts, the winter of 1842 to 1843, the residents of Copper Harbor vanished."

Bill took a deep breath. "An interesting tale, for sure. But what makes you think we're in for it again? What does that even mean, 'the Earth eats one of its young'?"

Steph's shoulders slumped. "I'm not sure. But we can't wait around to find out," Steph insisted. "It's been 177 years since the last disaster. Things are going to fall into place sooner or later and we need to gather as much information as possible before we're staring down the barrel of a gun. And the current meteorological models are predicting a very cold winter."

Bill pinched the bridge of his nose between his thumb and two fingers, massaging. "Seems you've done a lot of research. But I imagine that if you dug hard enough, you could find a hundred crazy theories or prophecies about what happened to Copper Harbor. As it is, it'll be mid-September before I have a slot open to take you out again."

"You must take days off?"

"Yes. Those are 'days off'. I'd like to use those to figure out what I'm doing with my son." She looked at him quizzically and he elaborated, bringing her up to speed on their recent reunion. "Once things open up I can lock you in for a couple of days. But I can't start canceling outings to look for a solution to a problem that probably doesn't exist."

Steph nodded slowly, closing her eyes.

The front door banged open and Brandon burst through, water dripping from his hair. "Dad! Help! Tril went down the sinkhole and passed out and I can't get her out," the words came in a monotone flurry, packed together so tightly that it took Bill a moment to comprehend. Then he was on his feet, crashing out the door, Steph tight on his heels.

All three piled into Bill's truck and took off, mud spraying out behind spinning wheels.

"I told you to stay away from that," Bill said in a scathing tone. Brandon said nothing and Steph stole a peek at Bill, also remaining silent. Bill kept shaking his head, his lips pulled tight against his teeth as he focused on the rainy street in front of them.

When they'd gone as far as they could by truck, Bill stomped on the brakes, sending all three passengers lurching forward before bouncing back against the seat. In a flurry, he jammed the drive-shaft to 'park' and shut down the truck, his door already open and one foot nearly to the ground. Without a word or look back, he started jogging up the hill to where they would find the entrance to the subterranean cavern. Steph and Brandon scrambled behind him, unable to keep up with the driven man.

Topping the hill, Bill instantly spotted the rope tied to the tree, the other end disappearing into the hole. He slowed and approached the hole cautiously, but there was still a determined purpose behind his stride.

"Son-of-a-bitch," he cursed. He looked down at the girl who was still dangling from her harness, arms and legs drooping downward in her unconsciousness. He reached for the rope and said, "I'll lift her up. You two grab an arm or leg and pull her in." He heaved and the girl's body came up to the level of the ground. Brandon dropped to his knees, took hold of a foot and pulled. Steph immediately grabbed the other leg. Together, they pulled the girl to safety and well away from the mouth of the hole.

Bill flipped Tril over and patted her gently on the face. "Tril. Tril!" He could see she was breathing. Then her eyes started to flutter and he redoubled his efforts. "Tril!"

Slowly her eyes opened, then quickly blinked in the rain that had barely slackened. He could see her confusion, and when she tried to sit up, she instantly decided that lying down was the better course.

"Tril, are you okay? What happened?"

She turned to look at him, water mixed with blood running down her forehead. "Mr. Hitze? I don't know. I thought I heard a voice or something, got dizzy... I think I was getting carbon dioxide poisoning or something. I started to climb up to get air and that's all I remember."

"A voice? Poisoning? Geez!" Brandon exclaimed, his head rolling back in alarm as he sat on his heels. "Is she going to be okay?"

"Take some deep breaths," Steph said.

Tril took a few very deep breaths and smiled. She looked at Steph, "Who are you?" Then at Brandon, "Hey, Brandon." Then at Bill, "Mr. Hitze? How did you get here?" She started to cough.

"She's loopy," Steph said.

"Get some clean air, Tril," Bill said. He took her wrist in one hand and felt her pulse, staring intently at her the whole time. "Do you feel okay?"

"I guess so." She sat up. "I'm still a little foggy." She wrinkled her eyes and frowned, then shook her head. Propping herself in a sitting position with both arms, she sat in the puddles of water and looked at the miniature stream that ran into what might have become her tomb.

"What voice?"

Her drunken eyes turned to Brandon. "What?"

"You said you heard a voice?"

After a minute of concentration, she said, "Yeah. I think. But weird." Bill could see her trying to pull the memories forward. "It was deep, like the deepest man's voice ever." She shook her head. "I dunno. I was probably hallucinating already."

Brandon stared at her and a visible shudder racked his body. "I'm sorry I didn't get you up faster," he said.

A snarl distorted the girl's face. "Not your fault, you idiot. You got me up. Everything's fine."

"Still," he said. As he knelt there next to her, he awkwardly wrapped one arm around her shoulders in a pseudo-hug. Eventually, Tril hugged him back. Bill tapped his son on the arms, scowling at him. Brandon took the cue and released her. "What was down there?" he asked.

Tril's eyes brightened, flashing with the excitement of a child on their birthday. "It was pretty cool. This dark rock all the way down. Mom calls it Copper Harbor Conglomerate. Anyway, the chamber opened up more, about ten feet in diameter. At the bottom was another hole. The petroglyph rock was partially blocking it."

"Another hole? Where?" Bill asked.

"At the bottom of this hole. It was pitch black down there. I couldn't even see with the light. And there was an awful smell coming up in, well, puffs. Like it was breathing up at me."

"Breathing?" Steph asked.

"Like that. I think somewhere down there the water must have been getting in with the waves and pumping the air up through the hole. Sounded like it."

Steph cast a meaningful glance at Bill.

"Oh yeah. There was writing on the rock, the one with the Viking ship on it. I took some pictures with my phone."

"Writing?" Steph said. "Can I see?"

Tril showed the professor the photos she'd taken, a victorious smile on her face.

"Can you email those to me?"

"When I get home, I can. Give me your email address."

"We can do that later. Gather up this rope," Bill commanded. "We should get Tril to the emergency room, so she can get checked out. I'll call your folks from the hospital."

"We can call them from here. They can take me, Mr. Hitze," Tril said. She pulled out her cell phone and walked around until she had a decent signal and called her parents. "They're on their way," she said.

Bill caressed his forehead. He would have taken her to the hospital, but Tril's parents would probably be waiting by the time they hiked back to the road. He wondered how they'd react to this near disaster. They didn't seem to get too worked up about stuff, but this was their daughter. Would they be angry with Brandon? If they were, he wouldn't blame them.

As they gathered up the ropes, Tril measured the distance between the mark Brandon had made and where she had been tied at the end. About sixty feet. Tril nodded in satisfaction and put the ropes away.

Bill and Steph each took one of Tril's arms as they walked back to the road. She seemed solid on her feet, but her mind was still wandering.

"The next chamber must be at least as deep as the first, if it goes all the way to water," Tril said. "I bet it curves toward the lake."

"You aren't going down there again, so don't worry about it," Bill stated. "And you and I are going to have a talk, Brandon." The young man wilted.

Steph caught Bill's eye but said nothing.

Ken and Diane Post were waiting by Bill's truck when they stepped onto the road. They ran forward and hugged Tril, asking her if she was okay. After she relayed the story of what happened, they thanked Brandon, then Bill and Steph for helping her. Then they loaded her in their little four-wheel-drive SUV and headed towards the emergency room.

Watching them go, Steph pulled Bill close so she could quietly say, "The Earth sure did 'regurgitate' up that 'young' lady after 'eating' her."

Bill deflated. "Shit."

After seeing how accepting, though alarmed, Tril's parents had been with the story of their adventure,

Brandon hoped his father's anger would subside. But the silence during the ride back home sucked away his hope like dust-bunnies up a vacuum hose.

Brandon's next big hope was that Dr. Crowe would stick around until his dad chilled out a little. But like all unsympathetic adults, she talked quietly with his dad for a few seconds, gave Brandon a small wave and a weak smile, got into her truck and left.

Bill looked at Brandon. "Get in the house."

Brandon took a deep breath and did as he was told. He braced himself mentally for the trouble he was in. Not that he should be in *that* much trouble. He didn't go down the hole. And he had almost gotten Tril out by himself. When he couldn't, he came and got help, like a responsible person.

Bill closed the door quietly. "I told you at least twice, to stay away from there." His words were like a razor-blade, a lot of danger packed into a simple looking package. Treat it carelessly and you'll be left bleeding out on the floor. Bill took a deep breath and his eyes hardened. "You could have been killed. You don't know how stable that rock around the hole is. What were you thinking?"

"We're fine," Brandon said.

"That isn't the point," Bill said. Now the volume was increasing. "In case you haven't noticed, you don't know squat about the outdoors because all you've done is play video games. You can't just go climbing around in caves that open up. The air can be toxic and you don't know it until it's too late. That could have killed Tril." His emphasis on the word 'killed' made Brandon's stomach churn.

"I'm not a complete idiot," Brandon said, his own voice rising. "I stayed on top."

Bill turned away in disgust. "Oh good. So, if it had caved in, then what? I told you to stay away from that hole."

What the hell did his old man want him to do? He's the reason Brandon was up here, north of no-where, in the first place. "Fine. I guess I'll just stay home and play video games 'cause it's safe."

Bill spun on him, pointing a finger at him. "No. You won't. You're done with video games for a week. Until you learn to follow the rules."

"What? That's bullshit!"

"Watch your mouth. You want to shoot for two weeks?"

Brandon glowered but could see that arguing was useless. Playing video games and kicking around outside was all there was to do up here. He had to get away from his dad. He went to the door and started to open it.

"Where are you going?"

"What do you care?" Brandon responded, letting the door slam shut behind him.

For a minute Bill considered going after Brandon. Instead, he flopped down on the couch and sighed. This parenting wasn't easy. Might it have been easier if he'd been doing it full time the last ten years? It wasn't worth asking the question.

Brandon was stubborn and clearly didn't like being here. Now, when he finds someone to hang out with, he does something reckless and dangerous. It was good for Brandon to be out and about rather than on the TV or games, but Bill felt a keen biting in his gut when he thought of his son in danger.

He knew that Trillium Joy was a bright girl who knew the outdoors. And her parents were both retired professors or something and very outdoorsy. But it was obvious she was still a young girl and there were things she didn't know, despite spending most of her time in nature. Kids are always doing stupid shit, as was evidenced by the constant barrage of bad news on TV. It wasn't because they were bad; just not wise.

Crap. Had he over-reacted with a week of no games? Now he was second-guessing himself. Brandon had at least done the right thing and had come to get help. He'd put some trust in his father and gotten punished. Gah! Too late now, it was done. But he would have to try and use the time to take Brandon out himself and teach him a thing or two to keep him safe. Maybe get to know him better.

When Brandon came back, they'd have a talk. A calm talk. He could explain why he had grounded him and that he just wanted to keep him safe. Hopefully, he would understand that.

Bill rubbed his forehead, reluctantly moving on to the next pressing matter, the one he didn't want to think about. But there it was, standing in front of him, arms akimbo, chest puffed out, legs shoulder-width apart; that stupid prophecy. As dumb as it was, what had just happened certainly seemed to match it. The words had seemed impossible, that the Earth would 'eat one of its young' and 'regurgitate' them. It had sounded like complete nonsense, and so singular that nothing like it could ever happen. Yet Tril had been swallowed up by the Earth and spit out again. Dammit.

Didn't Ernest say something about the coming winter being predicted to be a harsh one? Wonderful.

Though a lot of the Copper Harbor residents left for the winter, he and Brandon would be here. And too many people he knew and liked would stay as well. Could he afford to ignore what seemed to be happening? Maybe he and Steph would find something that would shed light on what had happened back in 1842 so they could prevent it from happening again.

Maybe he needed to use his days off to ensure the town's survival.

Brandon jumped on his bicycle and rode away from the house, prepared to ignore his dad's voice should he come out and yell at him to come back. But there was no volley of commands pursuing him and he rode away unfettered.

Water splashed away from the front tire of his bike as he drove through unavoidable puddles. It reminded him of when he and his mom had first moved to Minneapolis and the first thing she dug out was his little bike so he could ride around in circles on their small concrete driveway in front of the townhouse they rented. Then, he purposely aimed for the puddles, picturing a bomb going off as the droplets sprayed away in a circle. Now, he couldn't avoid them.

Just like he couldn't avoid his dad. Why did his dad have to be such a hard-case? It's like he didn't know how to be a parent. *Do this, don't do that. You did this too much. Are you an idiot?* What a pain.

Where was he going to go now? The only person he really knew was Tril and he'd feel like a moron showing up there again after ten minutes. She probably wasn't back from the hospital in any case.

Then he had a thought. Something that may give him something to do here in the middle of no-where that he might like. And maybe he could even make some money.

His dad probably wouldn't like it, but then it seemed like his dad wouldn't like anything he did anyway.

CHAPTER TWELVE

Brandon was riding around looking for the largest house in town when a very nice, white, four-wheel-drive truck slowed down next to him. When he glanced at it, the darkly tinted passenger side window slid down with an electric whine. Jeff Jansen peered out at him from behind the steering wheel.

"Hey, Brandon. I thought that was you. Hold on a sec." The truck stopped and Jansen waved Brandon over to the open window.

"I'm glad I spotted you. I need a hand unloading this landscaping stone." He gestured to about twenty plastic bags piled in the bed, apparently filled with decorative rock. "I can pay you for your time. Then maybe I can show you around the place."

This is just who Brandon was looking for. Maybe he could get in on helping design the next phone app that hits as big as 'Rabid Turtles'. "Sure," he answered. "Where do you live, again?"

"Just throw your bike in the back and climb in. It isn't far," Jansen said.

Brandon hoisted his bicycle up over the side of the truck's bed, slamming one of the pedals against the top of the shiny, white fender. It left a scratch. *Oh, nice!*

Good way to start, idiot! He figured he'd just screwed up any goodwill that Jansen might have for him. As he climbed into the cab, his face sullen, he told Jansen what had happened.

"Don't worry about it," Jansen said. He gave Brandon a big smile. "It's just a truck."

Brandon couldn't believe his good fortune. Who had such a cool attitude about what must be a 65,000 dollar truck?

"I'm sorry. You don't have to pay me to unload. I kind of owe you."

Jansen waved his hand dismissively. "Naw. Forget it. Shit happens." He pointed up the road. "This is it, right up here."

Brandon looked at a beautiful house that sat near the top of one of the slopes overlooking the harbor. The huge wooden door, complete with black iron hinges that reached arrow-shaped face-plates across its face, was framed by thick pillars crafted from rough-cut tree-trunks. These supported a roof that projected out to shelter the front porch from the rain and snow. Above this was a big, triangular, glass window that reached to the pinnacle of the steeply slanted roof. Through this window, Brandon could see a wrought-iron chandelier with candle-shaped lights that gave off a warm glow in the gray afternoon. The house extended to both sides of the door, a single story to the right that featured a picture window, and two stories to the left which then angled forward from the house with an attached three-car garage.

"Wow," Brandon exclaimed. "Nice house."

"Thanks," Jansen said through a smile. He wheeled into the wide driveway and pulled in a circle so the truck was facing down the driveway again. Then he backed it up to the edge of the yard.

"We gotta carry them around to the back of the house. But you look strong. Shouldn't be a problem." Jansen jumped out and before Brandon knew it, he'd opened the tailgate and lifted the bicycle carefully down onto the pavement. Then he smiled conspiratorially at the young man and hoisted one of the bags of stone onto his shoulder, grunting. Brandon mimicked him. "Follow me."

It only took about twenty minutes for the two of them to unload the truck, though Brandon was taxed by the end. The bags were heavier than they looked. He took some solace in noticing that the man he was helping looked at least as wiped out as he. Both of them were sweating profusely, even in the cooling late afternoon air.

Jansen led Brandon into the garage where, next to the empty stall where he parked his truck, there was a stylish sports-car in one stall and a snowmobile and four-wheeler in the third.

"My toys," Jansen said simply. Then he escorted Brandon into the house.

Brandon was amazed at the extravagance, having only seen amenities of this quality in the home of his wealthy friend down in Minneapolis. And that, he'd only seen once. He thought it much like being in a fancy hotel. Granite counter-tops, or marble, he didn't know which, dark, rich, wooden floor throughout most of the first floor, with what looked like hewn stone in the entryway. Thick wooden beams spanned the cathedral ceiling above the family room that reached to the peak of the big window above the front door. A stone fireplace on the back wall of the house climbed to the roof as well. He couldn't help but think of the dinky little house he'd be going home to where he could bounce a ping-pong ball off one wall of the family room and it would hit the opposite wall before hitting the ground.

"Wow. This is really nice."

"It's as much an investment as it is a home," Jansen said. "Either I'll get married and bring my wife here, or I'll end up selling it for a profit. Win, win." He called Brandon over to the picture window that looked out the front of the home. From that vantage, they could look down at the harbor, the waters of which were black with broken streaks of white where it rolled in the gusty late-summer breeze. "This kind of view could sell the house *you're* living in."

Brandon looked at his host but the man just continued to stare out the window with a satisfied grin on his face. He chose not to say anything, though he felt as though he'd just been insulted. An insult based on truth.

"Come on. I'll show you my office and game room where I do my work. It's pretty cool."

Jansen led him to a staircase that descended into a finished basement. The stairs emptied into another great-room where four garden-level windows lined the left wall. There were three doors along the right wall. At the far end of the room was a huge screen, movie theater-like, though a scale smaller. Eight comfortable chairs were aligned for viewing, four in front, four behind. And like a theater, the front seating was at a level lower than the rear. To either side of the array of chairs was a set of two steps that descended to a sunken floor where the front row viewers sat.

"That's the game and movie area," Jansen said.

"Holy cow. That's awesome!"

Jansen nodded then pointed to the center doorway, the only door that stood ajar. "That's my office." He stepped in and turned on the lights. Brandon followed and saw a desk facing out that was covered with papers and another, long, built-in desk and bookshelf along the right wall where a computer was situated. This desk was also littered with books and papers. Brandon looked around, silent.

"This is where it all happens," Jansen said. Then the cheery smile slackened and the corners of his mouth twitched. "But I haven't even come close to 'Rabid

Turtles' again. Gotta come up with something new." He laid a hand on Brandon's shoulder. "That's where I was hoping you could help out. Too bad your dad doesn't want you working with me."

Brandon's heart leaped and fell in an instant. "He doesn't really pay that much attention to what I'm doing," he said hopefully.

Jansen chuckled, leading Brandon back into the theater. "I don't want to cross your dad. Don't worry about it. I just thought it might be fun for you."

"I'll talk to him. I'd love to help out."

Jansen grunted. Then he walked down in front of the viewing chairs and motioned for Brandon to join him.

"You ever play video-games on a fricking-huge-screen TV?"

Brandon shook his head, the smile tickling his ears.

"Come on," Jansen said pushing buttons on a remote and handing Brandon a game controller. "You're gonna love this."

CHAPTER THIRTEEN

"Maybe they were trying to get to Isle Royale," Bill said. The vessel's gentle rock was accompanied by the squeal of the rubber bumpers that were being squeezed between the dock and the boat's side. He saw Professor Stephanie Crowe's eyebrows knit in thought. She'd been relieved, yet unsurprised, when Bill had offered to take her out on one of his days off.

"Why do you say that?" she asked.

Bill pulled out a paper map that showed all of Lake Superior. Isle Royale was a long green shape in the northwest edge of the lake. There was also a penciled dot just to the northwest of Copper Harbor. "If you trace a line between Copper Harbor and where we found the body," Bill pointed at the spot, then continued in a straight line right to where it intersected Isle Royal. "Look where it leads." He stabbed the map image of the island with his finger.

Steph seemed to be thinking, certainly not throwing out his theory as baseless. "Okay. If that's the case, why? Why would they try getting to Isle Royale in the middle of one of the worst winters in history?"

"Like you said, fleeing from something. That one guy's head sure was..."

"But why not just go down to Houghton? They had dog-sleds, they had trails and snowshoes."

Bill shrugged. "I don't know."

Steph's face lightened slightly, the morning's autumn sun shining on her dark hair. "Do you happen to have a down-imaging fish-finder or just a 2D sonar?"

"Both. But I usually only use the 2D. Why?"

"I have an idea that might speed things up for us. Let's test your theory." She looked around Bill's boat, checking that she had the Lakefly and all the necessary gear to run it. "I'm ready to go if you are."

Bill nodded and cast off. Then he set a course for where they'd found the body. As they sped across the water, white foam launching away from the surging bow, Steph sat in the passenger seat, looking forward, her face uncharacteristically stoic.

"What's up?" Bill asked.

She glanced at him, then down at her hands. Without looking up she said, "I got that petroglyph inscription translated."

Bill waited for her to continue. When she didn't, he said, "And?"

Steph drew in a deep breath, let it out in a huff and with a weak smile said, "It said, 'Take your ships and flee before the ice. It comes in winter. Winter means death. Flee or die.'"

Bill stared at her, unsure of what to make of that. "That doesn't sound good." Steph shook her head. "Are you sure?"

"There was no question. The writing was clear enough to make out and there weren't any alternate translations."

"We've come out here to find answers," Bill said, nodding at the expansive lake. "Hopefully, we'll find some."

Brandon smiled to himself as he pedaled. The plan he and Jansen had devised was working perfectly. During the remainder of the summer, Brandon went over to Jansen's house two or three days a week and helped him work on a new game Brandon had presented. Jansen had even gone so far as to formally hire him, making him sign employment paperwork for the Department of Homeland Security and the IRS. He had to sign some sort of forms about intellectual property and something else about not talking about their work. Jansen told him it was all a bunch of formalities. In the end, Brandon was getting paid to work on a game! Sure, it was minimum wage, but it was awesome. He'd even get to take breaks to play video games on Jansen's huge TV.

Maybe it wouldn't be so bad, living up here in the wilds.

In their first couple of workdays, Jansen had already taught him some basics about programming, though he knew most of the concepts already, having taken a computer class in school back in Minneapolis. But Jansen taught him some of the specifics for working with phone apps. He even had Brandon do some of the easier programming and testing. By the end of summer or early autumn, they'd have a working game that Brandon could 'beta test'. That meant he'd get to play it and see if there were any bugs in the code.

As he biked his way to Jansen's opulent house, he envisioned making a career with the man. Of course, he'd have to tell his dad. Eventually.

Jansen had always known he was a genius. Hiring that kid was a stroke of brilliance. The idea Brandon had come up with would set Jansen up with at least another million, if not more. The best part about it was that Brandon agreed to work for an hourly wage, giving up any rights to the royalties. All the profits from this endeavor would go to Jansen, while he'd end up paying Brandon barely a thousand dollars. Certainly not more than twelve-hundred. He'd have to find more dumb kids to work for him.

Once this game got to market, he'd be done with Brandon. He didn't want to teach him so much that the kid could go off on his own and compete with him. Nope. That's not smart business.

The best part about all of it was he'd used Bill Hitze's son, right under his nose.

"We're here," Bill said, eyeing his GPS.

Steph told him on the way out how she thought they could test his theory of the town fleeing to Isle Royal. If one had gone through the ice, others would certainly have as well. She believed that if they used Bill's fish-finder in 2D sonar mode, they would see if there were any anomalies on the floor of the lake. Then they could use the down-imaging mode to get a better resolution as to what it might be. If they were still uncertain or had located something interesting, they could launch the Lakefly and get video feeds from the bottom. Bill thought it was an excellent idea, though he wasn't anxious to find more bodies.

Dr. Crowe had received funding to further explore the possibility that the first body had been from the missing population of Copper Harbor as it would start to answer a very intriguing historical mystery. If there was something to this Native American legend, the best way to figure out what they were up against was to try to locate more of the missing. And it was as likely as not, others could be found in the depths of the Great Lake.

"Okay. Set a course for Isle Royal and let's start scanning."

Bill clicked on the fish-finder and a colorful display of lines started to trace across the screen from right to left. It was mostly white as that was the empty water below them. Then, near the bottom of the lake the ground appeared as a mix of yellow, red, green and purple, the colorful band rising and falling as the depth varied. However, at present, the bottom appeared very flat and not changing much at all, though it appeared to be getting deeper as the boat moved to the northwest.

"I really wish I could get my hands on that axe-head," Steph said suddenly.

"We might be able to find it again. I wrote the GPS coordinates down."

"I'm just not sure how we'd get it up. I don't think the Lakefly could carry something that heavy, even if it had the means to grab it."

Bill continued watching the fish-finder. "We might be able to figure something out."

"Like what?" Steph asked.

Bill looked at the pleasant woman. "I dunno. Maybe attach a kind of lasso to the Lakefly and have it drop it over the axe-head. Something like that?"

She looked at him and her face beamed, eyes sparkling. "Something like that just might- Whoa! What's that?" She pointed at the digital display that showed a distinct change in the surface of the lake floor.

Bill turned back to the monitor and saw the lakebed surface suddenly rise slightly, then fall back down. It did this twice more. "Probably some rocks on the bottom."

"Turn us around and let's look at it with the down imaging," Steph insisted. "Just to make sure it isn't anything important."

Flipping a switch, the monitor changed to a mostly black image, the bottom a shade of light brown. As he swung the boat around, he saw something pictured that caught his eye. Judging from the look on Steph's face, she noticed it too.

"Is that some sort of pack?" she asked. "It looks like a big pack! Stop!"

Bill shifted to neutral and they stared together at what most certainly looked more like something man-made than a pile of rocks. But there was something slightly off about it. A side looked very flat and it stuck straight up from the lake bed. It gave him the impression of-

"A dog-sled?" Steph asked. "Okay, we're launching the Lakefly right here. Take down the GPS reading." She turned and started setting up her transmitter and video monitor while Bill jotted down the coordinates of their location. "This is so exciting," she said. Her face was positively radiant. "This could be huge." Then she gave Bill a smile that melted his insides. "And it may be because of your theory."

"I...uh...answers, I hope." Bill stammered. His brain had apparently melted at her smile too. He'd wanted to say he hoped they would get answers to what might happen during the winter. He wanted to be prepared.

"Even if this is a wild goose chase, and nothing happens to the town, I'll definitely make sure you are included in my paper. You've been instrumental and this is a big discovery."

Bill had heard that publishing was a very big thing to researchers and her comment proved it. For a split-second, he hoped he wasn't being played, that she'd made up the whole prophecy thing just to get him out here. He filed the thought away for later.

She put down the remote control and grabbed one end of the remote submersible. "Can you help me get this in?"

Bill leaped forward and the two of them lowered the Lakefly into the gently rolling water. Steph picked up the controls and had the little submarine diving in a heartbeat, its long antenna trailing out behind it.

Anxiously, the researcher and the fisherman watched the video feed as the device dove into the 300 feet of water. The monitor image got darker and darker until it was all black. Steph flipped a switch and a beam of light illuminated the screen as the search lamp of the Lakefly clicked into action. For several anxious minutes, they watched as nothing but the occasional speck of debris passed through the field of view. Bill jumped with excitement when a big lake trout swam past, apparently checking out the alien light in its domain. Steph, however, was not phased by the appearance of the fish at all.

At last, the bottom came into view and the couple shifted forward on their seats, leaning forward in anticipation. The excitement dissipated as Steph worked the miniature submarine around in a circle with nothing to see but a sandy lake floor.

"What the heck?" Steph said. "Something is down here, but where is it?"

"Just keep expanding the circle. We know something is there. We'll find it," Bill said. His experience as a fisherman taught him that sometimes you just had to be patient and persist.

Finally, the light fell across a shape that rose from the bottom. Steph slowed the Lakefly down and approached it.

"That isn't a pack," Bill said, his voice heavy.

"I'd say not," Steph answered. "But it is what we came here looking for."

Through occasionally flickering static the image of a body needed no imagination to discern. It looked to be dressed in heavy winter wear, not of the current vintage. Steph maneuvered the sub over and around the body, recording notes on a hand-held digital recorder that sat on the seat next to the monitor. "Hard to tell for sure, but it looks female. No apparent trauma that I can see." She looked at Bill who shook his head, confirming her statement.

She returned to the circular search pattern, still not having found whatever they'd seen on the fish-finder. The Lakefly continued its slow cruise and then another shape, this one more like what they'd seen, materialized out of the darkness. As she steered in closer it was clear to see that there was a large pack, partially buried, sitting atop a dog-sled that was falling apart. They stared at it together in silence as the light fell across the bodies of the team, still harnessed.

Finally, Steph said, "Dog-sled all right. Way out here."

Bill just stared at the screen.

Steph resumed her search and in a short time discovered another body. This one was male and the barrel of a long-gun protruded from the mud and sand next to him. As she continued, she found body after body, all dressed in heavy winter attire. They located three more dog-sleds, the four sleds together forming the shape of a small square. Bodies within the square were largely female or children, while men's bodies were scattered outside. Guns and various axes and weapons of all sorts were scattered throughout the watery mass grave. When the count had reached sixteen bodies, Steph had seen enough and started to bring the Lakefly to the surface.

A grim silence enveloped them.

"I thought I'd be excited to make such a discovery," Steph said, her voice sounding deflated. "But there is something decidedly wrong about this. I feel more like I've uncovered some horrible truth that shouldn't have come to light."

Bill nodded sullenly. "It's an important discovery, Steph. Discovering the truth doesn't mean you created it."

She smiled weakly. "But what did create it? We still don't know."

Bill grunted, then squinted his eyes and made a circular motion with his finger as a thought struck him. "Looks like they were circling the wagons."

Steph looked at him, a puzzled expression on her face.

"The way things were laid out down there. It was like they circled the dog-sleds into a defensive position, like in the old west."

Steph's eyes raised and she stared out across the sparkling water. Then she nodded. "Yes, but none of these bodies were mangled like the first one we found closer to shore."

Bill shrugged. "I guess we raised as many questions as we answered, huh? So, what's next?"

"We'll have to get those bodies raised so they can be examined and laid to rest. We should be able to do some DNA testing to determine if they are ancestors of the folks we know descended from Copper Harbor."

"How soon do you think we'll get that stuff?"

"Not soon enough. The earliest we'll be able to get results from testing will be next spring or summer. I hope. Until then, I'm just hoping we can get all of these bodies recovered so I can examine their attire and some of the weapons. This will be a major operation with legal and ethical questions that need to be answered. I'm not sure we'll get any of them up yet this fall."

Bill's head dropped. Already halfway through September, the lake would soon become too perilous for such an operation. What if something down there could provide a warning or an answer to what had happened so many years ago? Steph looked similarly frustrated.

The Lakefly broke the surface and Bill and Steph quietly pulled it aboard and stowed it away for the ride back to shore.

"How far out here are we?" Steph asked.

"About sixteen miles," Bill replied. "If they were headed to Isle Royal, they had a long way to go."

Steph nodded her head, her eyes distant. "None of those bodies appeared to have been traumatized. Looks like they all drowned. If they had formed up a defense, don't you think we would have found signs of an attack?"

Bill considered that for a minute. "Unless, when they got everyone so close together, the ice finally broke."

"Yeah. I don't know. At this point, we have to look at what we know. First, fourteen miles out we find a body that was clearly attacked or traumatized in some way. It appears he had an axe with him. Then, two miles farther out, there are a bunch more bodies, armed, that don't appear traumatized and that were traveling with at least four dog-sleds. The first guy we know is from the appropriate time frame to have been one of the missing residents of Copper Harbor. The others look like they are as well, though we don't know that.

"They must be more of the missing people. Why else would there be a mass of bodies out there with no boat? And there were kids with them." Steph grimaced at the memory of the smaller bodies. "Armed. They were running from something. I just can't figure out why they came out on the ice. Why not just head to Houghton, like you said?

"What could cause an entire village, that was clearly well-armed, to flee recklessly out onto the ice?" Steph questioned aloud.

Bill threw his hands up. "Something freaking awful. And we might get the answer this winter."

Brandon was in the middle of mowing down mutant-zombie-Nazis when his dad came in from another outing with Steph. He didn't know what they were up to now and refused to care. His father looked at him in surprise.

"Not working today?"

Brandon paused the game and stared at the screen, his heart skipping a beat. He looked up. "What?"

"Jansen doesn't have you working today?" his father repeated.

"I-"

Bill scowled and crossed his arms across his chest. "Do you think I'm a complete idiot, Brandon? I know what you've been up to, working for Jansen on some video game or something."

Brandon was dumbfounded. How had his dad found him out? He'd been so careful, so nonchalant. He'd only told Tril and asked her to keep it a secret. Had she blabbed? Surely, she wouldn't do that.

"Jansen's been bragging about it around town," Bill said.

"I'm making good money and-" Brandon started to protest.

Bill held up his hands, silencing him. "Listen. I told you Jansen is a shit-heel. But you won't believe me. I'm glad you're getting paid to do something fun. But mark my words. Do not trust that guy."

"He's paying me..."

"I've warned you. Everyone has a choice. And every choice has a consequence. Remember that."

CHAPTER FOURTEEN

Over the closing weeks of autumn, Steph was able to arrange for the recovery of the bodies, but they had only managed to get three, a man, a woman and a child, along with three weapons before the weather turned too unpredictable to proceed. Unfortunately, the good weather didn't return in time to continue before the State Police said they would not go out on the water until after the spring thaw.

Steph was allowed to take the musket, sword, and axe back to her lab at the university, along with samples of the clothing from each of the deceased. She was able to look at the bodies long enough to determine that they had not been subjected to horrific or traumatic injuries, most likely having drowned.

Through a wickedly cold and snowy November and well into December she worked on the specimens she'd gathered. The DNA tests had been sent out to a lab with the optimistic hopes they would be completed by the end of February. From what she could tell, everything about the find pointed to these people being from the area around the time of the mysterious disappearance. All through this process, Bill was involved in some way or another. First with finding the bodies, now with helping her track down living relatives of the disappeared so they could ask if they ever received any oral histories. Frequently they dined together to discuss their findings.

"So, I'm really leaning towards a conclusion," Steph said one night, sipping a glass of wine as they waited for their ordered meal. Bill nodded anxiously, waiting for her to continue. "I'm almost certain those people are all from the missing Copper Harbor population. I'm certain the DNA tests will prove it."

Bill dropped his forehead onto the table, then looked up. "I was hoping you had a theory about what was after them."

"Sorry," she gave him an impish grin and reached for her wine.

Bill's eyes narrowed as he considered her demeanor. "There *is* a real prophecy, right? A threat to the area?"

Steph choked on her wine and quickly put the glass down, wiping her chin with her hand. "Yes! Yes!" she said. "Of course. I'm sorry, it's just that, even in light of that whole possibility, I still am excited about finding out where the people went. The professor in me."

Bill sat back against the booth's seat. Then he huffed out a weak laugh. "I'm glad to know you weren't lying. But at the same time, I kind of wish you had been."

She reached across and took his hand with both of hers. "I wouldn't lie to you, Bill. This is too important."

Bill looked at her smaller hands grasping his, smiled and met her shining, brown, eyes. "We still have a bigger question." Then his smile melted into pursed lips. Squinting at Steph he said, "What were they running from? And why go out on the ice? Especially where they had to know, or at least suspect, it was getting too thin."

Steph released his hand and grasped her glass. She took another sip and shook her head slowly. "I still have no idea."

"What do the native legends say about it? That it was too big or something?"

"That it was too big, or too strong, too powerful. Something they couldn't defeat."

"If they ran out onto the ice, that means there was something that was preventing them from going south to Houghton. Something, or someone, they couldn't get past," Bill said.

"An army of some sort?" Steph said.

"Maybe. They could have had sentries watching the ice on both shores of the peninsula." He shook his head. "Naw. Someone would have known about a force that big. And why would they have been there in the first place?"

"An alien army?" Steph shrugged, even as she posed the question.

"That's as possible as anything because we have no clue," Bill's voice raised at the end of his sentence, frustration breaking the surface.

Neither one spoke, both looking around the Houghton restaurant in which they sat. They had discovered a clue to the whereabouts of the population that vanished over 150 years ago. Just a clue. An ominous clue. If there was something to Steph's prophecy, they needed so much more.

"We're going to have to look around the area, see how hard it would be to cut off access to the south," Steph said.

"There are a couple of natural barriers, but there's plenty of room to go around those. Unless those ways were blocked somehow," Bill said. He thought for a minute. "But when the team from Houghton went up, they didn't mention any obstacles, did they?"

Steph shook her head. "There were some downed trees, but nothing they felt was unusual. They didn't know anything was wrong until they got to town and found it empty. I'm sure there are still two or three buildings up there that were around back in 1842. We should take a look at them."

"Jotnar's Tavern, I think, has been there since the dawn of time. It's been modified, but there may be something of the original place there still. And I think old Paavo Silkula's place may be original. Looks like it is."

Steph snickered and leaned back as the meal arrived. After the waitress departed, she said, "I'll come up tomorrow and we can look around. Is that okay?"

"Perfect."

Settled into his new home, Brandon spent most of his time on schoolwork, testing his new game, and hockey practice. He was glad the high school had a team, a good team. With the brutal weather, he and Tril didn't spend nearly as much time outside. Well, he didn't. He suspected she still did, the way she talked about snowshoeing and cross-country skiing. She must go on trails because in most places the trees were so packed together, it looked like you could hardly move between them.

But now that they were on Christmas break, Tril seemed bound and determined to drag him out into the cold with her. And when he said cold, he meant COLD. For the last several weeks the temperature had not gone over 12 degrees Fahrenheit, and lately, it had been hovering around zero. Though he hadn't lived here since he was five, he heard enough grumbling from the long-timers to know that even they thought it unseasonably chilly.

He glanced out the window at the old-fashioned thermometer his dad had mounted on the windowsill. Through a steady stream of snowflakes, he read the gauge. Minus 3. Of course, today was the day he was going snowshoeing with Tril. Ouch.

His dad walked into the kitchen as Brandon was putting his breakfast dishes in the washer.

"You're up early for a vacation day," Bill said. He wiped the sleep from his eyes and poured a cup of coffee from his coffee maker. "It's only nine o'clock."

"You're up late," Brandon retorted.

"Steph and I were talking kind of late last night." Bill looked at Brandon, his eyes cautious, measuring. "She's going to come up today."

Brandon had bristled the first time Bill told him he was going out to dinner with Steph. But after talking to her a bit more, and seeing how warm and genuine she was, he'd lightened his attitude. They seemed to be working hard on the whole 'mystery of the missing village'. And dad was getting paid for some of what he did and that helped out. Unfortunately, the memory of Brandon's mother was still fresh, and raw, leaving a void in his soul that couldn't be filled. Steph sometimes treaded on the borders of that void, and it angered and scared Brandon, though he knew it shouldn't. No one would replace his mom. She'd wanted him when his dad didn't.

Brandon decided not to care. In a couple of years, he'd be on his own. "Why?"

Bill sat down at the little kitchen table, taking sips of his black gold. "We have a theory that the town fled onto the ice and fell through."

Now Brandon sat down. "Fled?" Bill nodded over his mug. "From what?"

"That's the question. We're going to look around at some of the old buildings, some of the terrain and try to figure out why. They should have just headed to Houghton."

Brandon looked out the window at the snow that was coming down harder than it had the last three days. "You have enough snowshoes? I need a pair today."

Bill's eyebrows jumped. "Going snowshoeing? Tril finally convince you?"

"Yeah. I wish it wasn't so cold."

"Dress in layers. You'll warm up in no time. There's a spare pair of shoes in the mudroom."

"Thanks, but isn't Steph going to need some?"

"She's bringing her own," Bill answered. "We'll probably be out tromping around at some point. Maybe up on some of the overlooks." He turned a serious expression on Brandon. "Stay away from the hole. It may be covered over with all this snow and you could-"

"We aren't going up there. We're going to be in the woods by her place. I think."

Bill nodded in satisfaction. Then an oddly contemplative look captured his face. "If you want, see if Tril wants to come to dinner tonight. The four of us could go to Jotnar's."

Brandon's mind took a dump. Suddenly he couldn't quite process anything. His dad wasn't acting like a guy who hadn't wanted custody of his son. And was he asking him to double-date? He knew Steph and she seemed nice enough. She'd been to the house several times to talk with his dad and go over data or whatever. Slowly his mind returned. Tril would probably be fine with the idea. Nothing seemed to shake her.

"Okay. I'll ask."

Bill almost smiled. "Right. See you here sometime this afternoon, or no later than five?"

Brandon nodded. It might turn out to be a weird day.

"I'm glad you made it," Bill said. Steph had just climbed out of her truck, dressed in a big winter parka, leather mittens (locally known as 'choppers'), and a wool-knit hat with ear-flaps that could be tied down under her chin, complete with a tassel on top. Boots that looked over-large for the woman reached to mid-calf and were topped with white, gnarled, wool-like fiber. Black snow-pants were draped over her arm. She was not going to be cold today.

"So am I," she answered, cheerily. "It's really coming down. Plows are falling behind. I had to use four-wheel-drive the last six miles because the road hasn't been plowed. There's already a good foot on the road."

That was odd. The plows seemingly ran non-stop when it snowed like this. Then again, it had been snowing for four days straight. Up here in the upper peninsula of Michigan, the lake-effect snow could pile up so fast the plows would have trouble breaking through it if they didn't periodically clear the roads. No doubt they'd have the road clear by the time evening rolled around. He glanced skyward and was rewarded with a barrage of snowflakes that caused him to squint. *Hopefully*, the roads would be clear.

"Where do you want to start?" Bill's words puffed out of him in billowing white clouds.

"Let's do the outside stuff first. Want to make sure we get that done in the daylight. Plus, then we can warm up looking at the architecture."

"Sounds good. Come on in and put your snow-pants on. I have to get dressed."

Bill escorted the professor into his little dwelling, making sure the door was secure behind them to keep out the cold.

Brandon had been gone for half an hour already. Hopefully, he'd dressed warm enough to not freeze to death, but he trusted Tril to keep track of how cold they both were. She wouldn't take unnecessary risks in this weather.

Bill was surprised at how easily he made casual chit-chat as they both donned their winter clothes. Because Steph was already wearing most of hers, she ended up waiting a couple of minutes for Bill. But in no time, they were out the door. Bill had his compass and a backpack filled with paper, kindling, lighter, candle, multi-tool, water jug and some candy bars. He noticed that Steph had a pack of her own, doubtless filled similarly.

"Let's take my truck," Bill said. "It has higher clearance and we might need it before too long."

Steph agreed and they threw their packs in the cab and their snowshoes in the bed.

"We'll head up to Brockway Mountain Road. We can see a lot from up there," Bill said. He started the truck and headed in that direction, a little west of town. The heavily falling snow reduced visibility to about 200 yards, but the snow was dry and flew over the moving truck without melting on the windshield. Bill turned on the headlights to help others see them in the obscuring, white flakes. Thankfully, the wind looked to be slight or non-existent. A high wind in this kind of snowfall would cut visibility to zero instantly. The road inclined steeply and the truck's engine revved as it shifted to a lower gear, searching for power.

"What do you think?" Steph asked.

"There are three elevated ridges that run parallel, east and west. Brockway Mountain Ridge runs into Copper Harbor and the other two are both south of town. That means there are basically three routes they could have used to flee by land. The first and second, west along the shoreline and west along the southern edge of the Brockway Mountain ridge, would be visible from the overlook up ahead." He peered out the windows of the truck and shook his head. "I don't know about today, though. The third, go straight south across Manganese Lake and then either west through the flat land or continue south through Estivant Pines and then head west. The south edge of Brockway Mountain would be the tightest choke-point, the shoreline the second, and south across Manganese Lake, the third."

He pulled the truck into a parking lot high on the ridge where a walkway and platform had been built as a scenic overlook for tourists. He didn't bother pulling into a space today as he was sure they'd be the only ones here. Leaving the motor running, they climbed out and stomped through the deep snow, foregoing the snowshoes as they didn't have far to walk.

Bill looked out around them at white streaks in the air. Every now and again the snow slowed enough that one could see the general lay of the land below, but only what lay within a half-mile or so. It was good enough for his purposes.

He pointed to the north. "You can just see the west end of the harbor there. Anyone who wanted to escape along the shoreline would have to pass between that and this ridge, tight, but doable."

"How far is that?" Steph asked.

"Maybe a half-mile. I doubt if it's more than that." He turned and looked south. The ridge they were on dropped steeply into a narrow valley to Highway 41 before rising again up to another ridge. The trees on either side of the highway were tightly packed together.

If they were anything like that back in 1842, no dog-sled would have been able to pass through them without staying on the trail. He pointed to the ridge on the other side of the highway. "That other ridge is tough to climb. Both of these are. Damn near impossible with snow." He turned back toward the lake.

"Once on the lake, they could have just paralleled the shoreline," Steph said. "But they went straight for the island."

"Quickest way to put as much distance between themselves and Copper Harbor as they could," Bill added. "You can't see it now, but over there is Manganese Lake." He pointed to the southeast. "We'll head-"

He stopped talking when the ground started to tremble, accompanied by a low rumble. He looked at Steph, his eyes narrowed. "Did you feel that?"

Steph nodded. She looked around, tilting her head like a curious dog. "Did you *hear* that? Sounded almost like thunder."

"I didn't see any flash," Bill said.

"No. It wasn't thunder. Just sounded kind of like it. Felt almost like an earthquake."

"Yeah. Little one." He scanned the area quickly and said, "Never felt an earthquake up here before, but let's get off this ridge. Whatever it was, I think we're safer down near town."

"What was that?" Tril asked. Her voice was muffled by her scarf.

Brandon looked around and shivered, though not from the cold. "Felt like an earthquake with thunder."

"I've felt thunder shake things, but it had to be right on top of me and a ton louder. That was relatively quiet, like a storm twenty miles away."

"Do you have earthquakes up here?" Brandon asked. Not wearing a scarf, his words dusted the air between them like smoke-signals.

"Not so far. But that did kind of feel like one."

The kids looked around through the heavily falling snow. As far as they could see, which was only about 75 yards, there were only trees. The snow clung to skeletal branches, piling high on each limb, part of the reason visibility here was so limited. Evergreens took on the appearance of marshmallow-creme covered confections. On second thought, they looked like some of the weird flora from a Dr. Seuss book, their boughs hanging low, loaded with great, white piles of snow. Walking under one of the burdened trees was asking for a cold, wet surprise down the back of the neck. Unlike farther from town, the trees here were spaced far enough apart that the breeze that had picked up was lending a noticeable angle to the trajectory of the descending snowflakes.

"I don't know what that was," Tril said, closing the book on the mysterious rumble. "Come over here."

She walked over to one of the larger trees in the forest. Brandon followed. "What do you notice about this tree?" she asked.

Brandon examined it. Looked like a tree. A big one. "This is a really big tree."

Tril gave him a smile of feigned patience. "In relation to the world around it, do you notice anything?"

Brandon walked all around the ancient oak, looking up at its massive canopy and scanning its rough bark. "There's snow on the trunk on this side, but not the other?"

"Yay," Tril exclaimed. "Perfect. I'm glad you got that. Now, do you know why?"

"Because the sun melts it off the other side?" Brandon ventured. What was she getting at and why?

Tril pursed her lips. "I don't think you tried. Do you think the sun is melting anything when it's below zero?"

The young man frowned. Of course not. The snowflakes stung his face as he gave the question some actual thought. He turned his back to avoid the cold breeze that made the melting snow on his face burn his cheeks. He looked at the forest in front of him and saw snow-covered trunks staring back at him. An idea tickled his brain. He turned around and saw brown trunks everywhere.

"Oh. Duh. The wind."

Tril graced him with a triumphant smile. "Yep. And around here, that usually means the snowy side of the tree is on the north-west, cause that's the way the wind is usually coming from. If you're lost, walk north and you'll hit the lake. South too, but it's a longer walk. You hit the lake, people won't be hard to find if you head west on either shore."

"Good to know," Brandon conceded.

"And if you hit a road, stay on it. Some people crossroads and end up lost all over again."

Tril reached into her pocket and pulled out a compass. "Of course, if you bring one of these along, and you should," she gave him a stern look, "then you won't get lost to begin with."

"You seem to know a lot about the outdoors," Brandon said. He had to admit to himself that he was envious. It seemed so much cooler when she taught him survival skills than when his dad did. When his dad told him stuff, it just sounded preachy.

"I hunt and fish a lot. Wouldn't want to be lost out here without having supplies enough to survive until someone found me. Not hard to roll an ankle or something." She pointed to the pack on her back. "Water and jerky. Enough for both of us."

Brandon felt like an amateur. He didn't have a pack or a compass. His dad had taught him that much, yet here he was, bereft of any equipment that may save his or Tril's life. Guiltily, he looked at his friend. "I can carry that for a while."

To his surprise, she smiled and shrugged the pack off. She swung it over to him and he slipped it on. Must have been a gallon or two of water in it, because it weighed more than it looked.

"Follow me," Tril said.

She trod off through the incredibly deep snow, sinking mid-calf deep, even with the snowshoes. Brandon followed in her tracks. The tough walking had his heart beating and his hips burning in no time. He unzipped his coat, letting some of the heat escape. One thing he remembered his dad telling him is that sweat, on a day like this, could become a deadly enemy. At the very least, an uncomfortable one.

"How do you know where you're going?" Brandon asked.

She pointed to another massive oak tree, four trunks forming from one thick base and angling outward to form a leafless canopy that must have been fifty feet in diameter. "You see that tree? I know that tree. Over to its left, about ten yards is the 'gray rock'. You can't see it now because it's buried."

Brandon looked at her in amazement. "You know where a specific rock is?"

"I spend a lot of time out here. I like to hunt and just wander around."

Brandon suspected she was pulling his leg and dropped a gaze on her that said as much.

"You don't believe me?" she asked. "Come on." She tramped over to within about ten yards of the tree and started kicking snow away with her snowshoes. Brandon walked over and watched, skeptical.

"I'm guessing this might take a while," Brandon chided.

The aluminum frame of Tril's snowshoe clanked against something buried in the snow. "Nope. Here it is." She cleared the snow away to reveal the top of a big gray boulder.

"You've got to be kidding," Brandon said.

"This is as much my home as my house is," Tril said.

Brandon nodded. "You're something. Lead on."

With a smile, Tril started off again. Brandon glanced back at the 'big oak' and noticed the dark brown trunk. He turned forward again and realized they must be walking south-east, based on the snow-plastered tree trunks that lay before them. After about ten minutes of stomping through snow that lay at least thirty inches deep, she stopped and pointed. Brandon traced the invisible line from her arm to where the land sloped steeply upward. A small, dark shadow stood out blackly in the fresh, white snow. It looked like a hole in the hillside.

"What's that?" Brandon asked.

"My cave," Tril announced.

"Cool. Can we go in it?"

"I try to stay out of it in the winter. Bear might be hibernating in there."

Brandon tensed. "A bear? Right. That'd be bad."

Tril nodded. "But we can check it out this summer. It's pretty cool."

"How deep is it?"

"I don't know," Tril answered. "I haven't gone all the way back yet. A long way. I haven't had an exploring partner like I do now. Mom checked it out and said it's very stable and has fresh air. She just doesn't want me going too far back without someone around."

"Yeah. Let's definitely check it out this summer."

Brandon was happy to have something to look forward to.

The thick falling snow made it impossible to go faster than thirty miles-per-hour, not that they were in a rush. But Bill noticed the difference in the accumulated snow that was piled up on the road as they descended now compared to when they drove up the hill. With an elapsed time of half-an-hour, the snow must be falling at a rate of 3 or 4 inches per hour. And the plows hadn't come yet. If they weren't up there soon, Steph may not be going home tonight. The thought warmed his insides a bit. He sneaked a glance at her and saw the perpetual smile and sparkling eyes. No worry there. Just happiness. Maybe even joy. She sure was a pleasure to be around.

They spent the next couple of hours driving around the area, a feat that was getting more treacherous with every flake of snow. Bill wanted to see all of the logical passages out of town so they could try and figure out how they could become impassible. But each path looked so large that it seemed unlikely, if not impossible, that any one of them could be closed without a barrier. And that would have been noted when the search party arrived back in January of 1843. Which could only mean that there hadn't been any physical blockages, just an existential one, death.

Bill stopped the truck at the west end of Lake Fanny Hooe, the long lake that ran east-west just south of the harbor. He looked at the pass between the gentle hills. Though in deep snow like this, he wouldn't want to try climbing those hills, the pass didn't appear to pose any obstacle of its own accord. And he couldn't imagine what kind of animal could patrol all three passes with such speed and acute perception that dog-sleds couldn't slip by on the trails that must have run through each.

He shook his head. "I don't know. It seems like they should have been able to go through any one of these routes."

"Something that flies could patrol all three passes pretty easily. Even with snow."

Bill leaned forward and gazed up at the leaden sky. "That would have to be one big, frigging, bird." He turned to Steph. "But that would answer a lot of our questions."

Steph leaned forward and peered through the frosty windshield, looking skyward and then at the surrounding terrain. "I'm sorry we couldn't figure this out."

"Nothing says anything is even going to happen. We learned what actually happened to the missing people, if not why." Steph's lips drew into a weak frown. "Nothing has happened yet, and we're almost through December."

The look on Steph's face showed she wasn't convinced. As the echo of the words faded in his mind, Bill realized that he wasn't either.

CHAPTER FIFTEEN

"If you have a map, I'll show you where that cave is," Tril said. She flopped down on the couch.

"I imagine my dad has one here somewhere," Brandon said. He went into the small third bedroom that served as his father's office/dump-all-your-paperwork-in-heaps-here room. A quick scan of the papers scattered in disarray convinced him that finding a map was not simply a matter of spotting it sitting on a desk somewhere. He paged through some of the stacks on his old man's desk but found nothing but bills and records about his fishing charter and hunting guide business. A three-drawer file cabinet against the wall caught his eye. He opened the top drawer and took a quick read of the labels on the folders that were crammed together in hanging file pockets. One immediately drew his attention.

On this particular file, at least two inches tall, were black letters spelling out something he hadn't expected to find. Two words that he had never heard his mother utter. Words he thought belonged only to other kids, kids whose parents both loved them. Kids who hadn't been rejected by their fathers. Yet here they were.

Custody Battle.

He pulled the file out and looked at the first page, a bill from an attorney that showed a sum Brandon couldn't imagine his father could afford. This was followed by an estimate of "additional expenses based on the motions made by former spouse to prevent visitation rights." This number was three times what the bill had been.

Brandon sat down heavily on the office chair and looked through more of the file. It didn't take a genius to see that his father had very much fought for visitation but had been denied that and custody. He found a letter on fancy letter-head from his mother's boyfriend, Nick. Clearly, Nick was going to spare no expense in making sure Bill was bankrupted by any legal battle he pursued in order to have time with his son. He was in the middle of reading it when there was a knock on the door.

He looked up and saw Tril standing there, looking sweet, gentle and concerned.

"Are you okay?" she asked.

Brandon swallowed hard, rubbed his eyes with one hand as he stuffed the papers back in the manilla folder and spun his back to her, cramming the folder into the drawer where he found it. "Yeah. Fine. Ah, no map."

With a patient smile, Tril pointed at the wall of the office where Bill had pinned a big map of the county. As she took it down, she said, "My dad calls it 'male pattern blindness'. I see you have it too."

Brandon rolled his eyes and shook his head. "Duh."

Watching Tril lay the map out on the kitchen table, Brandon came to the realization that a double-date with his dad didn't seem so awful.

The kids were at the house when Bill and Steph arrived. Oddly enough, Brandon wasn't making Tril watch him play video games. They were scrutinizing a map they had laid out on the table. Bill stomped the snow from his boots as he took off his gloves, hat and coat.

"Glad to see we didn't have to rescue you this time," he said. The kids looked up, wide-eyed until they saw the mischievous grin on Bill's face, then their shoulders relaxed. Steph swatted him on the shoulder.

"Tril showed me another cave," Brandon said, weirdly scrutinizing his father.

"Really? You guys didn't learn the first time?"

"We didn't go in it," Brandon said. "She's showing me where it is on the map." Finally, he turned and looked back down.

"Sounds interesting," Steph said. She hung her coat on a wall-hook near the door and stepped lightly over to the table. "Where is it?"

Tril pointed to a spot on the map near the base of Brockway Mountain. Bill walked over and looked to where Tril indicated. His brow furrowed.

"I didn't know that was there," he said.

"And the hole that I went down is right over here," she moved her finger a short distance to the top of Brockway Mountain. "We were wondering if the two might be connected." They stared at Bill expectantly.

He shrugged. "Could be. They aren't that far apart. But don't go climbing in there. You could have died last time."

"Okay," Brandon said.

Bill glanced at his son, having expected more of an argument.

"We won't," Tril said. "Not until this summer. If they are connected, the air will have filtered out by then for sure."

Bill's stomach clenched. These damn kids were bound and determined to kill themselves. He couldn't imagine what it had been like when they were five-years-old.

Steph laughed. "If you go spelunking next summer, we'll have to make sure you are properly outfitted. I imagine your parents could set you up with some gear." Bill turned a horrified look on her. "What?" she said. "Don't fight it. Just make sure it's done safely."

"God in heaven," Bill said. Then he examined the map again. "If those are connected, that side of the ridge may not be very stable. Speaking of which, did you two feel that little earthquake?"

The kids' faces filled with excitement. "Yeah," Brandon said. "You felt it too?"

"Where were you when it hit?" Steph asked.

Tril considered the map, her hand over her lips. "Right about here," she said.

"Not that far from where we were," Bill said. "A little south of us."

Steph looked at Bill. "That's foreboding."

"What?" Brandon asked.

"Nothing," Bill said. "Who's hungry? Let's get over to Jotnar's before we're snowed in."

CHAPTER SIXTEEN

Something awakened Paavo Silkula in the deep hours of the night and he shivered. Had it been a dream, a sound, a smell? It was like being gently shaken from one's sleep by a worried lover. He pulled the big blankets up around his neck. His eighty-four-year-old body liked the warmth of his small cabin-like house, but it seemed this damned cold winter was sucking the heat out through the walls. Usually, he could keep the fire burning low and slow and it would put out the perfect temperature for most of the night. Not tonight. Not the last couple of weeks. Temperatures of twenty and thirty below were not unheard of, but not for weeks at a time. And not in December. Lately, he'd had to keep the fire burning hot. The problem with that was the wood was consumed quickly. And when the fire burned down, it didn't take long to get cold.

And so Paavo shivered. With resignation, he threw off the blankets and rolled out of bed. He ambled through the door into the main room of his home, where the embers of a dying fire cast a wicked red glow. He reached into the wood-box and found only one stick. Dammit. He'd forgotten to fill it up before he went to bed.

Now cold and angry, he donned a heavy winter parka, high, insulated boots, hat and gloves and a spirit of resolve. Paavo didn't want to open that door, but he had to bring in at least two loads of wood to make it through the rest of the night. The stubborn old Finn knew his flannel pajama bottoms wouldn't keep out the cold for long, but by the time he was done, he'd be so wide awake anyway, he'd enjoy warming himself by the fire.

The weak wind stabbed into his cheeks as soon as he stepped into the dark night, his breath being sucked from his warm lungs. The snow had slowed, maybe because the air was too cold to hold enough moisture for the heavy stuff. He cursed at the frigid air and dropped his head deeper into his coat. The pile of wood he'd stacked all along the front of his cabin, within close reach for extreme nights like this, was already depleted. The bulk of his supply was in the darkness around one side of the home. Not a long carry, but too long on a night like this. Before he had taken two steps, a low, brief rumble emanated from the forest that shrouded his property. Paavo stopped and raised his head, trying to free his ears from the confines of his coat so he could hear better. He scanned the dark trees, looking for anything that could explain the sound and listening for anything else. It had almost sounded like a bear's *wuff*, which was out of the question as any black bears around would be in full hibernation. Still...

Probably a big pile of snow falling out of a tree, he thought.

He shuddered and walked as quickly as his old body would carry him, determined to get the wood inside so he could warm up. The illumination from the front porch light didn't reach around the corner of the building, but enough light reflected off the unusually deep snow that he had no problems seeing what he was doing. In record time he'd filled his wood carrier, a rectangular piece of canvas that wrapped around the logs, handles at both ends so it acted like a sling. He headed inside. Before he had escaped the darkness, he heard the strange sound again. But this time a slight tremor accompanied it. Paavo cast a quick glance in the direction of the sound but didn't stop to stare. He got inside as fast as he dared to walk.

Grumbling, he unloaded the wood and then threw three of the four pieces in the fireplace. The fourth he put in the wood-box. He thought about the unusual sound he'd heard outside. It wasn't odd to hear trees "popping" when they got very cold. And when a large deposit of snow built up high in the branches of evergreen trees, it would sometimes avalanche down with a thump. But that didn't seem like what he'd heard. Wolves? They were afraid of humans and would growl if they felt threatened. Maybe it was a frost quake. With a deep frost in soil that was very moist, the ground itself could make snapping or groaning noises, along with a vibration. As uncommon as frost quakes were, it seemed the most likely reason. Rolling up his carrier, he braved the cold a second time, anxious to be done with the chore.

Again, as he piled wood on his carrier, a deep grunt resonated from the forest behind him. Sure now that it wasn't snow falling out of trees in great masses, or a figment of his imagination, the old man turned and stared into the darkness.

A heavy overcast made sure that no moon or starlight illuminated the area. Tree trunks were black sentinels that rose up from the deep layer of snow, but only those within thirty feet were even identifiable. Paavo's eyes strained to see any other shapes in the snow, anything that looked like a bear, unlikely though that scenario was. Nothing looked even remotely out of place. Then, slightly to his left and deeper in the forest, his attention was drawn to something. A movement?

A pile of snow cascaded from one of the big white pines that towered over his cabin, dumping part of its load down Paavo's neck. It had been almost as if he'd shaken the tree himself, causing the avalanche. But he hadn't and couldn't have caused it, not a tree some eighty feet tall with a thirty-inch diameter trunk.

His old heart increased rhythm, taking him back to his younger days when he would deer hunt and see his prey slipping through the bushes, stepping closer and closer. But here, he was decidedly not the hunter. A chill, deeper even than the sub-zero temperatures, crept out of the dark. Something moved, high off the snow. But with measured, precise, stealthy movements. He tried to focus on the source but found himself taking in a huge dark void, barely distinguishable against the blackness of the woods. Finally, he was able to discern a massive shape that blotted out the trees and snow behind it, despite the limited visibility. Whatever this monstrous thing was, it was alive. Paavo could feel it. Never in his eighty-four years had Paavo Silkula feared for his life.

Until now.

He stood there, transfixed by the shadow, staring. Fleeing was futile. That was a certainty. But he had no weapons, only a hunk of firewood clutched between numb hands. The old man took one, then two steps backward, inching toward the safety of his cabin. Raising the stick of wood, he shouted, "Get the hell out of here," trying to sound as intimidating as he could.

The blackness seemed to be coming at him from between several trees, formless and foreboding. The deliberate slowness of its advance made Paavo think of the shows he would watch about lions stalking their prey through the long grasses of Africa. At once the darkness was obscured by clouds of flying snow, the white plume rising up and then surrounding the old man as it fell around him in a heavy deluge as though he stood in the path of an oncoming snow-blower. He felt the snow bite into the exposed skin on his neck, face and wrists, the extreme cold a minor distraction in the face of this unknown doom. The piece of firewood in his hand felt silly, small and useless. He doubted it could hurt whatever was coming for him, even if he threw it with all his might. But throw it he did, as soon as the massive black shape rushed at him through the trees.

The octogenarian blinked out like a candle in an avalanche without ever seeing what stalked from the cold night.

The fire in Paavo Silkula's cabin burned to cold, gray ashes, with no one there to tend it.

CHAPTER SEVENTEEN

This was doubtlessly the most brutal start to any winter Michigan Conservation Officer Samuel Powers had experienced in the Keweenaw, of which there were eight. The second week of November, the temperature plummeted to ten below zero. Then, two days later, it warmed up enough to snow about ten inches. Followed by another cold snap, to fifteen below. And another warm-up with even more snow. The cycle continued without interruption, already dumping over sixty inches of the white stuff on Copper Harbor. Now, the temperature seemed to level off at zero degrees, but the snow was falling at an alarming rate. Even with the extreme temperatures, Lake Superior was slow to freeze so there was plenty of moisture being scooped up by the westerly wind, only to be dumped on land as massive amounts of snow. The snowpack, the depth of snow on the ground, was already over thirty inches. If this kept up, Copper Harbor could become snow-bound.

Luckily, the plows in the Keweenaw were equipped with gigantic snow-throwers that had three augers reaching five feet high and eight feet wide. But the plows were old and getting harder to maintain, particularly with heavy use.

Sam stared out the window at a steady snow, his feet cozying deeper into fur-lined slippers and threw on a thick, warm robe. His days off weren't a lot different from workdays in the winter months. During summer, he and his subordinate, Greg Travis, were busy all the time, keeping historic Fort Wilkins running, and monitoring the local hunters, trappers and fishermen. But in winter, the fort was closed, and hunting and fishing ground to a halt. Trappers still worked their lines, but he knew where most of them plied their traps and none of them had been a problem.

As he got the coffee-maker running, he glanced out the window. Though it was still dark, even at 8:15 in the morning, he could see that it was snowing again. Unreal. He wondered how much would fall before it quit. A peek at the thermometer let him know it was still barely above zero, not ideal for outdoor activity.

The temperature made him wish he had a wife, someone he could share body heat with. He knew he had better make another fire. His propane heat kept the place from freezing, but he didn't want to blow through the fuel too fast. After he got a nice fire going, slow-burning, he donned his clothes; long-johns and jeans, woolen shirt over a long-sleeved tee, and then his outdoor wear. A quick two-minute snowmobile ride would take him to Jotnar's Tavern. He enjoyed getting his weekend breakfasts at the only local eatery that was open all winter. And they served up a great meal.

Snowflakes swirled around the windshield of the snowmobile as he cruised along the packed trail. There was at least ten inches of new snow and visibility was limited to about fifty yards, so he took his time. He stopped the machine on the crest of a snowbank and looked up and down the road. In both directions he could tell that the passable roadway was shrinking, the snowbanks creeping in from both sides. The snowblower would have to come through soon because the regular plow wouldn't be able to push the banks back any farther. He could already see where the tires of two trucks had bit into the banks in order to pass by one another. If that kept up, someone was bound to get stuck. Hugging the side of the road, he rode the quarter-mile to Jotnar's.

"There he is," Ernest declared when Sam walked in. "How's it going this snowy morning?"

Sam stomped the snow from his boots and shook it from his shoulders. Taking his hat off he answered, "Hungry, Ernest. Hungry." He glided onto one of the bar stools, draping his coat over the empty stool next to it.

"You beat Paavo in this morning," the barkeep said. He poured a cup of coffee from the ever-full carafe and placed it in front of his first customer.

Sam checked his watch. Eight-thirty. He was pleased to have arrived first this morning. It meant he didn't have to pay for the coffee. That old coot was an early riser so it was a rare occasion that Sam wasn't paying for both their beverages. "Maybe he's going into hibernation." That elicited a chuckle.

"He'll probably be here in a tick," Ernest said. His eyes met Sam's for a heartbeat, neither man willing to consider the possibility that old Paavo hadn't awakened at all. The feisty octogenarian was respected and treasured by just about anyone who'd spent more than five minutes talking to him.

Sam nodded. "I'll have the ham and cheese omelet this morning. And juice."

Ernest walked in the back where he passed off the order to Suzy, his long-time cook and wife of forty-five years. When he returned, he said, "Damned lot of snow we're getting. And could it stay colder just a little while longer?"

"Got that right. I could use a break from it. Maybe some twenty's and sunshine. I'd like to get out cross-country skiing, but this is just a touch on the cold side." As if just talking about the weather could give him a chill, Sam sucked at his hot coffee, his hands clasped around it for warmth.

A snowmobile pulled up outside and Sam and Ernest both exhaled a breath of relief. Sam heard the outer door open, boots stomping, then the inner door swung open. He turned to show Paavo his smile of victory, but it turned to a confused grimace when he saw the concerned faces of Tril and Brandon.

"Sam, something's wrong. Grandpa Paavo is gone," Tril said.

He knew that Paavo wasn't Tril's real grandfather, but a lot of folks in town considered him such. "Gone?"

"And there was blood," Brandon added.

Sam and Ernest exchanged a glance as the ranger took his feet, leaving his belly sitting on the stool. "We'll be back. He couldn't have gone far," he said to the barman. In a flash, he was bundled up and was following the kids out the door.

Tril and Brandon climbed on her machine and sped off toward the old man's cabin, Sam close behind. When they arrived at the home, Tril stopped short, not pulling into the yard. Sam followed suit and climbed off into knee-deep snow.

"Over here," she said, walking around to the woodpile. "Brandon, could you check inside again?" Brandon disappeared into the little log cabin as Sam went with Tril. She kicked at a pink splotch in the snow, about two feet in diameter. Bright, red blood appeared in the track she cleared.

"Shit," Sam uttered under his breath. "Okay, don't move." He scanned the immediate area, looking for signs of who had done this to Paavo. He could see where the kids had tramped over the first time they came by this morning, but no other tracks.

"We just came by this morning to make sure he didn't need help hauling wood in or something and he was gone."

Sam nodded as he looked around.

"What's that?" Tril asked. She was pointing at a big divot in the snow, about two feet by four feet.

Sam wrinkled his forehead, trying to decide what he was looking at. Something had been there. Had some animal bedded down there and jumped Paavo when he came out for wood? "Almost looks like an animal bed," he said.

"Nope," Brandon said, returning from his check of the cabin's interior. He walked up behind Sam. "Fire's out. Been a while cause it's cold in there."

Sam looked up. "How cold?"

Brandon shrugged. "I could see my breath."

"Been out for several hours then. Dammit." He looked around through the falling snow, the cloud-grayed light casting a gloomy feel. "How far did you look for him?"

"When we found the blood, we left right away to find you," Tril answered.

He nodded, reaching for his handheld radio, then cursed. Saturday. His radio was back at home. "Go round up some folks, we need to get a search going right away."

Tril and Brandon nodded and took off. He knew Tril would have a crew assembled in no time. Right now he needed them out of the way while he assessed the situation. He didn't want the kids here when he found Paavo's body.

He kicked more fresh snow from around Tril's boot track. Damn, that was a lot of blood. He looked around for signs of a trail where Paavo may have wandered. Maybe he'd hit himself with the axe and stumbled off in shock. That had to be it. He wouldn't have gone far, not in this deep snow.

The ranger started a spiral search centered on the bloodstain, believing he'd find Paavo's tracks, even in the deep, fresh snow. He'd have been shuffling through the snow if he was injured, leaving an obvious channel. His first circle around the scene came up empty, aside from the animal bed. He spiraled out farther and found nothing. If Paavo had taken two steps and fallen, Sam would have tripped on his body. But he hadn't. He'd noticed Paavo's truck in the drive when they'd arrived, and the friendly old coot's snowmobile was under the lean-to attached to the back of the cabin. Where the hell did he go? Sam continued working his search pattern, now more confused and afraid for his old friend.

Another deep depression, like the first, sat in his path. Another animal? Deer frequently bedded down, leaving melted holes where they'd been, but this was too big. Wolves? But when they left, they'd leave deep paths in the snow and there were no such paths. It was as if Paavo had been scooped up by a giant bird of prey. And though Sam had heard of a golden eagle attacking a man, it hadn't, couldn't, carry him off.

"Hellfire and corruption," he said.

He left his search and went into the cabin. Though warmer inside than the zero-degree weather outside, it was as Brandon reported. He blew out a breath and watched as the steam floated away, disappearing in the dimly lit room. After stepping over to the fireplace, he picked up the iron poker and stirred the coals. The smallest red embers emerged from a deep pile of white ash. It'd burned itself out probably four hours ago. Which meant it hadn't been stoked for one or two hours before that. He looked at his watch, twenty minutes after nine. So Paavo had disappeared around three or four in the morning. If they found him, the poor old guy would probably have frostbite, and that was if he was properly dressed when he went out. A glance around the cabin confirmed that his coat and boots were gone. *Thank God, there is some hope*, he thought.

He made a half-hearted search through the common room in case Paavo had left a note. But he found what he expected, nothing.

A snowmobile roared up to the cabin and shut down. Sam heard Matti Tervonen's voice calling, so he went out.

Matti saw him at once. "Ernie told me what was going on. Need help?" The huge brewer took a long swig from a can of energy-drink, finishing it and stuck the empty in a bag on his machine.

Sam explained what he'd found, and what he hadn't. Matti pivoted his head around, eyes squinted. The image made Sam think of what the old fire towers must have looked like; a high wooden structure with a ranger atop, scanning the horizon, looking for smoke, the tell-tale sign of a forest fire. Just then he was glad the monstrous brewer wasn't a violator, he'd hate for him to be on the wrong side of the law. He took Matti over and showed him the blood and deep indentations in the snow.

"Huh," Matti said. He stared down at the weird hole in the snow and stepped into it. "This is pretty big."

"At first, I thought it might be a deer bed, but you're right, it's too big. There's another one over there." He pointed to the second. "That's as far as I made it, so far. I can't imagine where he went."

"What do you want me to do?" Matti asked.

"Go around the cabin and see if you find anything, blood, whatever."

Matti set off and Sam resumed his search pattern where he'd left off. After two more circles, he found a third 'bed'. He turned back toward the house and noticed the 'beds' were in a pattern not unlike footprints. Or perhaps a big animal leaping forward, each jump taking it from one side to the other as though it didn't quite know which way it wanted to go.

The sound of snowmobiles grabbed his attention and he saw several volunteers arrive at the front of Paavo's little home. He trudged through the snow to greet them. First to arrive was Bill Hitze with that professor from Houghton, what was her name? Stephanie? Greg Travis, Sam's young protege arrived in his department four-wheel drive, complete with a hunting rifle, and tossed some snowshoes and snow-pants to his mentor. Then he handed him a hand-held radio. Matti came slogging through the snow as Jeff Jansen pulled up on his $16,000 snowmobile, wearing another $1000 worth of winter gear. The arrogant guy immediately started strapping on his top-of-the-line Northern Lites snowshoes. Sam really didn't care for Jansen, but he had to appreciate the man's willingness to help out. Maybe Jansen did have room to care about someone other than himself. Tril and Brandon returned, Brandon holding a pair of snowshoes in one arm as he clung to the rear of Tril's machine.

"A couple more people should be coming shortly," Tril said.

Sam surveyed the array of white faces that looked expectantly at him. He didn't know why, but just then he felt more than ever that they were all part of the same family, despite his being the only African-American in the community. These were good people and they were here to help someone who may be in dire need. He would not let them down.

In short order, he had them broken into teams with assignments. They would have the area around the cabin searched in no time. He just prayed they would find some lead. He also prayed they didn't find Paavo, bled out and frozen, somewhere. The teams got to work, Greg Travis joining Sam.

"I was looking at these weird depressions," Sam explained. The two rangers walked to where Sam had found the third of these and Greg looked around, snowflakes accumulating on his wool cap.

"Are there more of these?" Greg asked.

"Maybe," Sam answered. "If there's a pattern or direction, should be one about..." He walked away from the cabin, examining the snow. "Yep. Here's another one."

"What the hell?" Greg said. "Was something jumping through here?"

Sam shrugged. "Beats the hell outta me. Must have been big, whatever it was. Scuff through the snow on your way over here, see if you find any blood."

Greg walked toward Sam, sweeping the snow away with his snowshoes on each step. When he had covered about half of the distance, a red glop flipped through the air and landed in the undisturbed white. Both rangers stared at the grim revelation.

"Get the others. Looks like we need to do a line and head off in this direction." Sam swallowed hard as Greg headed off to coral the other teams. He didn't want this to be a recovery operation, but he wasn't holding his breath.

How had that blood gotten way over here? There were no tracks. Wait. He couldn't assume that, not with how the snow was falling. Paavo's tracks could easily have been covered in the last six hours. These dips in the snow might just be how it was drifting when the wind picked up. Or maybe with his wound, the old guy was periodically falling. He stared to the north, the direction Paavo seemed to be moving, and wondered what had happened to the old guy. They had to find him.

With all twelve people once again assembled, he set the whole crew up in an east-west line, spaced five yards apart. Everyone was to sweep snow away as they walked, looking for any more blood. It would be slow going, but necessary.

After a half-hour, Jansen called out, he'd found more blood. As he was to Sam's right, Sam gave the order for everyone to shift one position to the right so the line was centered on the find. As they were repositioning, Jansen said, "I don't see any tracks. How'd he get way out here without leaving tracks?"

"They'd probably be buried by now," Sam said. He'd noticed two, maybe three more of those strange dips in the snow, but they were nowhere to be seen now either. If those had been caused by Paavo falling, they should have found his body. Unless he recovered enough to walk to the road and get help.

Jansen looked up into the sky, squinting against the flakes. "It's like the blood dripped out of the sky."

Sam followed his gaze skyward, thinking.

"It's like a giant eagle grabbed him," Jansen said.

Sam scowled at him. "Except there isn't such a thing. Never has been"

"Thunderbird," Jansen said, referring to the Native-American myth.

"You have to quit living in fantasy land," Sam said. Seeing the line was once again ready, he gave the order to resume.

The team trudged forward slowly, snowshoes sweeping the snow before compressing it and moving on. Everyone wore a grim expression, knowing deep inside that Paavo was dead, but wanting desperately to defy logic and expectation and find the old man cuddled up against a tree, shivering with a treatable wound.

When they reached the road, Sam checked his watch. 1:30 PM. He signaled to everyone to gather around. No one smiled and tears glistened in Tril's eyes. "We should get something to eat and then continue. Gonna be dark in four hours. I want to resume by two o'clock. Will everyone be back?"

A couple of the folks shook their heads, clearly having lost hope. "Would those who aren't coming back please check around to see if he showed up somewhere, looking for help?" The acquiescent nods displayed the pathetic amount of hope Sam had in making the request.

With that, everyone turned to return to Paavo's cabin, following their tracks through the woods. No one moved. It was a little more than a half-mile, but in that deep snow, it'd take them until two just to get to their snowmobiles. Sam looked up the road. It was clear the last time the plow went through was early in the morning. An undisturbed layer of snow laid at least eighteen inches deep.

The falling snow showed no signs of slowing.

Sam had thought they would have found Paavo by now. Dammit. Now they'd lose time walking to get food, but the search was strenuous and people needed fuel.

"I guess we'll get started as soon as we can. Let's just head back to town."

The group strode down the road in two lines, side by side, switching off who broke the trail as those at the back had much easier walking on the well-packed tracks of those who went first. Everyone continued to look around for signs of their old friend. As they walked, Sam pulled out his cell phone to call the Sheriff's department. After punching the 'call' button, he got a message that there was no service available.

"What?" Greg asked, walking next to him.

"No service. We should have something here, at least one bar."

Greg squinted up into the white and gray sky. "Maybe the snow is dampening the signal?"

Sam pulled out his handheld radio and tried to raise any other law enforcement. Greg turned down his radio when Sam's voice came across. But they heard nothing but silence after three tries.

"Well, shit," Sam said. "I'll use a land-line when we get to town."

It took almost thirty minutes to cover the half-mile back to town because of the snow. *And*, Sam thought, *everyone is going to have to change into dry clothes*. His own were drenched with sweat, a deadly situation in cold, snowy conditions like this.

Sam, Greg and Matti yanked off their snowshoes and went stomping into Jotnar's Tavern. Ernest looked up, concern on his face. Sam shook his head and the old bar-man grimaced.

"Suzy," Ernest called to the kitchen, "Couple of big grilled ham and cheese sandwiches. On the double, please." Ernest's wife peered out from the kitchen window, saw the grim-faced men and made a sad frown as she turned to cook the order.

"I'll help you," Matti said. He disappeared into the kitchen and Sam saw him reach to embrace Suzy, the little old lady obscured by the gigantic arms that enveloped her.

"I need to call the Sheriff," Sam said. He walked over to the phone mounted to the wall at the end of the bar. The ranger put the receiver to his ear and frowned, pulled it away to examine it, then back to his ear. He scoffed aloud. "Phone is dead."

"This is unbelievable," Larry James said to himself. His gloved hands gripped the steering wheel of the big plow and he leaned forward in an attempt to see through the heavy falling and blowing snow. In his twenty years of driving a plow in the Keweenaw, he hadn't seen weather like this. And up here it was nothing to have forty inches of snowfall over two or three days. But by his estimation, they'd received thirty inches in the last ten hours with no signs of slowing. They were definitely on pace to break the local record snowfall of 390 inches set back in the late seventies.

And the cold. Dammit! Stuck right at zero or less.

Webs of white frost encroached from the edges of his windshield, reducing his visibility to what was directly in front of the big truck. Both side windows of the cab were completely covered by the frozen moisture of his breath, despite the heater blowing full blast.

He stole a glance at the speedometer. Thirty-five. Shit. On highway 41, one of two roads that ran up to Copper Harbor, he would have liked to maintain at least forty-five to ensure the plow blade threw the snow onto or over the shoulder. At this speed, the snowbank would edge close to the road, making a narrow passage for vehicles. He hoped his buddy to the north, on Highway

26, was having better luck, but with that road twisting along the Lake Superior shore, he highly doubted it.

Suddenly, out of the blinding white, a huge gray shape emerged, directly in front of Larry's truck. He slammed on the brakes. Too late. Even at this speed, with the limited and varying visibility, he didn't stop in time. The cab rattled and the seatbelt grabbed him, pinning him to his seat. He saw the plow blade jar upward at an angle he'd never seen it in before.

"Aw, dammit!" He peered through the misty windshield, trying to identify what he'd hit. Not able to make it out, he donned his hat and gloves and stepped out of the truck.

Outside the confines of the truck, he could see the form of a cell tower laying across the highway, stretching off to his left. It had fallen across the telephone lines as well, one wooden telephone pole shattered and broken completely. What a mess. The plow driver stared at the girders of the tower puzzled. The wind was strong, but not nearly strong enough to topple the structure. It didn't matter, he wasn't getting through. Roy, up on 26 would have to clear out Copper Harbor.

Larry climbed back in his truck and started a several point turn, trying not to get stuck in the process. Finally, he was headed back to Calumet. There was nothing he could do until that tower was removed and his plow repaired.

He got on his radio and called for Roy. After the second try, he heard Roy's voice.

"Hey, Roy. 26 is the only way to Copper Harbor right now. Cell tower is down across 41. How's it going up there? Over."

The response was split up by static. "Huge drift... six... ten feet tall... far as I can see, which isn't far. No way... today... They're stuck... Over."

"Roger. See you at the garage." Larry put the radio mike back in its cradle.

It would be a day or two before plows could break through to Copper Harbor. Good thing those were hearty folk up there.

CHAPTER EIGHTEEN

It was 2:30 P.M. by the time everyone made it back to resume the search for Paavo Silkula. Sam and Greg had retrieved their trucks. Sam wanted a vehicle they could transport Paavo in if he was injured. The rest of the team had come in on snowmobiles, one with a tow-sled, also in case they needed to transport anyone wounded. Or dead. They were down to eight people now. Sam was surprised to see Jansen had returned. He stood talking with Brandon and Tril while Bill tried to conceal his contemptuous glances at the man. Luckily, the fisherman's attention was being diverted by the always pleasant Stephanie Crowe. Sam quickly set the line with Greg at the right end, Bill at the left, himself and Brandon at the center, with Dr. Crowe and Jansen to his left, and Tril and Matti to the right. Bill gave him a thankful look as they prepared to set out and Sam smiled back. It was no secret that Bill and Jansen didn't get along, and Bill wasn't crazy about Brandon's hanging around with Jansen.

Sam didn't need any more drama right now.

He was glad to see everyone had taken his advice to bring a firearm because he hadn't ruled out the possibility they were dealing with an animal attack. The only ones not armed with either a rifle or sidearm were Dr. Crowe and Brandon. That was probably just as well since he didn't know if either could handle a firearm.

The little team went to work, moving north toward the lake. Sam could only surmise that maybe Paavo had experienced a mental event on top of his injury and he had walked right across the road. Or if it had been an animal, it wouldn't go out on the big lake and they'd find it in short order. But that just seemed extremely unlikely. He glanced over at Jansen, then peered at the sky before he shook the nonsense from his head. Thunderbird!

It took them another two hours to reach the lake, the sky darkening slowly. By the time they turned around and performed a half-hearted search on the return to the road, darkness had claimed the peninsula. Sam thanked everyone and sent them on their way, everyone depressed and frowning.

Dread filled Sam's gut. Dread because he felt he'd failed his friend and community, and dread because as hard as he tried, he couldn't accept the theory that Paavo had injured himself splitting wood and wandered off to die. Which meant he'd either been murdered or attacked by an animal. The evidence for either scenario was scarce. All they had was blood. A significant amount at the cabin, and then a spattering here and there. The amount back at Paavo's house didn't look like a fatal blood loss, but it did represent a significant injury.

Could someone have kidnapped him? Jumped him and carried him off? Maybe someone from out of town? What ransom could be paid? Did Paavo have anything of value that kidnappers could demand? They would have to contact someone and Paavo didn't have any living relatives that Sam knew of. And he still had one major problem with this theory.

Those weird 'tracks'.

Greg Travis plodded through the snow with his snowshoes. Even with the weight distributing shoes, he sank nearly up to his knees. The walking was hard and slow. As the only other park ranger in town, he decided to continue looking around for Paavo, west of the search line the group had taken. The darkness and falling snow obscured the view of anything more than ten feet away. His flashlight had fresh batteries but even without it, he'd be able to find his way back to the road and town. In the year-and-a-half he'd spent here, he'd become one with the land.

He tugged at the ties of his hood, pulling it tighter over his mad-bomber hat. The combination did a great job, but when the hood loosened, the icy air circulated around to the back of his neck and sent a shuddering chill into his shoulders and back. Greg hadn't thought it was going to get any colder today. He was wrong. His lung-moistened breath froze into tiny, nostril-tickling icicles on the hairs of his nose as he exhaled, and left a white frosty trail down the scarf drawn over his mouth. Without the scarf, each breath he took would send an ache through his exposed teeth, similar to biting into ice-cream.

The young ranger stopped to shine his light around, looking for any sign of Paavo. It was still hard to wrap his head around what he was doing out here; looking for an old man who had apparently been carried off by some wild animal. That crazy, but likable old coot, Kearse, was popping off about that old legend of the disappeared settlement from the 1840s. No one was buying it of course. There had been some sort of tracks leading away from Paavo's cabin, going off through the woods. And for some reason, he really believed they were tracks, though what kind, he didn't know. But when they'd gotten into the open, they had been obscured by the windblown snow that drifted and white-washed everything in its path. Not even he, a ranger who prided himself on his tracking abilities, was able to find the trail again. Whatever it was, it had escaped. But the tracks had been either coming or going in this direction, toward the lighthouse on the little peninsula at the east end of the harbor. Though a long way from where the tracks disappeared, it was easy to cover this little bottle-neck by himself and eliminate it as an area of concern.

A concern for what? What had killed Paavo and dragged him away? He was sure that the poor old man was dead, based on the amount of blood they'd found.

But all of the predators that Greg knew about in these parts, would have left the remains of the body lying there, not carried it off with them. And the predators in Michigan's Upper Peninsula did not make a habit of threatening, much less killing, humans. The only ones he believed even capable were mountain lions and wolves. Bears were hibernating and the black bears in the area ran at the sight of humans unless they had young nearby. Mountain lions were scarce, though they knew some were roaming around. But the tracks they found were nothing like a loping cat. A couple of wolves could have killed him, but again, there would have been something left. The only thing left was an animal not native to the area. A grizzly or polar bear perhaps. Neither of them could have carried Paavo away without it being obvious by leaving a blood trail and hunks of the poor man behind.

He ran a thumb under the sling of the 30.06 rifle he had hanging over his shoulder, pulling it up higher so it didn't slip down his arm. It gave him a sense of power, though if there was a huge bear running around, it probably wouldn't save him from becoming its next meal. Not that he thought there were any predatory intruders here. He wasn't sure what to think.

Greg worked the flashlight beam around the trees that surrounded him, looking for blood or indentations in the snow that could be the strange tracks from the cabin. Nothing, though it was hard to see very well with the flurry of snowflakes flashing through the light. He could only look at the area directly around his feet, within a five-foot range. He sighed. This was useless. In the dark and snow, and with how much snow had fallen since the kids had reported Paavo missing this morning, their only hope was stumbling across the man's body. And that wasn't worth wandering around in this cold.

A vibration tickled up his legs. He stopped. He turned around and shone the light through the trees, seeing nothing but falling snow on a background of black tree trunks. He strained his ears, trying to hear something. But nothing was there. Silence.

Resigned to failure for the time being, he turned and headed in the direction of the nearest road where the walking should be easier. To his right, maybe 200 yards away, invisible in the dark, was the light-house. The metallic tower that hosted the working light was dark. The original, historical light tower was shorter and served only as a tourist site now.

Another shudder trembled his legs. What the hell? He was sure he felt it that time, but what was it? Earthquake? Seemed unlikely. He'd never heard of such a thing here in the U.P., but that didn't mean it couldn't happen.

He jumped when a 'whump' sound came out of the dark, like slamming a pillow onto a pile of sand. He took a moment to catch his breath and relax. It was a sound the ranger recognized as a load of snow breaking loose from its perch high in the branches of one of the evergreens and landing heavily in the deep snow on the ground. He resumed his trek toward the road, but faster now.

The ground shook again, followed by more snow falling from the boughs, closer this time. He clicked off his flashlight and stuffed it into a pocket. Then he switched on the headlamp he wore over his hat and pulled his rifle from his shoulder and held it ready. The light showed forth from his forehead, giving him enough visibility to navigate. Quickly he scanned a tight circle around himself. Seeing nothing, he took off at a hard pace toward the road.

Two more rumbles and more falling snow. Behind him, somewhere. Now he was sure something was back there. He cursed the feeble headlight he wore and got an idea. Veering to his right he started to trot as well as he could on snowshoes in the deep snow, his destination set.

A grunt sounded from behind him. He risked a glance back and saw nothing. In the heavy snowfall, it was impossible to judge the distance to the sound's source. He was afraid it may be a lot closer than he'd like. He started to run.

And the ground started to quake, rhythmically, a slow but steady cadence. He had to make it to the lighthouse and take shelter. Something was after him. He could hear tree branches cracking and snow being shaken to the ground.

Another grunt.

What the hell is out there? His heart was pounding from the exertion of running through the snow and he could feel sweat pour down his back. The trees fell away from his light and he knew the lighthouse was only about fifty yards in front of him, though he couldn't see it in the dark beyond the snowy white streaks illuminated by the headlight.

The ground continued shaking, branches, and now it even sounded like tree trunks, shattering and snapping behind him. Something big was on his trail and it was getting closer.

The side of the lighthouse suddenly loomed up out of the black. He found the door and slung his rifle, digging through layers of clothing for his keys that gave him access to all the park buildings.

A loud roar sounded from the trees and Greg could hear wood splintering. He jammed a key in the padlock and popped it open. He tugged on the door and it opened a couple of inches, blocked by the deep snow.

"Dammit," he raged.

The ground shook like a great carpenter was pounding on the earth with a sledge-hammer, over and over, trying to split it wide. Quickly he kicked off his snowshoes and used one like a shovel to move snow from the door.

Another sound, like a long, low growl emerged from the woods, maybe a hundred yards away.

Greg heaved on the door and it opened just far enough that he could slip inside and pull it shut behind him. Pulling his gun-free he ran up the stairs to the lantern room. The room was circular, with the huge lamp and lens situated in the middle, glass panes all around. He found the breaker switch and flipped it on, turning to look in the direction of the threat.

The blinding light started its sweep, starting at the seven o'clock position. When it rotated around to the three o'clock position, it should shine right over whatever hunted Greg.

He slipped out the glass door onto the catwalk that encircled the lantern room and dropped into a prone position, bringing his rifle up, ready to fire. He took no notice of the biting wind and snow that whipped around his face. When the huge beam of light swept across Greg's field of view, he saw a massive shadow coming through the trees, just at the edge of the clearing that surrounded the lighthouse.

"What the hell?" he said aloud.

His heart started racing. He knew whatever had been coming was big, but this was huge. Dinosaur huge. Images from the movie Jurassic Park intruded; a ravenous T-rex coming to tear up people, devouring whatever it found.

The lighthouse ray came around again and enough of the light filtered down through the flakes that Greg thought he saw... a face? The creature was only about thirty yards away now, growling like a prehistoric bear. It had to be thirty feet tall! He pointed his rifle in the direction of the monster and squeezed off a shot.

On the next revolution of the powerful lighthouse beacon, Greg caught a glimpse of a horizontal tree trunk coming at him with incredible speed, like a giant baseball bat. It was the last thing Greg Travis would ever see.

CHAPTER NINETEEN

If Ranger Sam Powers hadn't been outside Jotnar's Tavern after having dinner, thanking Matti for his help during the day's search for Paavo, he wouldn't have seen the old lighthouse beacon. A muffled gunshot sounded. Then the light went out in a flash of sparks. He and Matti stared in the direction of the historical landmark, snowflakes melting on their cheeks.

The air clouded with Matti's exhalation as he spoke, "What was that about?"

Sam stared in the direction of the lighthouse. Greg had gone out that way to look around for signs of Paavo or whatever took him. It had been a little over twelve hours since the kids had discovered he was gone. All tracks were basically gone, buried in the falling and drifting snow. Had he found something and turned on the light? Why wouldn't he have just radioed?

Sam looked at Matti and shook his head. "I dunno."

He pulled out his handheld radio and keyed the mic, "Greg."

Nothing.

Again. "Greg, you there?"

Silence.

"I'm going out there. See what's up."

"I might as well come with you," Matti said.

They climbed into Sam's four-wheel drive and started up the road. They hadn't gone more than two hundred yards when the truck stopped moving.

"Oh, you've got to be shitting me," Sam said.

"Where are the damned plows?" Matti asked.

"I haven't seen one all day," Sam answered. He tried working the truck from forward to reverse to forward, rocking it to see if he could get moving. It was no use. They were high-centered, the snow so deep the truck's frame was supported by it, putting little or no weight on the wheels.

"We can take one of Ernie's snowmobiles and my machine," Matti said, opening his door.

They made the quick trek back to the tavern, walking in the stranded vehicle's tracks. Sam could see the tracks already had a fresh coat of snow accumulating in them. This was one hell of a snowfall.

Matti opened the door to the tavern and shouted into Kearse, telling him they would be using a snowmobile for a little while to go check on Greg. Then they both tightened their hoods and walked around back where the snowmobiles were buried under a foot of snow. They quickly cleaned them off and cranked them up. Matti signaled for Sam to lead the way and they took off up the street.

Once past Sam's truck, the road looked like virgin snow in the arctic. In the darkness and limited visibility created by the falling snow, they blew right past the road that led to the lighthouse. They'd only gone about a quarter-mile beyond when the road curved and Sam realized their error. He pulled a tight turnaround and explained to Matti who merely shrugged.

Going slower, and paying closer attention, Sam found the road with no problems this time. It was less than a mile to the lighthouse. They reached Greg's park service truck which was axle-deep in snow and empty. Sam pushed on without stopping. Without warning, Sam's machine suddenly dropped into a deep hole in the snow. He gunned the throttle and popped back up onto the deeper snow and stopped. Matti had stopped on the other side of the hole, his snowmobile's headlight shining over it, casting the crater in dark shadow.

"What's this?" Sam asked loudly, to be heard over the idling snowmobiles.

Matti shook his head. He scanned around. "Looks like one of those weird tracks like we found at Paavo's." Then he pointed farther up the road, to the left of where Sam's headlight shined. "Looks like another one."

Sam climbed on his machine and motored up to the next indentation, Matti following close behind. They stared down at the deep depression in the snow. Dread filled Sam's heart. What the heck made this? And where was Greg?

With a sense of urgency, he headed toward the lighthouse, driving as fast as he dared, Matti's headlight illuminating the snow to either side of Sam's snowmobile, chasing the shadows back to the trees. The frightening tracks continued along their path, heading straight for the lighthouse.

When they pulled into the little yard that served as a parking lot for the historical site, Matti pulled up beside Sam and angled his machine away slightly to cover more ground with the headlights. They shut the motors off but left the lights on. Sam could see the padlock was missing from the door, though it was shut.

He pulled out his flashlight and shined it at the top of the tower. "Holy shit," he muttered. The lantern room was gone, its metallic roof resting crookedly where it used to be.

"What the fuck happened here?" Matti asked. He stared up at the destruction.

Sam shook his head and went to the tower door, yanking it open. "Come on." They needed to find Greg, hopefully holed up inside.

"Greg," he called from the doorway. There was no response.

Together, he and Matti climbed the stairs. At the top, they had to push debris away so they could mount the last couple of steps. Even then, they had to crawl out from under the tower's roof before they could stand. There was no sign of Greg.

Matti looked at Sam, an unspoken question floating in his eyes. Sam shrugged, frowning. They looked down at their snowmobiles from the catwalk and then Matti pointed to the right, just on the edge of the light. "What's that?" He indicated a dark shape protruding from the snow.

"Looks like the stock of a rifle," Sam said. He led them down and out into the yard and over to where Greg's 30.06 was stuck, barrel down, in the snow. He scanned the area with his flashlight and gasped. "Oh no."

The snow was pink where it covered fresh splashes of blood around a dark pile that was quickly becoming buried. Sam walked over quietly, struggling in the deep snow, each step sinking up over his knees. He wanted to see that pile and didn't. Each slow step was both a blessing and a curse, keeping him from a horrible truth. Matti stayed where he stood, staring, a grim frown on his face.

Sam took a hesitant step and reached down to wipe the snow from Greg's mangled torso. He easily recognized the man's black coat, but little else. Greg's head, arms and lower body were gone. A hollow cavern opened in Sam's stomach as he looked down at what was left of his friend. It almost looked like the young ranger's head had been... bitten off. The flesh appeared to have been sheared through cleanly, but not by any sort of cutting weapon. Where Greg's arms and legs had been, the injuries were similar. He turned back to Matti who met his gaze with a glassy stare.

Their search for Paavo was over. The old man hadn't hurt himself with an axe and wandered off. He'd been killed. Killed and taken by the same thing that had mangled Greg and destroyed the top of the lighthouse. Looking back at the bloody mess he noticed the huge tracks that led away.

"Tracks go west," he told Matti.

"You really want to find what made them?"

"Matti, the harbor is only about a hundred yards that way. Either it's still there, or it went into the water."

Matti looked west, into the dark and falling snow. "Let's get the hell out of here."

Sam nodded.

The short ride back to town went quickly, without mishap and without running across any more of the big tracks. They pulled up in front of Jotnar's Tavern and ran inside. At only eight-thirty, Ernest was preparing to close early due to the weather and lack of customers. Matti blurted out what had happened to Greg.

The old tavern owner narrowed his eyes. "It's happening again. It's a hard winter."

"What?" Sam asked.

"The whole town is gonna disappear," Ernest said.

"Oh shit, Ernest," Sam said. "Not now. We have a problem. Try the phone again."

Ernest walked to the end of the bar, picked up the handset of his telephone and put it to his ear. He held it out, examining it, before listening to the earpiece again. He shook his head as he replaced the receiver. "Still dead."

Sam dug his cell phone out of a pocket hidden beneath layers of winter clothes. He poked 9-1-1 into it and hit send. After a moment of silence, he too looked at his phone. He held it aloft and frowned. "Dammit. No bars at all."

"The snow?" Matti asked. Then he tried his phone with the same result.

"Maybe."

"Try your radio again," Ernest said. "That thing has to be good for something."

Sam shook his head. "This thing is low power, only good for about a mile, mile-and-a-half." Despite his statement to the contrary, he tried to raise the Sheriff's office, the nearest law enforcement outpost, and got no response.

"Tomorrow we'll send someone down to the Sheriff's office. Hopefully, the plows will have come through by then. Where the hell are they, anyway?"

"What do we do 'til tomorrow?" Matti asked.

"Get home and stay inside. Whatever this is, it seems to be killing people who are outside. And it seems like maybe it's just working in the dark. Thanks to this storm, no one will be going out tonight. Ernest, can we use the tavern as a command-post tomorrow?" Ernest nodded, wiping his bar down. "Okay. Let's meet back here at first light, about 8:30."

"Love these long winter nights," Matti said sarcastically. "Ernie, I'll see you in the morning."

"Don't call me 'Ernie'. I'm not a damned muppet!" Stress made Ernest ornery. Then the old man nodded and waved his hand dismissively. "Yeah. See you in the morning." He caught Matti's eyes with his own. "Be careful."

Ernest's residence was located just behind the tavern and he kept a path cleared between the two so he and his wife could walk back and forth. His snowmobiles were for recreation and days like this.

Sam and Matti headed outside, each jumping on a snowmobile and heading home as fast as they dared in the whiteout conditions. Somewhere out in the dark, something hunted.

CHAPTER TWENTY

Sam had to make a stop before he went home. He drove straight to Bill Hitze's house, hoping he'd find Dr. Crowe there as well. She certainly couldn't be driving out tonight.

A solid pounding on the rickety storm door was unexpectedly answered by Tril. The young woman had shed her winter layers and was in a sweatshirt and sweatpants.

"Hey, Mr. Powers," she said. Her voice was monotone and devoid of emotion. She opened the door, ushering the ranger inside.

"Tril. Didn't expect to see you here."

"My folks were speaking at a conference but are stuck in Chicago 'cause of the snow, so Mr. Hitze asked if I wanted to stay here tonight."

Sam nodded. Good ol' Bill, watching out for her, just in case.

Bill and Steph were sitting on the couch, sipping something hot and smelling a lot like hot buttered rum. Brandon sat up from where he was laying on the floor and Tril walked over to sit in the easy chair.

Upon seeing Sam, Bill stood. "What's up, Sam?"

He glanced uneasily at the two kids. "Do you and Dr. Crowe have a minute to talk?"

"Sure. Come sit at the table. You want a drink?"

Sam nodded. "Please." He pulled off his boots and coat and took a seat at the little kitchen table. Steph joined him as Bill poured another hot drink. Sam couldn't conceal his concern and sadness. Steph reached across and put her hand on top of his.

"What is it?" she asked.

He glanced again at the kids.

"You want some privacy?" Bill asked.

Sam blew out a long breath. "I guess not. They will have to know, sooner or later."

Steph frowned. "Know what?"

The kids, their curiosity peeked, came and stood by the table, waiting.

"Something happened up at the lighthouse..." Sam described what he and Matti had discovered, choking up when he mentioned Greg's remains, the emotion finally blooming from the seed it had first been. Tril started to weep, not only for Greg, but for her friend Paavo. Her quiet sobs were the first domino as silent tears slid from everyone's eyes. Brandon took her in a hug and Bill grasped Steph's shoulders as he stood behind her. Steph took Sam's hand in both of hers, fixing her wet, concerned eyes on his.

"There's more," Sam said. "This part is a little... speculative." The four waited in silence, not sure how there could be more. "It looked kind of like Greg's head had been... bitten off."

Steph's eyes immediately jumped to Bill who took a seat beside her.

"That body you two found out in the lake. Wasn't its head gone?" Sam asked.

Steph nodded. "I'm not a medical examiner by any stretch, but I kind of thought it looked like it had been removed, uh, cleanly. From here, to here." She traced a slight arc, starting from one clavicle and draping over to the other clavicle, like she was describing where a necklace would hang.

"That's how it was with Greg," Sam said, caressing his forehead.

Quietly, the adults looked at each other, the unspoken question looming in the air. Brandon and Tril looked on, confusion playing on their faces.

Sam finally had to voice his thoughts. "Dr. Crowe, do you think whatever killed Greg is the same thing that killed that guy you found?"

She withdrew her hands and frowned, deep in thought. Bill stared at her. "I don't know how that would even be possible. Our guy died, what, almost 180 years ago?"

"Maybe not the exact same thing. But the same type of thing?" Sam pushed.

"I guess it's possible. But what the hell could it be? Didn't you say the top of the lighthouse was wrecked? What could have done that?"

Sam shook his head, dejected.

"Something is killing people," Bill said. He hesitated. Then, "Looks like it probably got Paavo first. Now Greg. And Greg had a gun. Whatever it is must be sneaky or really tough, or fast. Sam, what kind of tracks did you see?"

"Big ones. Never seen anything like it. Kind of like a man would walk, but no boot prints or toes. Nothing like that, just big, oblong tracks."

"We need the State Police." Bill went to the phone mounted on the wall and put the receiver to his ear. He replaced it on the cradle with a frown. "Dead."

Sam nodded. "Same thing at Jotnar's. Figured they were all down. Cells aren't getting anything either and my radio doesn't reach the Sheriff's office. I figure someone can zip down there tomorrow on a snowmobile if the plows haven't come through yet."

"Why wait?" Steph asked.

"This thing kills in the dark. At least, that what it looks like." No one spoke for a long moment, each a captive to their own thoughts. Then Sam said, "We're meeting at Jotnar's in the morning, around 8:30. Spread the word tomorrow morning. Don't go out tonight."

"What are we going to do?" Bill asked.

"Haven't decided yet. Maybe we'll all just convoy down to Calumet or Houghton, get everyone safe. I'll get some support from the State Police and the Sheriff's office, come back up here. Until then, stay inside." He stood up and started donning his winter clothes.

"Thanks, Sam. Be careful," Bill said. They walked to the door and Sam left, Bill closing and locking the door behind him.

He turned and looked at Steph and the kids who were wide-eyed and pale. His gaze focused on the black-haired professor. "So?" he said.

"I don't know. Seems likely that whatever killed Greg killed that guy you found, except that it isn't logical."

Bill nodded. "Not at all. What the hell could wreck the lighthouse too? And Sam has no idea what kind of tracks he saw? He knows all the animals up here."

"Dad, what are we gonna do?" Brandon asked.

Bill saw that both kids were terrified and fighting to look calm and adult. "We'll stay in tonight and go to the meeting in the morning. Tomorrow we'll probably all head to Houghton, check in to a hotel."

"You're welcome to stay at my house," Steph offered. Bill nodded his thanks.

"Steph, you familiar with shotguns?"

She nodded. "Kind of. No expert, though."

"Okay. I have a pump and a semi-auto. I'll give you the pump, if that works?" She nodded again.

"Brandon, I'll give you the semi-auto. And a crash course on gun-safety and how it works."

Brandon swallowed and nodded. Tril placed her hand on Brandon's back.

"I think we should be ready to head straight to Houghton tomorrow morning. I don't want to hang around here until they kill whatever is out there."

"If they *can* kill it," Steph whispered.

CHAPTER TWENTY-ONE

The whole town was represented at the meeting that morning at Ernest Kearse's tavern and eatery. The parking lot was full of snowmobiles, the plows still strangely absent. In all, about thirty people were there. Most of them ordered some sort of breakfast so Matti was pressed into service to help the one waitress that was typically more than adequate. In the kitchen, Ernest and Suzy were noisily cooking away, pots and pans clanging and the grill sizzling. The whole place smelled of hickory smoked bacon, eggs, toast and maple syrup. Ernest would only serve 100% pure maple syrup, nothing less would do. Matti and the waitress, Tammy, hustled around with plates in both hands and pitchers of coffee. Though the talk was hushed and concerned, there was enough of it to make the place sound like a bar after work.

Matti saw Sam raise his hands for quiet. Then the ranger said, "I'm sure you've all heard that Paavo went missing and we weren't able to find him. But last night something else happened that you all need to know about." He went on to tell about the lighthouse and he and Matti going out there and finding Greg's remains.

There were gasps and muffled screams of dismay.

"What have you been drinking, ranger?" came a voice out of the crowd.

"It's true," Matti yelled above the din. "I heard the gunshot and I went out there with Sam. Whatever killed Greg left some big-ass tracks."

Sam's face scrunched up, then relaxed. "I know the tracks of all the animals up here, but I've never seen anything like that."

"Did you call the police? No offense Sam, but sounds like we need more than just you."

Sam nodded emphatically. "I agree. But all the phones are out and my radio doesn't reach the Sheriff's office. Which brings me to my next point." He went on to say that two volunteers were on their way to the Sheriff's office in Eagle River, about fifteen miles away, to tell them what was going on so they could get help.

Matti heard everyone start talking at once. People were afraid of whatever was out there. He said, "This thing has only attacked at night. You should be safe enough today."

"Why don't we all just get the hell out of here?" another voice asked.

"That would have been my plan, had the plows come through. But we don't have enough snowmobiles. Whoever goes to the Sheriff can also see about getting plows up here so we can drive out of here. If that doesn't pan out, then we may have to shuttle people on snowmobiles. But yes, I think you all should get out of town. Anyone who has the means to leave, please feel free-"

He was interrupted by the tavern door slamming open and two snow-covered figures shaking the snow to the floor. Joe Harris and Mary Pinanen stood there looking at the assembled town-folk. Sam looked at them, clearly surprised.

"Highway 26 is blocked," Mary said.

"Blocked?" Sam asked.

"Couple of big trees across it," Joe said. "Like they were stacked there. Not a mile out of town. We're going to go down 41. Just wanted to report first."

"Was the road plowed on the other side of the trees?" Bill asked.

"No. Not as far as we could see," Mary said. "But in this snow, we could only see about fifty, maybe seventy-five yards past it."

All eyes turned to Sam. "Huh. Wasn't expecting that. Well, get going and keep your eyes open. Hopefully, 41 will be open."

Mary and Joe headed back into the snowy outdoors. Their machines started and could be heard driving away.

"You think someone is trying to block the roads out of town?" someone asked.

"No," Sam answered without hesitation. "Trees probably just fell under the snow and wind. We've seen that happen enough up here."

"Don't see any other trees down," the voice muttered. It didn't look like Sam had heard it, but Matti did. If that was true, it was a good, and disturbing point.

"The trail was groomed before we got all this snow. Should be able to use it," Jansen said. He was sitting by himself at a table against one wall.

"Yeah," Sam said, "but if someone gets buried on the trail, there's really no way to get around them." The ranger was talking about the hazard of a snowmobiler going through deep, unpacked snow, when the snowmobile's track digs the machine into a hole, rather than propelling it forward. Once 'buried', getting moving again can be near impossible and requires a ton of labor. Stopping in this kind of snow can exponentially raise the chances of 'burying' your machine. The roads are solid at their base, whereas the trail is still just packed snow at its best. Trying to run through the woods would be equally difficult as maneuvering in the deep snow is trying enough without having to steer around trees. And just outside of town, the trees are so close together that driving through that with a snowmobile was near to impossible.

Matti said, "I think we should stick to the roads for now. If we end up walking, we'll eventually get to where it's plowed."

"Which brings up a good point," Sam said. "If we have to ride out of here, make sure you bring your snowshoes with ya."

"What's the plan then, Sam?" someone asked.

"We'll wait until we hear from Mary and Joe about the roads and Sheriff's office. I'd expect them to get the road cleared in a hurry knowing we want to evacuate town. Once the road is cleared, everyone get out of town and wait for the all-clear."

"Sam, you said that you and Matti heard Greg shoot before the lighthouse was destroyed. Did you find any blood?" Jansen asked. Sam shook his head and Matti saw Jansen and a few other people frown. "Is he a good shot?"

"He's a fine shot," Sam said.

"How'd he not hit something big enough to destroy the light at the lighthouse?" This was followed by some affirming grunts.

"We don't know how big it is, how fast it is, and it was dark with only a moving lighthouse beacon to give him any light, and he probably knew it was coming for him. How'd you all shoot in those conditions?" Sam said, his voice taking an edge. "Having said that, I'd highly recommend you carry whatever firearms you have with you. Don't shoot anyone else. I'm guessing if you see this thing, you'll know it's a threat."

"Any reason to not leave?" Bruce Feeny asked, stressing the word 'not'. He was a small, grizzled man of about fifty. Next to him was an equally grizzled woman with a cup of coffee in her hands, his wife, Nora. The two looked like they'd lived in the wilds, surviving by their own wits for the last thirty years.

"If you have enough snowmobiles to get yourselves out of town, then I'm not keeping you here. But I don't want to leave someone here just because they don't have a way out. I'm staying until everyone is evacuated."

"See you all in Houghton," the man said, standing. He helped his wife getting her coat on.

The sound of a snowmobile, traveling fast, penetrated the lull in the conversation. The sound grew louder until it roared and shuddered to an eerie silence. The door to the tavern flew open and Mary Pinanen burst into the room.

"It got Joe!"

CHAPTER TWENTY-TWO

The last two days had been bad enough, now things were getting worse. Bill hadn't minded Steph having to stay the night at his house, but now he wished they were all somewhere, anywhere, else. And he felt he needed to protect Tril as well, with her parents out of town and unable to return. When Mary burst into the tavern, the look of terror on her face cut through the crowd like a scythe, leaving a poison of fear in every wound.

"Mary, what happened?" Bill asked before anyone else could speak.

"We were only about a mile down the road and there were trees all across it. As we slowed down to look for a way around, I could feel tremors, like short, little earthquakes. Then the trees flew apart on the road in front of us. We turned around and gunned the machines. It went after Joe. Chased him down and..." She covered her wind-reddened face with her hands, sobbing.

Sam was next to her in an instant, an arm around her shoulders. "What was it?"

Mary dropped her hands and looked around at everyone staring at her, her lips narrowing and pulling tight. Slowly, her head shook and she stared at the floor.

Bill had never experienced a silence this complete in Jotnar's, ever. He could feel and hear his own pulse as he waited for her to speak.

Finally, she said, "It was huge. A man? It looked like... a man. Kind of."

"How big was he?" Sam asked. If he'd been surprised by her revelation, he wasn't showing it, pursuing more details.

Mary looked up, her mind reaching back to see how big this monster was, trying to envision it again. "At least twice, no a lot bigger, probably three or four times as tall as we are. One of its legs was-" she opened her arms in a wide arc, like she was wrapping them around the trunk of an oak tree.

"A giant?" Bill asked. What the frightened woman described sounded like a monster out of 'Jack and the Beanstalk'. How could such a thing exist? He and several others looked over at Matti, who stood behind the bar, towering over everyone in the room. A man that made Matti look like a toddler?

"That's crazy," someone said. Sam instantly shushed them.

"It ain't crazy," Ernest's voice boomed from the kitchen door. "It's a damned frost giant! That's what it is."

Everyone turned to stare at the loremaster of the village. He had always hinted at strange tales when he told anyone about the disappearance of the town back in the 1840s. The hints circled around a massive creature that attacked the town, though most believed it was a rogue polar bear that had somehow migrated down during the harsh winter. Ernest had always played up the mysterious and unexplained nature of the event. Bill thought it was just for entertainment purposes. Now he wasn't sure.

"Dad?" Brandon asked. Bill shrugged.

"What the hell are you talking about, Ernest?" Jansen asked.

"You've all heard about the town's history, the whole population disappearing back in the winter of 1842. I've told the story a hundred times."

"But you're full of shit," someone said, eliciting weak chuckles.

"It's true," Steph put in. "The town did disappear. Without a trace until this past summer when Bill and I found evidence that some of them went through the ice on the big lake. And one of the bodies had been mutilated, like what happened to Greg."

"But we're talking about a giant?" Jansen said. He wasn't arguing, just unable to process what they were discussing. In that, he and Bill were alike.

Steph looked in Ernest's direction and the old man continued, his wife holding his arm, looking out at the crowd, her face stern and hard.

"My Grandmother told me stories that she'd heard passed down from her family. Back in 1842, someone had gotten word down to Eagle River that a monster, a huge monster, was storming the town. But no one believed it and it was forgotten. Never went into any official reports. By the time anyone got up here, the thing was long gone. Everything I ever found on the disappearance didn't fit an attack of anything we've ever seen before. They tried to force the explanation of a polar bear on the evidence, but it just doesn't fit. If it was a frost giant, that would seem to explain a lot."

Sam looked deflated. "What the hell is a frost giant, Ernest?"

"It's a giant! Apparently wakes up when it's shit-ass cold. Eats people or whatever it can get its hands on."

"If it's a giant, we should be able to kill it," Jansen said. "We've got rifles."

"They had muskets back in 1842," Bill said.

"What? Are you really assuming this is the same giant from almost 200 years ago?" Jansen asked.

Bill turned fierce eyes on Jansen. "It's a fucking *giant* you genius. Why couldn't it live that long? We didn't think such a thing even existed." Bill could feel his face beginning to flush. "And if they could have just shot it, don't you think they would have and then we'd all have known about it and the whole damned town wouldn't have disappeared?"

Steph took Bill's hand and patted it.

"Okay. Thanks, Bill," Sam said. "Good points."

"I say we get the hell out of Dodge," Bruce Feeny said. He and Nora were moving toward the door. Several others grunted in assent, standing up and pulling on their winter clothes.

"No!" Mary screamed. "Don't go. He'll get you. He ran Joe down like nothing."

"We'll take the trail up on the ridge. You said he was down on 41." Bruce replied.

Bill saw Sam grit his teeth and shake his head slowly. "Bruce," Sam said, "I think that's a really bad idea."

"This is a free country. You can't keep us here."

"No. But I don't want you two to get killed, either."

"We're going. Right, Nora?" Nora nodded, fire in her eyes.

"Anyone else coming?" Bruce asked. Over half the people there stood up to leave. "We all go at once, he can't catch everybody."

"If you get through, send help," Sam said.

Bruce nodded and escorted his wife of thirty-two years out the door, followed by the others. An entire fleet of snowmobiles roared to life, then slowly faded as the crowd raced away.

Of those that remained, a few people stared at the door, wistful, but full of fear. The rest simply looked down at the floor.

"I say we try to kill it," Jansen said. "How many rifles we got?" Most of the remaining people indicated they had one. He leveled expectant eyes on Sam.

"I'm not going hunting," Sam said. "But seems as we are not going to be leaving town, we can lie in wait for it. If it shows up, we give it everything we got. Who's in?"

About half the assembled raised their hands, including Brandon and Tril. Bill glared at them. "Brandon, you don't even have a rifle."

"Slugs will hurt it." He puffed out his chest, clearly not wanting to be emasculated in front of Tril.

Bill sighed. A one-ounce slug did pack a big punch, but he certainly preferred for both of the kids to stay with Steph at the house. He turned to the professor to get her support and saw her hand go up. She looked him square in the face.

"You too?" he said to Steph.

"Sam, you got an extra rifle?"

"You can use Greg's," Sam answered.

She gave Bill a triumphant grin. Tril, too, gave him a classic 'you're not my parent' look. Ah, shit. This had better work.

Sam saw both kids with their hands up and looked at Bill. Bill grimaced and gave an assenting nod.

"Okay, everyone who's not coming, go home and stay inside, in the basement, if you have one. Stay away from windows in case the lead starts flying."

A spattering of people stood and slipped into their heavy winter wear before filing out the door. The frigid air blew into the tavern, whitening its path as it arced in and settled to the floor where it swirled around feet. Bill watched as at least ten long-arms went with them, hoping those ten guns weren't missed when they faced the monster. Engines fired up outside and one by one, people rode off to their homes to hunker down and see what happened.

Bill looked at those who remained; a mix of sexes and ages ranging from Brandon at fifteen all the way up to a rugged old Yooper named Fritz who was apparently immune to death and remained active despite the aches and pains he complained about under his breath. He was glad to see Fritz there. The man always brought home a buck during deer season, his shooting skills seasoned and proven. Well into his eighties, the guy was one tough old cuss. Matti and Jansen were there too.

Ernest and Suzy would stay here at the tavern. Ernest, being dedicated to fishing, not hunting, didn't own a gun other than the pistol he kept secreted under the bar.

Bill counted; eighteen guns. sixteen high-powered firearms against a being that shouldn't even exist.

Sam looked at Brandon and Steph. "Slugs?" Brandon nodded. "Go for the body, not the head. Anyone who doubts their marksmanship," he glanced at Steph, "go for the body. Everyone else, headshots." No one questioned the ranger. He handed the professor his late friend's 30.06.

"Where should we set up?" Bill asked.

"It's too cold to sit outside for long so we're going to need to be able to go in and warm up." Sam scanned the group and addressed four people. "Can we use your places as hides? The corner of 41 and 26 seems a likely spot if he's working both roads." He posed the question to those who had homes or businesses at the intersection, Fritz being one of those. Getting consent from all he said, "Groups of four at each site. Bill, you and your crew go with Fritz, I'll tag on with one of the other groups. Each group should have two people outside at a time, somewhere the others can see them. Cycle in when you get cold. If someone sees it, or think they see it, raise your gun in that direction and yell. We'll all follow suit. If you're inside and you see rifles go up, get your ass outside, ready to shoot. Have your snowmobiles ready to roll in case we gotta get out of there or be prepared to get inside if you can." He surveyed the hunting party. "Questions? No. Okay, let's go."

They'd only ridden two blocks when they saw what looked like a junkyard for snowmobiles. At least ten machines were strewn in the middle of the snow-covered street, laying on their sides, upside down, some upright, but all of them destroyed beyond repair. As they drew near the first sled, Bill saw the blood that was smeared all over the seat and handlebars. More blood than he'd ever seen before. The snowmobiles all looked like they had been dropped from the sky to bounce and roll into the wrecked heaps they were now. There were no tracks and no bodies anywhere to be seen.

Sam led the group a block over to avoid the wreckage, both because it was difficult to maneuver around and because it had a chilling effect on the group going to lay an ambush. Bill was glad he did until they saw another pile of destroyed machines on the next street.

It appeared that none of the people who'd left the tavern with plans of escape had made it very far. How the hell did the thing catch them all? The thought scared the hell out of him and he felt Steph squeeze tighter around his waist as she sat behind him. He glanced back at Tril and Brandon and saw Tril shake her head in disbelief. Brandon was staring at the heaps of parts that had been highly engineered snowmobiles.

An uneasy feeling slinked its way under Bill's skin. Here they were, riding snowmobiles right where it looked like the monster was putting an end to snowmobiles and those who rode them. He looked around, eyes frantically searching, but finding nothing but fresh snow and more of it falling through the bitter air. He was more than relieved when they made it to their rendezvous. He took one last look around.

Somewhere out there was a monster.

Bill and Steph took the first shift outside, letting Fritz, Brandon and Tril stay in Fritz's little house. When he glanced at the big front window of the home, Bill saw Fritz chattering away with the kids. He was probably regaling them with stories of the past, or of hunting victories. Brandon had a dumbfounded look on his face but Tril was all smiles. Hunting stories.

The breeze was gentle but the cold it carried bit into exposed skin like the venomous fangs of a viper. Bill pulled his scarf up over his nose and it tickled the eyelashes on his lower lids every time he blinked. Snow fell silently in the gray daylight, the flakes flashing quickly to the ground in hard little crystals. If they had floated gently down as always depicted on a picturesque Christmas card, it would actually seem pleasant. But the flakes fell with a purpose; to bury the town in as much snow as possible in the least amount of time.

The whole town was quiet. No snowmobiles roaring about, no trucks, cars, and for some reason, no damned plows. Initially, some of the residents had used their personal trucks to clear some of the roads in town. But the drifting had come on too fast for anything but the big county trucks to handle. Now, with the threat of this 'giant', no one wanted to go out, so the roads would remain impassible.

Steph squirmed incessantly. She turned to Bill. "My hands are cold."

"Sling your gun over your shoulder and put them in your pockets. They'll warm up fast," he told her. The cold metal of a gun on a day like this could suck the warmth from your hands in no time, even through the best gloves. Bill cradled his rifle in the crook of his elbow where there was more insulation but he could still bring the weapon up quickly. "If you get too cold, we'll go in."

Steph nodded. She looked like an arctic explorer with a black balaclava covering her face that was white with frost from her breath, a fur-lined hood pulled tightly over her head, snow pants and big winter boots. Her dark, brown eyes were as cheerful as ever, even in these dire circumstances. He let his focus on her linger just a moment too long.

"Everything okay?" she asked.

He turned and scanned the area. "Yeah. Sorry. Just thinking how nice it would be if we weren't waiting for a monster."

The balaclava didn't hide the smile that reached her eyes. "Yeah. I wish we were out on your boat again. That was fun. And not nearly as scary."

Bill nodded and sighed. This was hardly the time or place for reminiscing or dreaming, no matter how much he wanted to.

Across the intersection, he could see two or three of the other hunters, waiting in anxious anticipation with their guns, slowly bobbing up and down on flexing legs to generate heat. Diagonally through the intersection were Sam and Jansen. The ranger a stoic, silent sentry, whereas Jansen was the distracted child who had to go potty. Sam was a good man. Jansen, not so much. Bill shook his head. Maybe he was being too hard on Jansen. After all, he was out here trying to help. And this wasn't exactly fun.

"I gotta go in," Steph said. She turned and stomped along the little path they'd packed between their post and the door to Fritz's house.

Bill fell in behind her. Fritz was out the door before they got there, rifle in one hand, holding the door for the professor with the other. But Brandon and Tril strolled out before Steph could walk into the coveted warmth of the house, the kids oblivious to courtesy. Bill decided to let it go, they had bigger worries.

"Stay alert," he said to Brandon as they passed. Brandon nodded, doing his best impression of an obedient soldier off to take point. And like a soldier waiting for battle, Bill wished both that it was over and that it wouldn't happen at all. Most of all, he hoped they could kill this thing.

Bill closed the door tightly behind him and took off his coat, hat and gloves. Steph had already shed her winter garb, except her boots and snow-pants, and was standing with her back to the fireplace with her hands reaching back to grab the heat. Bill stood next to her after throwing another log on the dwindling blaze. Bill was glad that Fritz had started the fire so they could warm up faster after coming in from the bitter air. Steph cozied up to him, pulling him close to share body heat. He reached around her with one arm and she snuggled in tighter.

"It is so cold out there," she said. They were both staring out the picture window where they could see Fritz and the kids. The shapes of the two hunters at the far side of the intersection were unidentifiable through the heavy snow.

"I haven't seen it this cold, this long, pretty much... ever," Bill said. "Wish it'd warm up about twenty degrees."

He realized then that he was holding her, holding this delightful, beautiful woman, as naturally as he'd hold his own child. And his heart was beating its normal rhythm. How had that happened?

"Do you think this will work?" Steph asked suddenly.

Bill continued looking out the window, feeling the comfort of the fire on his legs working its way up his back. "I sure hope so. Can't imagine anything being able to withstand a barrage of hunting rounds."

"Before this, could you imagine an actual man-eating giant?" Steph asked.

Bill looked at her and pursed his lips as a hollow feeling filled his stomach. "No. I guess not." For a minute he was despondent, fearful. What if she was right and this giant couldn't be killed? They all might die, right here.

He was looking at Brandon when he saw the boy raise the shotgun, joined by Fritz and Tril. "Let's go," he shouted, throwing on his coat and pulling his hat and gloves on as he burst through the door. He didn't notice Steph right behind him, focused on getting outside to address the threat to them all. But no one was firing.

Bill stepped in between Brandon and Tril, raising his rifle and looking up highway 26 toward Brockway Mountain and the snowmobile trail. He saw Steph pull up next to Fritz.

"Where is it?" Bill said.

"I can't see it," Fritz said. The old man lowered his rifle part way, peering off into the distance. "They said they saw something big off that way, but I don't-" His words were silenced by a tremor that rumbled through the ground. Another followed. Then another.

"Holy shit," Brandon muttered. "The ground's shaking."

"Keep your eyes peeled," Fritz ordered. "Don't stare down the highway, it could be circling around us. Keep looking around." The old man crouched forward, his rifle in both hands, ready to be raised to his shoulder, his head on a swivel.

The tremors picked up in frequency. Bill imagined the giant's pace increasing, each massive leg hammering the ground with avalanche-like force. But out in the whiteness of the snowstorm, he could see nothing of the monster.

A shot rang out, and a shout, followed by a cacophony of gunfire. Two teams, eight people in all, had their guns pointed up and into the gray light down highway 26. Bill's team raised their guns and watched as a huge area darkened, then sharpened into the shape of a massive man-like body. Gray, stringy hair dangled from a balding pate and he wore only a primitive pair of shorts and some sort of moccasin style boots. The boots and loin-cloth looked to be made of human skin. Dried, red streaks ran down from the corners of a gaping maw. The towering man-beast didn't slow, striding confidently directly at the band of warriors.

"Steph, Brandon, body shots," Bill said. Then he fired his first round at the head of the giant that stormed their position.

The air around him exploded as his team and the fourth team joined in the attack, the guns flashing in a dizzying display of light, the booming thunder from weapons of various caliber ripping snowflakes into mist from the soundwaves alone. From the corner of his eye, he could see Brandon frantically trying to reload his shotgun, having fired his four rounds with blinding speed, if not accuracy. His ear oddly focused on the slow, rhythmic pounding of Tril's 30.06 rifle, firing away in a measured cadence, not at all panicked. Through his scope, Bill saw the crude, cruel visage of a man. A bloody snarl contorted the creature's mouth revealing squarish teeth, not unlike Bill's own. The skin was light-gray and looked more like stone or dirty snow. The eyes, bluish-white, radiated anything but human compassion, hate, hunger and evil played in those devilish orbs.

Bill fixed the crosshairs of his sights directly on one of those massive eyes and squeezed the trigger. Over the sound of the gunfire, he heard a deep bass grunt. But the ground continued to shake.

He looked over his scope and saw the monster close on the group of shooters directly across the road, apparently unaffected by what was surely a head-shot, if not one directly to the eye. The four people scattered, jumping on snowmobiles. Bill knew one was Matti, the man's tall form easy to identify, even from a distance. He emptied his two remaining rounds at the giant and heard Brandon's Remington 870 roar four times in quick succession. All to no effect.

One of the fleeing riders sped into the middle of the intersection and the giant jumped forward, pulling the person from the snowmobile's seat with one massive, engulfing hand.

"Get inside," Bill ordered. He could see the other teams running for the shelter of the houses that now looked as safe as the first little piggy's house of straw.

But perhaps getting out of sight would help. It was clear that they wouldn't outrun the giant, snowmobiles or not.

Steph led the way, followed by the kids then Fritz. As Bill fell in behind, he watched the giant lift the yelling woman to his mouth and bite her head clean off, her screams stopping with dreadful quickness. With his other hand, he threw her snowmobile at one of the other fleeing hunters. The machine crashed into the racing sled and its rider flew into the snow, struggled to stand up and tried to run through the knee-deep snow. Bill reached the door and turned back in time to see the giant grab this second unfortunate soul. The beast must have squeezed then because he heard the cracking of bones and saw blood and meat explode from within the giant's fist.

"Get in the basement," he heard Fritz ordering, followed by the pattering of boots running down the stairs. The ground continued to tremble.

Bill charged into the basement and found himself looking his son directly in the eye. He could see the unspoken terror and hopelessness he felt reflected there. Steph and Tril didn't appear to be faring any better. He knew he should say something to reassure everyone, but he wasn't sure they were going to live and couldn't think of a good lie. Only Fritz had a steely look of determination on his face and Bill took some comfort from that.

"Do you think they got away?" Tril asked, her voice hollow and quiet.

"It got two of them, but I suspect everyone else is hiding like us," Bill said. Steph looked at him in alarm, her eyes widening unnaturally and pursing her lips. He noticed the look and shrugged as if to say, *no use hiding the truth.* She shook her head slightly and wrapped an arm around Tril.

"We shot that sumbitch a hundred times," Fritz growled. "I can't imagine he'll live long with that much lead in him."

"I hope not," Brandon said despondently.

"Don't count on it," Bill said.

"Bill!" Steph exclaimed.

"What? I shot it in the eye and it didn't even twitch. I don't think the guns were doing anything to it."

Steph rubbed her forehead. "We must have hurt it. That thing was hard to miss."

"I know I hit it," Fritz said with a snarl.

Bill looked at the little hunting party. The truth couldn't be avoided and he wouldn't dance around it. "They probably shot it with fucking muskets back in eighteen-forty-whatever, and they got wiped out." He took a breath to calm himself. "I'll go look and see if we drew blood. If we did, then maybe it'll die or we can kill it with guns."

"You're not going out there?" Steph asked.

Bill looked around the small, dank cellar and frowned. "Ground isn't shaking," he said. Everyone stood still and looked at each other, shaking their heads.

"Maybe it's dead," Brandon said hopefully. After seeing his father's skeptical grimace, he amended, "Or just gone."

"It could be waiting. Like an ambush," Tril said.

"Yes, Bill. Don't go out there," Steph said.

"That fucking thing doesn't ambush, sweetheart," Fritz spat. "Didn't you notice it just walk right at us as we were shooting at it? If it wants us, it'll just come take us." He slapped Bill on the shoulder. "Come on. I'll go with ya."

He stomped up the wooden stairs, not waiting for anything. Bill glanced at Steph, "We'll be back in a few minutes." She nodded silently and he turned and followed Fritz.

The two men stopped at the picture window and looked out at the intersection. The sky was still gray and issuing forth flakes at an alarming rate. Every now and then the wind would whip the falling snow into little cylinders of twirling white. Diagonally across the crossroads, Bill saw someone moving, gun in hand.

"Someone's out there. Let's go," he said.

They slipped through the door onto the boot-packed path into the yard and headed to the site where the gun-team had been attacked. The other figure was moving in the same direction. As they slogged through the deep snow, getting closer to where the giant had been, Bill could finally identify Sam by his forest-green winter coat and hat. They came together in an area where

246

it looked like a herd of elephants had decided to roll around in the snow, the giant's tracks. Sam's face was grim.

"Holy shit," the ranger said, shaking his head. "That didn't go well."

"Understatement of the century," Fritz said.

"We had to have hit it," Bill said. "Didn't look like it felt anything."

Sam shrugged as he looked around in the snow. "I emptied my mag into its head."

"I shot that big sumbitch right in the nuts and it didn't even flinch," Fritz said.

Bill threw a confused and surprised look at the rugged old man. He was glad he was on Fritz's good side. He walked around in the snow scanning for any sign that the monster had been injured. A splotch of crimson shaded the pure white of the freshly fallen snow. "Here's some blood." He looked around.

"That's Carolyn's," Sam said sadly. He dropped his chin to his chest, wilting.

"Carolyn, huh? Who was the other?"

Sam took a deep breath. "Think it was Bob."

"At least they went together," Fritz said. "Nothing wrong in that."

Bill's head spun. Why was this happening? Good people getting cut down by some awful monster from God-knows-where. The three men stood quietly, each considering the circumstances and paying silent tribute to the young couple. Thank God they didn't have any kids. But it was wrong that they should be taken in what, their early thirties?

"Where'd he go?" Bill asked. He turned in a circle, trying to determine where the gargantuan tracks went.

Sam pointed. "Off towards Brockway. Where he came from," he said, referring to the high ridge west of town upon which a seasonal road served as the snowmobile trail during winter. He walked in that direction, examining the snow near the monster's trail. Bill and Fritz slogged behind, Bill half-heartedly, Fritz like he was following a still-living Hitler. The old guy had his rifle in both hands and was scanning the horizon with his pale eyes, teeth gritted.

After several yards, Sam stopped and shook his head. "Dammit. Guns didn't do anything to it. There's not even a hint of blood."

"I'm sure I hit it right in the eye. It didn't even react," Bill said.

By now some of the other hunters were emerging from their hiding places in the houses and approached the three men. Sam signaled for everyone to gather around in the middle of the intersection, waving at the houses where some hunters were cautiously peeking out the windows. After a few minutes the whole crew was assembled, minus four.

"Anyone know what happened to Matti and Jim?" Sam asked, referring to the last two from the team that took the brunt of the giant's assault.

"Last I saw, they were both on snowmobiles heading into town," Jansen said. "Where's the giant?" he asked, looking around with wide eyes.

"Not here," Sam said. "We'll feel him if he's coming."

"Did we get him?" Jansen asked.

Sam frowned. "No. I think all we did is piss it off."

CHAPTER TWENTY-THREE

Word was spread that there was another meeting at Jotnar's that afternoon, but it wasn't attended nearly as well as the one that morning. To Bill's relief, Matti and Joe were already there telling Ernest and Suzy what had happened. Most of the people in town had felt the tremors of the giant's running footfalls and some refused to leave their homes. Bill surveyed the folks who had managed their fear enough to come find out what was going on. Most looked worn and desperate, which is how he felt. Everyone pulled chairs out and arranged them in a semblance of a semi-circle so they could hear Sam and converse easier.

When Sam told them that the monster had been completely unaffected by the guns, there was a collective groan. Seated to Bill's right, Steph reached over and grasped his hand. When she did, he looked to his left where Brandon leaned forward, elbows on his knees and hands on his head. Just on Brandon's other side, Tril leaned back in her chair, arms hanging limply and chin on her chest, looking like she was going to flow out of her seat like melted ice-cream. Just then he really wished Tril's parents were here so he had one less thing to worry about. It was hard enough worrying about how Brandon and Steph were handling this mess. Though Tril was a tough little nut, this situation was far beyond even the adults in the room. He watched her eyes as Sam described the fight. To him, they looked cold and analytical, like she was taking everything in like she was sitting in high-school physics class. By contrast, Brandon looked like a kid who was taking an exam in a class he'd never attended.

"What are we going to do, Bill?" Steph whispered.

He turned to her and quickly raised his eyebrows and shook his head. "Hide? I dunno." Dammit, why were there so many questions and no answers? Why did she ask him, like he knew what to do now? He just wanted to get the hell out of here, but they couldn't do that because the plows were nowhere to be seen, there were no phones, and that big fucking monster seemed to stomp anything that tried to get out of town. With his free hand, he massaged his forehead and eyes before letting his fingers slide down to stroke his chin.

Questions assailed him. How did this thing get here? Where did it come from? If it is the same thing from 1842, how'd it survive? How do they kill it? *Can* they kill it? The questions and uncertainty threatened to overwhelm him. He sucked in a deep breath, Sam's voice a droning sound in the background. The only questions of any importance were the last two; Can they kill it? And if so, how?

A subtle tremor brought all conversation to an abrupt halt. Everyone looked around, uneasy, handling their firearms like a child clutches a teddy-bear close in a storm. More vibrations brought Bill and Sam rushing to the windows facing Brockway Mountain, invisible through the falling snow. They were quickly joined by nearly everyone in the tavern, people crowding next to the windows with macabre curiosity, wanting both to see the monster and wanting to see nothing but a winter scene. With so many people breathing on the cold glass, the windows started to frost, dramatically limiting visibility.

"Dammit," Sam muttered. Pulling on his coat and hat he strode to the door.

Without a word, Bill and the towering Matti followed him. Outside they could feel the ground shaking, but not like it did when the giant had been close. But the constant tremors convinced Bill that the huge creature was around and up to something. In town.

"Let's go," Sam said. "Slowly and stay out of sight of it, if you can."

Bill didn't need the last comment. He had no plans to be seen if he could help it. The men climbed on their snowmobiles, fired them up, and with a wave at the windows of the tavern, headed up one of the two main roads that ran through town.

"Where are they going?" Brandon asked. He turned worried eyes on Steph.

In her head, Steph cursed Bill for leaving them without a word. "Don't worry," she told Brandon. "They're going to see what's happening. They know what they're up against." She thought they were smart enough to stay well away from the monster, but part of her wasn't sure.

"Stupid," Tril said. "They're fucking stupid."

Steph raised her eyebrows. "Sorry?"

"They know they can't shoot it. What good is looking at it going to do?"

Brandon looked at Tril, his eyebrows scrunched together. He noticed that he wasn't the only one staring at the fierce young woman.

"It might help to know what it's doing," Steph said softly.

"Fuck that," Tril spat. Brandon had never seen her so vehement, a foul passion possessing her. Her eyes burned with rage and her lips were pursed so tightly they were turning white. "Ernest, you said this thing was an *ice* giant?"

The grizzled barkeep's eyes narrowed and he raised his chin. "I did."

"How does ice do around fire?" She said the last word like she was giving the command to a line of executioners.

Everyone in the room suddenly looked dumbfounded, gazing from Tril to one another. Brandon felt the smile creep across his face. How could they have not thought of that? Ernest was smiling wickedly.

"Young lady, you are frighteningly sharp," Ernest said.

Suddenly, everyone was talking at once. Ideas ranged from fire-arrows to Molotov cocktails to flame-throwers. The last idea was quickly thrown out as the guy who suggested it realized that, thankfully, no one in town had a flame-thrower. They were still brain-storming when they heard snowmobiles approaching.

Bill, Sam and Matti crashed through the door, breathing hard and wide-eyed. Sam surveyed the crowd and grimaced. Brandon thought he saw the ranger's eyes glisten in the tavern lights. No sooner had the thought gone through his mind than the lights shut off. The power was out.

Sam dropped his chin to his chest. "Dammit!" he shouted.

"What's going on?" Ernest asked.

"We aren't safe in our houses," Bill answered.

"Thing smashed the living shit out of Doug and Nancy's house. Pulled them out and left," Matti added.

"Doug and Nancy are dead?" a voice asked.

Sam shook his head. "He just carried them off. We heard them screaming."

"Why?" Steph asked.

Bill shrugged, his face ashen.

"We gotta kill that bastard," Tril announced.

"How?" Bill asked, unable to hide his annoyance.

Ernest started chuckling. "Oh, Bill. We've been talking since you've been gone. Miss Tril here pointed out that an ice giant may not react too well to fire."

Light returned to Sam's eyes and he immediately organized the group into a team of warriors bent on the destruction of their enemy. Brandon was both pleased and surprised when Jansen came up with the basis for their whole plan. But then, he knew the man was smart.

The lights of the tavern came back on, accompanied by the drone of Ernest's generator out behind the building.

Preparations for the attack on the giant began in earnest, everyone glad they wouldn't have to venture too far to get the supplies they needed. In a little over an hour, they had weapons and were prepared to set the trap.

CHAPTER TWENTY-FOUR

Eight people were chosen to set up the fire trap. The trap needed to be set up quickly, but as quietly as possible. Sam would lead the team that consisted of Bill, Matti, Jansen, who'd come up with the idea for the trap, Tril, who insisted that because she'd spawned the idea, she be able to help in its execution, Brandon, who demanded to come because Tril was allowed to go, and two hunters: Dr. Stephanie Crowe and Jim Booth. Since she had a fast machine, Mary Pinanen would lead the second wave made up of two snowmobiles with fire-bombers riding behind the driver. An enthusiastic Fritz would ride with her. They'd rush in to bash the monster with more fire and hopefully distract it so the others could get away before it raged into them.

Now that there was hope, Bill wished the kids and Steph would have stayed behind. But he knew Tril was very good with a bow, and her fire-arrows would provide good cover fire, should it be needed. And Brandon was young and strong and could chuck a Molotov cocktail farther than anyone other than Matti. Matti's presence just gave everyone confidence, the man was so huge and unflappable. Jim was also an excellent shot with a bow, having almost made the Olympic

256

archery team five years ago. He'd be armed with fire-arrows too. Steph, Bill, Sam, Matti and Jansen would build the trap under the watchful eyes of the other three. Steph had come up with the details of the trap and would ensure it was done correctly.

Everyone had a backpack full of essentials should they have to flee; lighter, candle, water, kindling, flashlight and some food. This was Jim's idea, having been stuck in the woods once or twice, he said you never knew when it would happen. And if you weren't prepared in the U.P., you could die unnecessarily.

Once the trap was ready, Tril would ride back to Jotnar's and assemble the rest of the ambush team who was still putting together fire-arrows and Molotov cocktails. Once everyone was on site, they'd bring in the giant.

At least, that was the plan.

Bill shivered at the sound of the snowmobile engines, sure it would draw the damned monster to them prematurely. The team of eight rode to the agreed-upon ambush site on five snowmobiles, each machine towing a utility sled filled with wood, gas cans, and a variety of flammable materials. Tril, Brandon and Jim all bore their weapons as they rode double behind a driver.

When they arrived, the machines were pulled into a wide circle, twenty-five feet in diameter. They were in the middle of a small side road, snow-laden evergreen trees they would use as concealment clustered closely on both sides. Houses lined both sides of the street, shut up and quiet except for the smoke spiraling upward from several chimneys. Everyone disembarked, Tril, Brandon and Jim setting up defensively away from the circle, watching outward. They all knew they'd feel the approach of the giant before they saw it, but no one was taking chances.

The remaining five quickly dispersed, unloading the wood and other flammables and arranging them in a circle with a three-foot opening on the side farthest from Brockway Mountain. Then they laid an "X" of wood and rags that intersected at the center of the circle. Steph examined their work, making sure everything was in contact as planned. With the snow falling, they knew the wood would be snow-covered by the time the monster arrived. Matti and Sam grabbed gas cans and doused the entire circle and "X" with fuel. Then they repeated it a second time.

The ground shook.

"Go, go, go!" Sam told Tril.

The girl jumped on a snowmobile and raced off toward Jotnar's. The rest of the team rushed to move the snowmobiles to pre-determined escape points should they be needed. Then they knocked the snow from the trees in several spots so they could hunker down within the concealing branches.

Tremors rattled down the street; one, two, three. They were growing stronger. He was coming.

"I'm going out," Sam said, arming himself with a Molotov cocktail.

"We're not ready yet," Bill hissed.

"We can't let him go anywhere but here," Sam answered and pushed through the evergreen wall. He trudged into the middle of the circle, holding a lighter in his left hand and the fuel-filled bottle in his right.

Bill looked across the road and saw Brandon handing Jansen his bow, a can of glowing embers on a board in front of the man. The boy gave his father a thumbs-up and a smile. Jansen was stoic and gave a slight nod of his head. Bill had wanted Brandon next to him, along with Steph and Tril, but strategy and tactics won out over emotion. To his left, away from where they expected the giant to approach, Tril arrived, spun her snowmobile around, jumped off and crouched under the trees. In front of her, just out from under the evergreens, a small can of charcoal burned, the igniter for every arrow the girl would launch. Directly across from Tril, Jim was set up with a similar can, watching up the road, waiting with a determined scowl on his face. To his right, closest to the circle, Matti knelt holding a long fuel-oil doused broomstick made into a spear in one hand, lighter in the other.

He handed a long-necked grill lighter to Steph and grabbed one of the Molotov cocktails out of the crate behind them. She would light the cloth hanging out of the bottles and Bill would throw them at the giant, fast as he could.

The ground started shuddering and Sam yelled, "Come on, you big bastard!" Bill looked and saw the ranger standing in the middle of the circle, defiant.

Snowmobiles roared in the distance as the rest of the team approached.

Vibrations came with a constant frequency and amplitude, each one feeling stronger and more foreboding than the last. A huge shadow clouded the street, growing darker and more distinct with every thundering footfall.

Tril knocked an arrow and held its tip above the ignition can. Across the street, Jim mirrored her.

The form of the monster emerged from the wall of falling snow, its full attention on Sam. With horror, Bill realized the giant was too close and moving too fast. He would be on Sam in a matter of seconds and Sam would not be able to get out of the circle, not in this deep snow.

"Now! Now!" he shouted to Steph who quickly lit the cloth of the bomb in Bill's hands. He turned and saw the creature reach a massive hand toward Sam's fleeing form.

A flash raced across Bill's face and the creature gave a roar of surprise as Tril's arrow stuck in its cheek, followed by a second that hit it in the chest. An orange streak, like lightning, marked where Matti's spear caught it in the side. Bill leaped up and flung his flaming bottle at the gargantuan form, seeing another arc through the air from Brandon. The bottles connected and burst into a liquid coat of fire, covering the monster's neck and chest. Jansen's flaming arrow caught it on one thigh. Another arrow zipped into the pile of wood and flames rose with painful slowness, growing to encircle the giant who now stood fully upright, swatting at the flames on his body.

Sam, miraculously out of reach, turned and flung his unlit Molotov at the beast's head where it shattered and burst into flame. Then he turned and ran toward Brandon and Jansen.

They watched as a mountain of fire burned around and over the big killing machine.

Four snowmobiles raced in, each with a rider, three bearing flaming spears, Fritz with a Molotov. Everything was flung at the monster as they sped past. All four found their mark and the spears dangled and bounced with the monster's movement.

Bill noticed then, to his surprise, that the monster didn't roar. Rather, it quit swatting like a man who'd punched a bee-hive and started systematically pulling arrows and spears from his thick hide, dropping them where they sizzled uselessly in the snow. Then it walked clear of the burning trap and casually wiped the flaming liquids from his skin, the fire already sputtering weakly.

"Run," Sam screamed.

CHAPTER TWENTY-FIVE

The overconfident group exploded with frantic motion; people crashing through snowy hedges, snowmobiles racing in indeterminate directions, flaming weapons discarded to lie smoldering in the snow. The giant started to rage, its huge arms flailing like crushing steel girders. It stepped back and forth, reaching for anyone or anything in reach. Somehow, everyone had escaped its wrath, fleeing in every direction. Black soil burst through the air as the monster grasped one of the evergreen trees and ripped it from the ground. He flung it in Sam's direction on the street. The tree hit the snow just behind the ranger, its branches catching in the snow and snapping it to a halt before it reached him.

"Go," Bill shouted at Steph, pushing her toward their snowmobile. He could hear the machines roaring to life all around the disastrous scene.

Bill looked across the road and saw Brandon climbing on the back of Jansen's bright orange snowmobile. He was carrying Jansen's bow and remaining arrows so the man could drive them the hell out of here. He hoped Brandon could hold on to the machine as well as the weapon. They took off through a yard, heading west, in the direction of the trail heading out of town. The last he saw of them, Brandon had managed to get one arm between the string and body of the bow, the weapon clinging to his shoulder. He'd have at least one hand to hold on with. Like a cannonball to the gut, he was hit by the fear that he may never see his son again.

Matti raced past on his snowmobile, stopping to pull Tril onto the seat behind him before accelerating up the empty road. No one was on foot, machines screaming as they raced through town as fast as they dared. Bill looked over his right shoulder and seeing the giant looking elsewhere, pulled hard on the handlebars, maneuvering into the street where the snow had been packed by the other fleeing sleds. One more glance back and he saw Sam and Jim flying in the direction Jansen had gone.

The giant turned and strode heavily in the direction Jansen and Brandon had fled.

He knew then that Jansen was making a run for it, with Brandon clinging behind. They would try to get to the trail, which made a switchback on its way up Brockway Mountain before it made a straight shot west, leading to the road that ran to Eagle River where the Sheriff's office was. His stomach clenched. There was a chance his son would escape with Jansen and they could call in help, but it was so risky. Seeing how easily the giant walked through this deep snow, and his immense size, made it seem impossible that they'd crest Brockway Mountain before he caught them.

Maybe they'd circle back around the monster and come back into town. Jansen should be smart enough to do that, right? He wanted to turn around and go after them, to make sure Brandon was okay. But he couldn't, not with Steph clinging to him. He couldn't put her at risk, even if he was willing to... what? Die? It was a strange thought; dying along with his son. But it seemed preferable to letting Brandon die.

He zoomed up to Jotnar's tavern and shouted to Steph to get inside. As soon as she was off the snowmobile, he squeezed the throttle, pulled a tight circle and headed toward Brockway Mountain.

Sam glanced to his right, letting the snowmobile slow momentarily. The big bastard was going after Jansen and Brandon. Jansen was obviously going to try to get to the trail to flee town. But he'd never make it. The switchback would make them sitting ducks for a creature that big. The giant didn't need to follow the trail and would just climb straight up and intercept them. *Dammit Jansen, turn around!*

With a sick feeling he realized the giant was moving too fast, he'd catch them even before they were halfway to the switchback.

Sam stopped his sled. "Jim, get off."

"What are you going to do?" Jim asked, having watched the dreadful scene develop himself.

"Distract him, if I can." Then Sam raced off, leaving Jim to run to the nearest house for shelter.

Jansen held the throttle down, but in the deep snow, an uphill grade and with two people astride, the snowmobile struggled to maintain anything but moderate speed. It wasn't far to the trail and he thought they could escape and tell the Sheriff what was going on. Brandon sat behind him, holding tightly to the passenger handle on one side and head tucked low to avoid the biting cold air.

Even on the snowmobile, riding on at least three feet of snow, he could feel the rumble of the monster's pursuit, the vibrations shuddering through the handlebars. He wondered if the giant's visibility was hampered by the falling snow as was his own. He hoped so.

The tremors grew stronger with each second and Jansen quickly realized their hope of an escape from town was futile. He sneaked a glance back and saw a massive dark shape cutting through the snowflakes behind them. His heart stuttered as he realized that any escape at all was slipping away. They were just going too slow.

His eyes slid across Brandon's huddled form before he turned forward. He pulled the handlebars hard to the left, abandoning his hope of making the trail. They had to lose the monster. They left the road and went flying between trees, his path now an unpredictable, hazardous route through the woods.

"He's catching us," Brandon screamed, his voice sounding distant in the rushing wind and whine of the engine.

Now alone on his machine and following the path of another snowmobile, Sam was able to go much faster. He'd lost sight of Jansen, Brandon and the giant in the time it took to off-load Jim, the falling, swirling snow filling the space between them like a billowing sheet on the clothes-line. But he knew where Jansen was going and the tracks spoke for themselves.

Still, he was slowed by the occasional hole on the path left by the gargantuan feet of the giant. The tracks were mostly to either side of Jansen's trail, but now and again one would touch the edge, causing Sam's machine to tip precariously to one side or the other, changing his direction until he regained control. At one point, one of the big prints was perfectly centered, like an open tiger pit waiting for prey. Sam noticed it just in time, leaning back and shifting his weight to his feet he accelerated to prevent the nose from diving into it. Instead, the sled dropped from under him, the skis in front reaching forward just enough to catch the far edge of the hole, enabling Sam to blast up the other side, the seat slamming into him as he dropped onto it.

Jansen's trail suddenly swerved off into the woods, running straight south. Good. He'd had enough sense to realize they wouldn't make it up Brockway Mountain. But they were still in trouble. That thing didn't seem to be abandoning the chase.

Before him, he saw a dark shape looming skyward through the falling snow and his pulse quickened. What the hell was he going to do? He had to get its attention. Though he may not escape it either, he knew he had a better chance than a machine carrying two people.

Jansen could see the giant's eyes, even with the heavy snowfall. It was too close. He couldn't get enough speed. He could feel the ground shaking through the seat and the handlebars now. The throttle was squeezed to its max and he was doing his best to pick a straight line through the trees. But it was no use, they were going to get caught.

Unless...

Sam saw Jansen and Brandon out in front of the giant now. Too close. The thing was nearly on them! *No, no, no!* He thought.

Then Jansen turned and thrust his left arm back, catching Brandon beneath the chin, sending the boy toppling off the seat to land in the snow.

Jansen sped away, leaving Brandon behind, helpless.

Brandon felt the impact of Jansen's elbow on his chin, the blow taking him by surprise. As he tipped backward, he reached forward, trying to grab onto Jansen's coat in an attempt to stay on the snowmobile.

What was Jansen doing? Why'd he hit me? I thought we were friends.

The sky flew across his field of view, skeletal tree branches against the gray light like cracks in a splintered windshield. With a grunt, he landed on his back, the bow mashing against one shoulder-blade. His momentum brought him back to his feet and threw him forward onto his face, the bundle of arrows flying as he instinctively stretched out his arms, the limbs sinking in the snow.

Desperately, he yanked his arms out of the holes they'd punched and flopped over to see the wicked blue-white eyes of the giant and one massive hand reaching for him.

"No!" Sam screamed and gave his machine full throttle.

From the corner of his eye, Brandon saw a snowmobile race up behind the giant and crash into the back of one leg, sliding up the calf and jarring to a halt behind the huge knee. The monster's gigantic fingers closed into a fist, just feet from Brandon, and the thing roared in rage or pain.

"Hide!"

Brandon heard the command and saw Sam's dark face as he stood in the snow behind the giant, his snowmobile sputtering to silence as the huge being kicked it from its wounded leg.

Brandon wasted no time in turning to run, only to bury his legs in the deep snow. Frantic, he pulled them up and churned his way into the forest, adrenaline powering every step. He ripped the bow from his shoulder and held it in one hand, like a racing baton as he fled.

A wail of agony echoed through the forest. Sam's voice. Brandon fought back tears as he ran, the labor of his flight bringing forth sweat on his back and chest. Sam's screams died with the selfless ranger.

Then Brandon noticed that things looked familiar. He'd been here before, with Tril. The cave! It was here somewhere. He took a breath and tried to remember where she'd shown him the cave. It couldn't be far. But he couldn't see more than fifty yards in any direction.

The ground shook and Brandon looked back at the giant. Though at this distance the beast was all shades of gray, Brandon could see Sam's headless body grasped in its right fist, the deep crimson of the man's blood dripping across the giant fingers, the only semblance of color to be seen. Brandon froze in place, hoping to avoid detection, but the massive eyes locked onto him.

He renewed his flight, hoping the cave would become visible before the horrible monster had him. He felt the pursuit shake through his legs as he ran. Where was that damned thing?

The giant closed the distance between them with horrifying quickness, his huge strides carrying him through the chest-high trees and calf-deep snow like a man walking through a field of wheat. It made a deep, resonant sound, like a laugh as it neared the fleeing boy.

"Come on! Where the hell is-" Brandon's words were abruptly cut off.

Bill sped up the road on the track they'd just packed down in their flight from the fire-trap. He had to help Brandon. If they escaped and made it down to Eagle River, the police or National Guard could come in here and rescue everyone. But he'd have to distract the giant in order for Brandon and Jansen to have a chance. If it was bent on catching them, they were dead.

He smelled wood-smoke as he neared their failed ambush. Before he reached it, he took a left on a cross street, went over one block, then turned right on the road he figured Jansen had used. He quickly found a well-packed snowmobile trail; more than one machine had traveled it. Then he noticed the big tracks running parallel to Jansen and Brandon's path. Shit.

A quarter-mile along the road, Bill saw someone step out of a house just ahead of him. Jim. He came slogging through the snow and Bill stopped impatiently.

"Sam went after them," Jim announced.

Bill looked forward to where the snowmobile tracks faded away in the ceaseless snowfall. A flash of orange on the next street caught his eye. That had to be Jansen headed back to the tavern. He was the only one around with an orange sled.

"Get on," Bill said.

Jansen and Brandon beat them back in time to get inside, the snowmobile was sitting empty in the parking lot. Bill jumped off his machine and ran into the tavern. The first eyes he saw were Steph's, and they were full of tears. He scanned the people, looking for his son, finding only sympathetic faces.

"What? Where's Brandon?" he asked. He fixed his gaze on Jansen.

Jansen's face dropped and his Adam's apple flexed as he swallowed hard. "It got him. I'm sorry, Bill. It pulled him right off the back of my sled."

Steph was there in an instant, ushering him into a seat. It was a gut-punch. Bill felt every ounce of strength seep from him and he could only stare at the ground. His arms and legs tingled and his mouth turned dusty. He could picture his son's face in his mind; not angry or defiant, but smiling and happy, both as a four-year-old and at fifteen. His eyes stung but no tears came. It couldn't be. His family was gone, his only son. When he had the strength to look up, he saw Tril, quietly crying with her face in her hands. Weakly, he looked at Jansen and thought he saw real remorse on the man's face.

"I thought we might be able to get to Eagle River," Jansen said, "but it caught up to us too fast. I turned around and tried to lose it in the woods, but..." his words trailed off.

Bill nodded slightly. He took a deep breath and realized that Steph was gripping his hand.

Fucking Jansen. If he'd wanted to try an escape, why didn't he do it alone? Instead, he took Brandon into a hopeless situation now his son was dead. Of course, if they'd made it out, he'd be indebted to the man. But Jansen took liberties that weren't his to take, he'd gambled with someone else's life, and lost.

The bottom fell out, dropping Brandon into a cold, stony hole. Looking around in the dull light filtering down he realized that snow had drifted over the cave entrance and he had run right over it.

A shadow suddenly blocked the light and he scrambled deeper into the cavern just as one massive hand reached in, knocking the remaining snow away. Fingers bigger than Brandon's thigh swept around the rubble, reaching, searching, but unable to dig deep enough to grab him. The giant's hand was just too big. He expected a roar of anger, but the hand just retreated, followed by the hammering of the ground as huge foot-falls trembled away, fading with each long step.

Brandon let out a sigh and his body settled against the ground like wet putty. Laying the bow aside, he stared at the dark ceiling only three feet above his face. Out of the frigid air, it felt considerably warmer in the shelter of the cave's entrance, but as he crawled forward to peer outside, he felt the cold flowing down around him and he shivered. The monster gone, Brandon poked his head up and looked at the snow-scape that surrounded him.

Nearby were several trees with dead branches and one tree that had broken about two feet above the snow, folding over at a forty-five-degree angle. He climbed out and quickly started gathering wood for a fire. He snapped one large branch and cringed at the deafening sound that lanced through the forest. Grabbing up what he could carry, he hustled back to the cave and crawled in, pushing the twigs before him.

The cave went straight back, horizontally, into the hill-side, allowing Brandon to build his fire in the entrance. The smoke would float up into the air while throwing heat back into the hole where he could be safe from the giant. He took some of the paper scraps from the pack on his back and set them on a rocky area he'd cleared of snow. Then he piled twigs and kindling on the paper and ignited it all with his lighter. God, he was glad he had the pack. If he ever saw that guy, Jim, again, he'd thank him profusely for recommending everyone have supplies.

He watched as tendrils of smoke rose in conflict with the descending flakes of snow. The flames grew, taking a flickering yellow shape. Slowly, he fed the fire with larger pieces of wood. Once he was convinced that the fire was established and could survive several minutes without tending, he crept out to find more wood.

As soon as he was out of the ring of warmth a chill shook him. Sweat. He'd worked up quite a lather when he was running through the deep snow. Now it cooled with dangerous efficiency. He wanted to get back to the cave but knew he needed a sufficient store of wood if he wanted to survive. Now that the fire was going, he wasn't about to let it die. He had to get it roaring so he could shed some of his clothes and dry them out. Keeping the wet articles against his skin would drain him of heat and energy, two things he couldn't spare. Especially since he didn't know how long he'd be stuck out here. The snacks he had in his pack wouldn't last long.

It took him a full hour of gathering to accumulate a pile of wood he was satisfied would get him through the night. His breath caught. The night. He was going to be out here, in this cave, overnight. Alone, cold and hungry. He sat there staring into the flickering flames, going numb with despair. How long could he hope to survive here? He had enough food for about a day, maybe two. Water was no problem with the snow he could melt in his bottle when it was empty. His father had taught him not to eat snow. Melting snow, even in your body, required heat, and that would cool your insides, something you definitely didn't want to do when you were trying to survive outdoors in the winter.

He wondered if his dad was still alive, and Steph, and Tril. What had happened to them? They must have got away. The giant had come after him and Jansen.

Jansen! That fucker had pushed him off the snowmobile and left him to die. The thought soured his stomach and lit a burning desire for revenge. If he ever saw Jansen again, the son-of-a-bitch would be sorry. What would the guy tell his dad? Surely, not the truth. If his dad found out what Jansen did to him, what would happen?

He didn't know.

Over the last couple of months, he'd carefully avoided making a connection with his dad, wanting only to make it to his eighteenth birthday so he could move back to Minneapolis and leave his father and the wilderness behind him. As he thought about it, he realized that his father had made several attempts to bond or get to know him or whatever. But recently, he'd given up trying, choosing instead to go out with Steph. Brandon had killed the man's hopes and intentions. All because his mother had told him that his dad had never wanted him, had never even tried to get visitation rights. But he'd seen evidence to the contrary. And now, because of his selfish, pissy, little boy behavior, their relationship was simply a peaceful coexistence.

He threw another hunk of wood on the fire, glad for the survival and outdoor lessons his dad had forced on him, though at the time he hadn't thought he'd ever need them. The man wasn't stupid and had known Brandon might need some unique skills living up here. If not for Tril's subsequent reinforcement of those lessons, he may have let them slip from his mind. Now here he sat, realizing how smart the old man really was.

And how much he wanted to see him again.

Brandon shed his coat and quickly pulled off his sweat-soaked t-shirt and long-sleeved T that was also wet. He put his sweatshirt back on, followed by the coat and set the two soiled garments to dry by the fire. Watching the steam float up from the shirts, he found himself wishing he had a better relationship with his dad. Sure, his dad was awkward and didn't really know how to parent. But even through that, Brandon had seen that the man cared about him. Maybe he just wasn't good at demonstrating it, or good at parenting. Now he may never see him again.

Suddenly the ground started shaking. The monster was coming. And judging by the steady repetition of footfalls, he was coming fast, with a purpose.

Brandon sidled deeper into the cavern, the low ceiling only a foot above his seated, hunched form. He pulled his flashlight out of his pack and shined it down the dark tunnel behind him. Tril said it went quite a way back there.

Movement from just beyond the fire caught his attention. As he watched, he suddenly realized he was looking at one big, blue-white eye that was staring back at him through the flames.

CHAPTER TWENTY-SIX

"Did you see Sam?" Jim asked Jansen. People were gathered in Jotnar's discussing the recent failure to bring the giant down.

"Sam? No." They moved off and talked quietly.

Bill moved to the window and looked out into the snowy, gray daylight. It had been at least fifteen minutes since Sam had dropped Jim and took off, hoping to distract the monster. He hadn't returned yet.

Probably wouldn't.

Just like Brandon.

He turned away from the window and found Steph right behind him, her eyes sympathetic and sad. She wrapped an arm around him and sat him down.

"How you doing?" she asked.

"Shitty," Bill said. "We gotta kill this fucking thing."

Tril approached quietly. "I'm sorry," she said. "It was my idea."

Bill looked at her, scowling. "Sorry?"

Tril nodded as a tear slid down her face. "I thought it would work. It was a bad idea and now..." she trailed off.

Bill drew in a long, deep breath. "Tril. It was a good idea. It just didn't work. We all thought it would. Nothing is your fault."

"Yes, Tril," Steph said. "You don't take the blame for anything. We didn't know that thing could withstand fire."

The girl slumped into a chair, her face sliding down her cheeks into a frown. "What are we going to do?"

"Kill it. It has to be mortal. We just have to figure out how." He distracted himself with thoughts of vengeance. He couldn't dwell on the pain. Didn't want to.

Matti and Ernest pulled chairs up and sat down. Ernest put a comforting hand on Bill's shoulder but said nothing. He looked at Steph and said, "So, professor, looks like we answered what happened to the missing village. Though I would have preferred not."

Steph nodded. "I just hope we can do better than they did."

"We will," Matti said confidently. He took a big swig of energy-drink and turned intense eyes on Bill. "Bill, you have any ideas of what to try next?"

Bill shook his head. "It looks like a gargantuan version of a person. I have to believe we can kill it. It's just really tough."

Steph turned to face the direction of Lake Superior, her face thoughtful. "Bill, remember those bodies we found in the lake?"

"Yeah." He frowned seeing her stare in the direction of Isle Royal. Slowly he started to shake his head. "No. No. The lake won't be frozen all the way. That's why the settlers went through the ice. Good thought, but no."

She turned back to him and smiled. "What happened to them?" Bill's face wrinkled in confusion, not following her. "They drowned, right?"

"Yeah," he said.

"Holy cow," Matti exclaimed. "I'm with ya. How heavy do you think that thing is?"

"A lot heavier than any of us, even on a snowmobile," Steph said with a wicked smile. "And from all outward appearances, it breathes air, just like us." She let the information soak for anyone slow on the uptake.

Ernest grinned.

Tril glanced up, a weak, unsure smile on her face.

Bill wrapped an arm around Steph. "That's a good idea. But it's going to be risky."

Matti said, "The snow on the lake is always packed harder because of the wind, and it won't be so deep. Snowmobile should be able to rip across it."

Bill nodded. "But how close will that thing be when he busts through? Will it take down the rider too?

And how far out will the machine have to go? They might go through just trying to lure him out there."

"I'll do it," Matti said, downing more liquid energy. "I'll use Jansen's snowmobile. It's the fastest one in town."

"Why would he chase one person out onto the ice? He could just stay here and kill or eat whoever doesn't go out there," Bill said.

Everyone was silent for a few moments. Then Matti said, "If he doesn't chase me, I'll just shoot down the coast to Eagle River."

Bill looked at Matti, meeting his intense eyes. Damn, the guy was fearless and confident. "That gives me an idea," he said. He told the little group what he was thinking and they all agreed.

Bill stood up and got the attention of all thirteen people in the tavern and told them his plan. It included eleven snowmobiles driving onto the harbor and going out onto the big lake. Five machines would go west along the coast directly to Eagle River. The other six would head east around the tip of the peninsula, then cut southwest to follow the other coast to safety. If the monster followed either team, they would try to lure it to thin ice so it would break through and drown.

"I hate to throw water on your plan," Jansen said. "But Jim was saying that the mouth of the harbor isn't frozen."

"What?" Bill exclaimed. How could that be? It should be frozen solid.

Jim nodded. "I got a look at it this morning. It looked like an ice-breaker had driven through from the light-house to Porter's Island and from there to Hunter's Point."

"What'd he do? Smash the ice? How deep is it through there?" Steph asked.

"Apparently not deep enough. Shit. Where's the next best place to get onto the big lake?" Bill asked.

"Agate beach?" Mary Pinanen said. She'd stayed with the team since watching Joe Harris die in their attempt to snowmobile to the Sheriff's office in Eagle River. "Or just east of the lighthouse. Everything else is too big a drop off the rocks."

"The beach may be too close to the giant's stomping grounds. He seems to be most active on the west side," Bill said.

"We'd be on the road almost all the way to the lighthouse," Fritz voiced. "In fresh snow."

Everyone ruminated on that thought.

"Single file. Fastest machine in front. Heading away from him? Should be on the lake before he can close," Bill said.

"Anyone need gas?" Ernest asked. Everyone shook their heads. He looked at his watch. "Going to be dark in half-hour. Better get going."

"Keep your headlights off until you know you're safe," Matti added.

"Good luck," Ernest said, wrapping an arm around Suzy.

Suddenly the eyes were gone and Brandon felt the ground vibrating as the huge monster strode away, leaving him with a racing heart. He crept closer to the fire and peeked out to make sure the giant was definitely gone. Convinced, he added two more pieces to the fire.

He wasn't sure why it had returned, then he looked at the smoke drifting skyward. Oh. A thought crashed into his brain and he felt a rush of hope. Smoke! Maybe someone from town would see or smell the smoke and send help. Then he looked out into the never-ending snowfall and realized that unless someone was within fifty yards, they wouldn't see anything. His heart sank.

Maybe he should start walking out. He discarded that idea before it even developed into a partial plan. Gathering wood was a challenge. How far would he have to walk to get back to town, exposed the whole time? Maybe if he had a... He crawled out of the cave and looked around. Sam's snowmobile was out there. Maybe it'd still run.

He went back and checked how dry his clothes had become. Deciding they were dry enough, he put them back on and bundled up again and set out to find the snowmobile.

The little convoy left Jotnar's parking lot and zoomed up the road single file. Jansen had the most powerful snowmobile and was in the lead, breaking the trail for the rest. On the packed track, the other machines would easily be able to keep pace as Jansen was slowed by the poor visibility as well as the deep, unbroken snow.

Bill figured it would take them no more than ten minutes to get to the lake. Once they were on the ice, they should be able to go faster as the wind would have reduced the depth of the snow and would have hardened what was there. Two teams of sleds heading in two different directions would prove too difficult for one giant to stop. He just hoped it didn't mean one team, or even one person would end up dead.

Every rider had a survival pack and a weapon slung over their shoulder, despite the ineffectiveness of the guns.

The snow hadn't let up at all, still falling like the end of the world was upon them. They'd probably gotten three inches in the last hour. Though the sky was still a dull gray, he knew that night was closing in on them quickly. This twilight time was perfect for keeping them obscured, everything seemed to blend together into indistinct images. But at the same time, he wished they could see farther so they didn't have to wait to feel the giant's approach. That'd put them too close to the beast before they started to flee. White flakes came at his windshield and face like little frozen darts, each one that struck his face sent a cold sting lancing through his skin. He pulled the scarf up higher and wished he'd grabbed his helmet. He would probably have frostbitten cheeks by the time he made it around the tip of the peninsula and down to Calumet. Scarf or no.

At the moment he felt invincible, an armed caravan slinking through the winter landscape under the cover of snowfall and fading light. Then a melancholy seized him as an image of Brandon presented itself in his mind. The sounds of the snowmobiles, the bite of the cold, and the dead gray around him all faded to nothing as he remembered. He'd done his best when dire circumstances had thrust Brandon into his care. But after being deprived of time with his son, he just didn't really know how to be a dad. When Brandon hadn't responded well to things he thought any boy would love, he was at a loss and eventually gave up. He should have tried harder.

Brandon had seemed to enjoy working with Jansen, talking about video games and such. It irked Bill, but he ultimately tried to be supportive, despite his dislike and distrust of Jansen. Maybe the kid liked the more intellectual challenges working with computers could provide.

He looked forward, seeing Jansen's form bobbing along as his machine pitched, sunk and rose as it plowed through the virgin snow. How had he gotten away when his son was plucked from so close behind the man?

He shook off the thought, bringing his mind back to the here and now, knowing he had to be sharp. Glancing at the scene around him he realized they were about to leave the road to cover the last two hundred yards through the trees that lead to the lakeshore. He peeked behind him and saw four of the eight machines trailing along, the others out of view but back there somewhere. He saw Steph clinging to the handlebars of the snowmobile she'd borrowed from Ernest, following him like they were on a sight-seeing cruise. He was glad to see she was faring well, not having driven a snowmobile before. He'd keep her with him, following in his tracks as they and three others made their way east on the ice.

Since Jansen had the fastest sled, he would lead the team west. He wouldn't be able to max out his speed while breaking a trail, but he could do it faster than the others. Those who followed him could go as fast as they needed once there was a packed trail. Their route was the most likely to be intercepted by the monster, running back past town on their way west. If the snow was wind-packed, even Jansen could open his machine up. The giant would be hard-pressed to catch that rocket.

This plan might work. This plan *had* to work.

For now, everyone would go as fast as they could and were to stick together unless the giant got close, then everyone would scatter and regroup at the tavern unless they had a clean shot along the ice to the next town.

Suddenly Jansen stood up on his sled and raised his left hand, coming to an abrupt stop. Bill mimicked the hand gesture which was repeated down the line to the last rider, all the machines closing the gaps before coming to a halt, everyone wondering why they were stopping.

Bill walked up and stood next to Jansen who was looking out at the lake that was only twenty yards away. Then Bill's heart sank as he looked at broken ice and open water that sat between them and an inviting, solid sheet of white farther out on the lake. He looked left and right and saw that as far as he could see, the ice along the shore was destroyed, making it impossible for them to leave land.

"Dammit!" he cursed. Jansen plopped down on the seat of his machine and a huge plume of steam issued from his balaclava as he exhaled heavily.

Steph stepped up next to Bill. "What-" She looked at the water and her eyes lost the sparkle that had been so hard to extinguish. "Oh no."

"Son-of-a-bitch broke the ice," Bill said.

"Maybe he learned from last time," Steph said.

That's when they felt the first rumble.

It took Brandon ten minutes to find Sam's snowmobile, most of the time wasted in trying to walk through the thigh-deep snow. It lay on its side but looked mostly intact. He struggled to right the machine but it seemed eager to return to an upright position, even if it was still listing dramatically in the snow. He climbed on, and standing on the running boards, shifted his weight, forcing it into a level attitude. Looking forward he could see the hood was cracked and the right ski was slanted inward at a slight angle, rather than pointing straight like the left ski. He jumped off and examined the bent ski. It was just bent, not broken. He might still be able to use it, though steering would be a challenge. *If* the motor would run, and nothing else was destroyed.

Taking a seat again, he reached forward and turned the key. The engine cranked but didn't fire. He tried again with the same result. Then again. And again. Brandon dropped his head against the handlebars, his shoulders slumping.

He looked at the trail the snowmobiles had made through the trees, undisturbed a few feet away from where Sam had attacked the giant. He made his way through the haphazard and loose piles of snow over to where he could stand on the track. Climbing up onto the path the two machines had packed, he was elated that it held his weight. He took two steps toward town before his foot broke through the surface and he sank in over his knee. Trying to pull himself up, his other foot joined his first, the trail just not solid enough to support his feet. It wasn't any better than walking through the unbroken snow. He'd never make it all the way back to the houses before the giant found him.

Bill didn't have to tell anyone to get moving, everyone felt the tremors and snowmobiles started peeling to the sides like the falling sparks from a fireworks display. Still, in the woods, the riders had to carefully pick their way through the trees, trying to get onto the open road to fly, or trying to get deeper into the cover of the wood, hoping they'd be concealed.

Jansen wasted no time and took off toward the lighthouse, somewhere off to their left, maybe trying to circle around behind the thing.

"Follow me," Bill ordered as he pushed Steph toward her sled.

Quickly he started breaking a new trail through the trees on their right. He'd circle to the road and they could zoom back to town and find shelter. Maybe. The ground was thundering like he was standing on a railroad trestle while a train rolled by. Each hammering pulse from the giant's steps felt stronger and more intense than they had during the last attack. He must be close. Bill stole a glance back to make sure Steph was following. Even in the failing light, he could see the whites of her eyes, wide with fear.

They'd just made it onto the road when a riderless snowmobile landed in the snow twenty feet in front of Bill, bouncing and rolling off to his left, the orange body breaking and throwing pieces flying. Jansen's machine. Dammit. They had to get away from here and fast. The trail they'd packed down could only be a hundred yards in front of them, then they'd be able to go full throttle.

The ground shook like nothing he'd felt before and he looked to his right, from where the snowmobile had been flung. Snow flew like it was being shot out of a snowblower and trees were exploding as the huge form of the giant stormed straight at them.

Bill glanced back and signaled to Steph to go as fast as she possibly could. Just then, her machine dipped into the fresh snow next to the trail, pulling her off balance, the whole sled banking to her right. Instinctively she squeezed the handlebars, desperate to stay astride the misbehaving snowmobile. But she still held the throttle under her thumb. The sudden burst from the powerful engine turned the drive-track into a digging conveyor, dropping the rear of the machine into a hole in the snow from which she wouldn't escape.

Bill stopped immediately and waved his arm. "Come on," he shouted to her, hoping she'd make it to him in time for them to flee. He saw her jump to the trail and start running toward him, the heavily packed snow precariously bearing her weight. Screaming reached Bill's ears, not from Steph, but from the giant's direction.

The sound of a male voice wailing. He turned and saw the monster smashing the last line of trees out of his path, the wood, branches and snow raining out like an artillery round had just burst among the flora. Jansen was in the giant's right fist, one arm free, one trapped next to his side. He hammered on the gigantic fingers with his free arm as he screamed. Bill was dimly aware that the giant hadn't squished the life from Jansen and wondered at it.

But then the massive creature was on them, reaching for Steph.

"No!" Bill yelled.

Another snowmobile zipped past, just behind the giant, smashing through the huge footprints, stopping once it reached the road. Bill saw Fritz stand up on the running boards and twist with his rifle raised, aiming at the giant's back. Two shots sounded in quick succession.

The monster ignored the bullets that struck it, grabbing Steph and spinning to face the old man who had slung his rifle back onto his shoulder and had one knee on the seat and was accelerating away. One big foot kicked out at him, an awkward movement that was slightly off target but connected with the tail of Fritz's sled, sending snowmobile and rider crashing into the trees where Fritz's head smacked an oak trunk, his body falling limp.

Then, in a whirl of white, billowing snow, the giant started to run back toward Brockway Mountain,

Jansen in one fist, Steph in the other, both of them screaming for their lives.

"Come on," Brandon muttered at Sam's snowmobile. He'd returned to the machine, knowing he couldn't walk out of these woods. "Why won't you start?" He examined the controls, looking for something, anything that could be a ray of hope. Then he saw the black knob with a cryptic looking symbol next to it and slapped his forehead. How'd he forgotten to use the choke? He vaguely remembered his dad saying you "had to choke it" when the motor was cool. He pushed the knob and it didn't move.

He felt a vibration shimmer up through the snowmobile. Then another.

Brandon pulled the knob and it slid out about an inch. Excited and angry with himself for forgetting about the choke, he turned the key. The engine sputtered and started to chug roughly, a cloud of smoke billowing out around him.

The trembling of the giant's approach was steady now, each footfall landing with alarmingly short intervals.

The motor started to die, its rhythm changing to a sporadic cough. "Oh, shit," Brandon uttered. He jammed the choke knob back in and the engine settled into a stable purr.

He looked in the direction where he knew the giant would come from. The horizon had slid closer than it had been even in the limited visibility of mid-day, now only ten yards away. The darkness beyond encircled the boy, creeping ever closer, like a slowly rising dark tide, threatening to engulf him completely.

A man's cries and a woman's screams reached through the ugly blackness of the darkening woods. The monster was coming. Dammit. If he'd gotten this fucking snowmobile running earlier he could have been long gone. But now he had to get back to his cave before the giant got him too.

Brandon squeezed the throttle and the machine moved forward, as tentative as its driver. He turned toward the cave, following his tracks and fighting to steer straight, the crooked ski constantly pulling on the handlebars.

He could still feel the pounding of the earth, but it didn't seem to be getting stronger. It was just a constant.

It only took him a minute to get to the cave. He pulled up in front of it, killed the engine and scrambled back into the safety of the shelter, the fire burning low at its entrance. A couple of pieces of wood had the flames flickering high once again, the heat flowing back to comfort Brandon. He focused on the shaking of the earth around him, a sign of the horrible creature's passage.

Then it stopped.

He listened, unnerved that the thing was stationary. Stationary where? Why? What was it doing? He wondered if it was sneaking toward his hiding place, hoping to catch Brandon when he poked his head out looking to see if the way was clear. The monster obviously knew he was here, having peeked in at him not long ago.

The footfalls started again, furious in their pace, but fading quickly. The thing must be gaining strength. It had looked ponderous when they shot at it during the first ambush. When they tried to burn it, it moved more like a linebacker, shifty and quick, but not altogether fast. Now it sounded like an Olympic sprinter and he shivered at the thought of something that big and evil being able to move with obscene speed.

He waited for several minutes, wanting to be sure the thing was gone before he started the snowmobile and tried to get to town. Then he wondered if that was even a good idea.

Shouting and screams got his attention. But they were not where he expected, not coming from the winter night, outside. They were coming from behind him, somewhere deep in the mountain.

The giant carried Steph and Jansen to a huge hole in the base of Brockway Mountain where it appeared the creature had rolled a massive stone away that had previously covered it. The monster crouched down as he walked into impenetrable darkness, his iron fingers locking her arms to her sides. She screamed and hollered, convinced that now that he had them in his lair, he would devour them. Though she couldn't see a thing, the acoustics let her know that the walls and ceiling were close. She felt her captor stand up straight again and then she was being lifted high before he relinquished his grip and her feet hit solid stone. The darkness and sudden freedom made her wobbly on her legs. A fetid stench assailed her olfactory senses and she regretted the need to breathe.

"Hey!"

Steph jumped at the sound of a voice in the complete blackness behind her. Next to her, she heard Jansen eke out a frightened exclamation. She turned and strained to see anything, but it was as if she were totally blind.

"Is someone there?" she asked.

"Yes," a man's voice said. "Doug and Nancy Schaefer."

"You're alive?" Jansen's voice.

"Jeff?"

"Yeah. It's me and Stephanie Crowe."

"Be careful. You're near the edge," Nancy said.

"Edge?" Steph asked.

She heard Jansen digging around in his pack. When he switched on his flashlight Steph covered her eyes like a vampire stepping into the sunshine. She squinted until her eyes, which had been straining in the complete darkness, adjusted to the introduction of light. Doug and Nancy groaned at the unannounced brightness.

"Dammit. Tell us next time you're going to do that," Doug said, shielding his eyes.

When her eyes had adjusted, Steph looked at their surroundings. They were standing on an oval-shaped stone shelf, about eight feet by twelve feet, within a massive cavern. The edge of the shelf was three feet from where she stood. Jansen shined the light over the edge and they saw that the drop was about thirty feet, three stories. Overhead, black stone arced up another fifteen feet to the ceiling of a round chamber roughly forty feet in diameter. The far wall was broken by a tunnel that stretched into the darkness. From what she'd heard, that was where the giant had gone after sticking them up on this perch.

"What's that smell," she asked, wrinkling her nose.

"Don't ask," Doug answered.

She turned to Doug and Nancy. "Why did he put us up here?" The couple gave each other a grim look.

"For later," Nancy said. "He's been eating..."

Steph's stomach dropped to her feet. "How do-"

"There were four of us before," Doug said.

"Who else?" Jansen asked.

"Tim Benson and Eric Jameson," Nancy said. Her voice was flat and lacked any hope.

"He's saving us for a snack?" Steph exclaimed. "But he hasn't been eating everyone. Some he seems to kill just for the joy of killing them."

Doug huffed out a breath. "I don't suppose you have any rope in that pack?" he asked, looking at Jansen. Jansen shook his head.

"So, you're stuck here too," Doug said. "'Til he needs nourishment."

CHAPTER TWENTY-SEVEN

"First Brandon, now Steph," Bill said. "Anyone seen Tril, or Mary or any of the others? I think Fritz is dead." He sat in a chair at Jotnar's, head hanging in defeat. Beside him, Matti had one hand on his back, trying in vain to lend strength to the broken man. Ernest and Suzy sat in front of Bill like concerned parents.

"Come on, Bill," Ernest said. "They could still be alive. You said yourself that the giant didn't kill them outright. And he carried Doug and Nancy off alive too."

Matti saw the tears glistening in both Ernest's and Suzy's eyes, once again feeling the loss for one of their friends. They were good people. Ornery, but good. They'd do anything for a friend, or even a stranger should the need arise. He patted Bill's back.

"He's right," Matti said. "That damned thing was killing everyone. Now it seems like he's just taking them." He hated how clinical he sounded, but facts were facts.

Bill looked up through bleary eyes. "But why? What the hell is he doing to them?"

"Doesn't matter," Matti said. "If they're alive, we can rescue them. We can leave Jansen there if you want."

That elicited a weak huff of a laugh from Bill and a "Great idea!" from Suzy.

Bill shook his head. "We don't know where they are. And even if we did, how do we rescue them from something we can't kill?"

"Quit sounding like such a chicken-shit," Matti said. "We just gotta think. You're one of the most resourceful guys I know. Start acting like it because we're running out of time."

The grieving man jarred at Matti's attack, looking hurt, angry, then thoughtful and finally, determined. It was the reaction Matti hoped he'd get when he spoke, though he knew he was being a bit of a dick.

"Okay," Bill said. "We have to figure out where they are."

"Big son-of-a-bitch like that should be easy to track," Ernest said through a malevolent grin.

"But we'll have to do it quietly," Matti said. "We can't get away from it on the snowmobiles. Maybe we can sneak away on snowshoes."

All four screwed up their faces in thought, skeptical, but hopeful. It was something they hadn't really tried, too afraid of being caught in the open and unable to get away. Though in truth, you couldn't escape it even on a snowmobile.

"It's the best idea I've heard," Ernest said.

They heard a snowmobile pull up outside and everyone turned anxious faces to the door. Snow crunched as whoever it was walked up and tugged on the tavern entrance. Mary Pinanen walked in, her face white.

"Mary?" Matti asked.

"It got them all," she said, the statement hitting like a sucker-punch. "I saw it carry off Tril and Jim. I found Gus's and Jerry's machines lying in the snow."

"Fuck," Bill spat.

"Were they still alive? Tril and Jim?" Matti asked.

Mary plopped into a seat and nodded, the tears of her trauma finally breaking free. Suzy went and sat next to the weeping woman and patted her shoulder. "Let me get you some coffee, honey. You look cold."

Matti glanced first at Ernest, then at Bill. "Still alive. He's taking them somewhere. West of town from the look of it. By Brockway Mountain. That's where he comes from and that's where he goes."

"Long walk in snowshoes," Ernest said. "We're in."

"We're going to have to bring more sets with us," Matti said. "Everyone needs a pair so we can trek the hell out of here."

Bill looked at Matti, intensely. "You're pretty sure we're going to find them and get away."

Matti grunted. "If we work things out ahead of time, why wouldn't we?"

Mary was sipping on her coffee, hands wrapped around it like it was the Holy Grail. Suzy had her arm around the woman, stroking her shoulder. Matti was so used to seeing the woman smiling and laughing that he barely recognized her. It made him mad to see her hunched over, spirit crushed. Bill hadn't been hard to kick back into action, as he struck most as a bit cold and unemotional. Mary was a real people-person, gabbing with anyone, always having a bright smile for you. She might be too far gone at this point. It was a lot for someone who loved people to witness some being eaten and others carried off, presumably to be eaten. He didn't know Mary very well, but just looking at her, he got the impression that she had given up. She couldn't afford that. He was sure they could do this without her, but she wouldn't survive without them. And he wasn't going to let her down. Working for Ernest and Suzy seemed to be rubbing off on him, making him feel like the next town patriarch, despite being only twenty-eight years old. This was his town and his people, no fucking monster was going to take it all away. They would win because they had to.

He sat down in front of Mary and patted her knee. "How you doing?" He gave her a sympathetic smile.

She grunted, shaking her head slightly, but she looked up at him, a wan smile on her face. "What the hell?" she asked.

He nodded and took a deep breath. "Mary, what we've been doing isn't working. That thing can catch us on our snowmobiles. It's easy enough to hear them." She watched him with questioning eyes, clearly detecting that he was going somewhere with this and she wasn't going to like it. "And we think he's taken the others somewhere and they are still alive." She pursed her lips and fought more tears. He took one of her hands in his. "We're going to try to find them and sneak out of here on snowshoes." Her eyebrows raised slightly and she huffed out air like she was having trouble catching her breath.

"Are you serious?" she asked.

"We can't kill it. All we can do is get away. The only way to do that is to sneak away. In the dark. Tonight."

Her face filled with despair. "It's freaking cold out there! And you want to try to walk all the way to Eagle River on snowshoes? Ten miles, in the dark, on a freezing night, through four feet of snow? No thank you."

Matti pursed his lips. Dammit. He couldn't leave her here to die, but he was asking for something incredibly difficult. "Mary, you'll die if you stay here."

"I'll die if I go with you," she said.

"You might, *might* die, if you come with us. You *will*, if you stay here. He's busting into houses to get people. We have to escape."

"Ten miles on snowshoes through deep snow is going to kill us."

"Ernest and Suzy are coming," he said. "If they can do it, you can. Plus, we'll switch off who's breaking the trail. That's the hard part. Everyone else will have much easier going."

He could see the wheels of her brain turning and her eyes stared at her hands while her mind drifted through the horrible memories of the last day, or maybe considered the possibilities that lie ahead. Whatever the case, her eyelids sank lower and she took a deep breath. "Okay. When do we leave?"

"Run home and get your extra snowshoes," he said. Everyone in town had extras. You couldn't be a proper host without them. "And meet us back here. I'm going to help Ernest and Suzy pack up some food and water."

She nodded dutifully and pulled up her hood and slipped on her mittens. Then, without a word, she walked out the door.

Bill shot Matti a conspiratorial smile and said, "I'll grab some extra shoes from my house and Sam's. Be back in a few minutes." Then he followed Mary out of the tavern's door, hoping he and Mary would make it back to the tavern alive.

CHAPTER TWENTY-EIGHT

Brandon stared at the splotch of darkness where his flashlight beam disappeared. Around it was rough, black rock, looking entirely too much like the gullet of some fearsome dragon, down which he must crawl. He was sure he'd heard screaming coming from back there somewhere. How and why? He didn't know. But now he had to find out. And the only way to do that was to scurry like some rodent in its tunnels, far beneath the earth. He glanced back out the entrance to his cave, the fire still burning warmly, fed with several new logs. Outside it was still snowing, still cold, and now nearly as dark as where he needed to go.

He could still go out and jump on the snowmobile and ride back to his dad's house. It wasn't that far and it'd be a lot warmer with more food. And he kind of missed his dad. In the past couple of months, he'd learned that his dad wasn't a complete asshole that just couldn't handle being a dad. For a moment he got a dread feeling that his dad might be dead, another victim of the giant. What would he do if he got home and no one was there? And what about Tril and Steph? What if he was the last one left? Oh shit. How long could he last? How long did he need to last?

Part of him wanted to run out there, jump on that snowmobile and zoom home and get some answers. He had to know what was going on. But a bigger part of him, one he didn't want to acknowledge, one that skulked around inside him like some all-devouring monster lurking below the water's surface in a swamp, that cowardly part, wanted to hide here and wait. Wait to be rescued and taken home where he'd be told everything would be fine. *Why'd mom have to die?*

More noise echoed to him from the depths of the hill-side. He turned and focused on the sound. Definitely more screams and shouting. People. People were back there somewhere. Maybe they'd found a place to hide in another cave. Maybe his dad was with them! And Tril. And Steph. They seemed like his family now. Except, he kind of liked Tril the way a man likes a woman. He didn't think of her as a sister.

He shook the distracting thoughts from his head and made up his mind. Strapping on his pack of gear, he wasn't even sure what all was in there, he started crawling on his hands and knees. The flashlight wiggled back and forth with each 'step' forward he took with his hands and he smacked his head into the stone ceiling more than once, not paying enough attention to what the light revealed. The air was cool, but not the frigid cold of outside, and he soon unzipped his coat and pulled off his hood and gloves. It smelled dank, like one would expect the earth the smell, but it was a rich, healthy dank, not one of rot.

Brandon hadn't crawled more than fifty feet when the tunnel split. To his left, the section branched off at a forty-five-degree angle and looked like it inclined, ever so slightly, whereas the path he was on continued straight and level. He chose to go left and pressed on. Just after he passed the intersection, he dug into the pocket of his jeans, buried beneath snow-pants that would probably be torn to shreds before long, and pulled out a nickel. This he laid on the floor of the tunnel that led back to his fire.

He wondered if Tril had come this far back. He wondered if he'd see her again. Or his father. A sharp rock bit into his palm, bringing him back to his mission. And now that's how he saw his predicament, a mission. He had to find the people and be reunited. His survival depended on it, as did his state of mind.

In front of him, the floor of the tunnel started to rise and heighten, eliminating the risk of bumping his head. He was relieved at the larger space, breathing easier. He hadn't noticed how claustrophobic he'd been feeling until coming out of the tight space behind him. His shoulders relaxed and he felt like he was taking in more air, though now it held a different smell. It didn't smell good, more like a dead animal. He desperately hoped he wouldn't crawl through whatever it was. That'd make him puke. The farther he crept, the stronger the stench became. He might hurl without having to schlep through something disgusting.

A murmur reverberated through the tunnel. Voices. It had to be voices. Somewhere in front of him. Brandon quickened his pace, anxious now to find someone.

Then the ground started to shake.

Steph froze when she felt the giant approaching. "Turn the light off," she commanded.

"Why?" Jansen asked. "Don't you want to know what he's doing?"

She realized that her instinct to try and hide in the darkness was wrong. The beast had carried them in here in the total darkness and put them right up here. He must be able to see something, even in the pitch black.

Jansen shined the flashlight at the hole in the opposite wall, the vibrations increasing in amplitude. The giant's hunched form slipped into the chamber and he stood up. Steph's heart started hammering, seeing the thing this close again, how huge he was, it was overwhelming. Even up on this shelf, three stories high, she'd be able to kick him directly in the cold, blue eyeball. Tril was gripped in one of the monster's hands, the other clamped around Jim Booth. They were silent but each wore a look of rage and defiance, as though their hate for this beast alone could cause it agony. He reached up and set the pair on the shelf with the others. Then he stood there, his massive eyes moving to each of the captives as though counting them. It was a calculating look that sent a shiver up Steph's already cold spine.

"Why don't you go fuck yourself," Tril yelled in the giant's face.

The resulting stare wasn't angry or insulted, but it looked comprehending. Steph shuddered again and reached forward to pull Tril back into the group. Tril looked at her and quickly wrapped her in a fierce hug. Seemingly unperturbed, the gargantuan turned and left the cave once again.

"I'm so glad you're alive," Tril told Steph. She wasn't crying, stronger than Steph felt.

"You too," Steph answered.

"Is Brandon here?"

Steph shook her head and saw Tril's shoulders slump. It only occurred to Steph at that moment that Brandon was surely dead, not having been brought here as a midnight snack. An emptiness opened inside her, sorrow at the loss of a nice young man, the son of her-what? Boyfriend? She supposed so. She and Bill had developed a friendship that was blooming into a romance. Thinking about it, she realized that she cared for him more than anyone she had ever met. And she was sure he cared for her. It was in the little things he did; the tolerances for her intellectual needs, taking her all over in his boat and putting up with her crazy theories. His saving her life when they got caught in a storm had really sparked something in her, awakening her realization that she was attracted to him for all the right reasons. As analytical and unemotional as he appeared, there was great depth to him. He wasn't cold at all. In fact, he was the most considerate and conscientious person she knew. Bill just didn't exhibit effluent displays of his thoughts and feelings. Despite his lack of embracing Brandon, he obviously loved the boy. She was sure he would do anything to keep him safe. But now it was too late for that. And she'd seen how hard it impacted him, even though he hadn't appeared overly distraught. Quietly she prayed that he was alive and bearing up through what he probably saw as another loss. Hopefully, it wouldn't become just that.

"Do you have any rope?" she asked.

"I lost my pack trying to get away," Tril answered.

"Jim?"

The man looked at her with a disgusted look. "No. He pulled it off of me. Maybe he's smarter than he looks."

"Well, that's great," Jansen said. "I'm probably the only one who didn't have any rope. I still have my pack."

"You have some food and water? And some fire building materials?" Tril asked.

Jansen's eyes narrowed. "We could make a fire that would last about 3 minutes," he said. "All I have is some kindling. You see any firewood up here?"

"We could use a sip of water," Doug said. He moved forward to dig in Jansen's pack. Jansen spun around, keeping his back from the thirsty man.

"Cut it out," Jansen snapped.

"We're not going to drink it all," Doug said. "Nancy and I just need a sip. We're parched."

"We might need that later," Jansen said.

"After he eats us?" Nancy asked.

"We don't-"

"Just give it to them, Jansen," Jim said. "We gotta stick together."

Grudgingly, Jansen pulled the pack off his back and retrieved the water bottle, pointedly taking a generous swig before reaching past Doug to hand it to Nancy. Doug rolled his eyes and waited for his wife to take her drink. Then Nancy met Jansen's possessive eyes as she proudly handed the bottle to Doug.

When Doug finished, he said, "Anyone else?" Getting no takers, he passed the water back to Jansen who angrily stuffed it into his backpack again.

"Might as well turn the light off," Jim said, "since you're so concerned about conserving our resources."

Steph hated the feeling of complete blindness she felt when Jansen turned off the flashlight. She felt Tril bump into her. No, not bump. The girl stayed in contact with her, lending more strength than she probably received in return. It was good to feel the young lady's presence.

"Is there any way out of here?" Tril said.

"The way you came in," Doug said.

"And it's too far down to jump. You'd break your legs, or worse," Jansen added.

"If we tie all our coats together, could we get low enough to jump?" Tril asked.

Silence.

"That seems like a good idea, kiddo," Steph said. "We can give it a try. Jansen, turn on the light."

The group of six people took off their coats and quickly set to tying the sleeves together. The net length of the 'rope' was just shy of twenty feet, leaving it dangling a good ten feet above the rocky floor. As they looked at their work, they all realized that it was brutally fricking cold without their coats on.

"Who's first?" Jim asked.

"I'll go," Jansen answered.

"Not you, dickhead," Jim said. "Doug, you feel like going? You're probably one of the heaviest and we'll need all the help up here to hold it. Then you can catch the others when they come down."

"Sounds like fun," Doug said unenthusiastically.

Jim and Jansen each grabbed the makeshift rope, making sure they had good footing near the ledge. Steph and Nancy grabbed the two men around their waists to help them brace for Doug's descent. Tril was relegated to light-bearer. Doug crawled forward and sat with his legs hanging over the edge with the coat-rope to one side.

"Geez, I hope this holds," he said. Then to his wife, "Love you."

"Love you too," Nancy answered.

Then he grabbed the coats and let his hips slowly slide over the edge, the stone doubtlessly gouging his back. He grumbled in pain and spun around, hanging his entire weight on their only hope for escape.

"So far, so good," he said.

The anchors held his weight with less effort than expected, the four easily outweighing the one. Tril shone the light down on Doug, reporting his progress. Finally, she said, "He's almost down."

Then, once again, with the inopportune timing of a case of diarrhea, the ground began to shake.

CHAPTER TWENTY-NINE

"Dammit to hell," Jim cursed. "Pull him up!"

The crew hauled back on the coat-rope, desperately trying to get Doug to safety before the giant came back. If he found one of them on the cave floor or in the process of trying to escape, he may kill everyone.

"No," Doug yelled and suddenly Steph was tumbling backward, Jim toppling onto her. She looked over into the shadows at Nancy and Jansen who were in a similar heap. Tril was shining the light down over the edge.

"He's down! Doug, hide," Tril yelled. She illuminated the cave floor so Doug could find a suitable hiding position, if such a thing existed.

The four bodies on the ledge jumped into action, pulling the coats up and quickly working to untie them lest the monster see their intentions. Each member stuffed their jacket on until only Doug's was left. Steph stared at it in her hands, knowing that somewhere below them the man must be freezing. But they needed it if the rest of them were to make it down. She handed it to Nancy.

"Put that on over your coat," she told the woman.

Tril stepped over and joined the others, the light illuminating the terrified expression on Nancy's face. "Everyone huddle at the back of the ledge. Maybe he won't notice Doug is gone."

"Where is he? Is he okay," Nancy asked as they moved into a shivering clump.

"Hiding," Tril assured.

The monster's footfalls grew heavier as he drew nearer. Then they lightened. Steph suspected it was because he was slowed by having to crouch to enter the cavern. The entrance must be small enough that it hindered the giant's movement.

"Turn off the light," she said.

In the total darkness she pulled Tril tight to her and felt the girl trembling, whether from cold or fear, she didn't know. She worried about Doug. She hadn't seen much in the way of hiding places down there, but she hadn't been looking for one. Thank God Tril had given him light to find a spot. She was a smart kid. If they made it through this and she was able to meet Tril's parents, she would have nothing but praise for the young lady.

If they made it through this... Shit. Her life had finally started moving forward again, having been stagnated both at work and romantically. Here she was with Jansen again, with whom she'd almost had a relationship before realizing that he was too self-centered to really care about anyone but himself. It didn't necessarily make him a bad guy, just a bad boyfriend.

She had been glad when he left the university, but it had scared her from pursuing any other faculty guys. And of course, the graduate students were off-limits. Not that there had been any she would have considered anyway.

Then, quite by accident, she met Bill. She wasn't looking for anything from him other than to be her charter to search for more evidence about the dead guy in the lake. Not only had they found evidence, but they also seemed to have found what happened to the folks from Copper Harbor, a major discovery. And she and Bill had hit it off. No pretenses, no games. Just the two of them, enjoying each other's company, like two saplings winding together as they grew, to become one complex tree with two different root systems.

She laughed at herself then. What a strange simile, thinking of the two of them being like two trees. Maybe it was time for a trip to the city and get out of the woods. She decided then that if they did make it out of this, she'd make that suggestion to Bill. Or rather, extend that invitation.

Steph felt the giant enter the chamber. Light wasn't needed to sense his presence. Somehow, the way he filled the space was tangible, subtle changes in the air pressure, the scuff of his huge feet on the stone, the whimper of whoever he had in his grasp. She felt the penetrating gaze fall upon the little group and prayed silently that Doug remained hidden. Her grip on Tril tightened and she could feel her tense, the two of them understanding that they were being scrutinized. Counted.

A deep, angry growl boomed forth. The monster's fetid breath, stinking of rotting flesh, blasted over them and suddenly two stumbling people were thrust into their midst.

"No!" Nancy screamed.

The two newcomers howled in terror, feeling hands grabbing them and hearing a voice so near in this dark prison set free their pent-up tension.

The giant moved with such quickness that the air in the chamber swirled. The stomping of his big feet on the stony ground as he searched for the missing meal was awful to feel and hear. Against her will, Steph envisioned Doug being crushed as the giant inadvertently stepped on him.

A man's cry of fear resonated from below. Doug. She could hear as his voice grew louder, being lifted into the air. "Nancy! I love-" The words were cut off in a sickening crunch followed by the smacking of the beast's lips. Then more crunching.

Nancy wailed and Steph heard her fall to her knees. She let go of Tril and bent to hold the grieving widow, stroking her hair and shedding her own tears.

A wet slapping sound signaled the end of the giant's meal, whatever had been left of Doug had been cast aside to rot. Then the cold, rotten breath blew into the group, coming in slow, steady currents as the horrible thing watched them.

"Lights, lights, lights," Jansen said.

Light flared into the cavern as Tril switched on the flashlight, shining it directly into the face of the giant showing his blood-smeared maw and icy blue eyes. Doug's fresh blood trickled down his chin and his upper lip bulged out as he ran his tongue across the front of his stone-like teeth, cleaning away the flesh that was caught between them. Steph helped Nancy to her feet and held the poor woman's head against her shoulder, not wanting her to see her husband's life-blood running from the giant's grisly mouth.

Then a massive hand was reaching upward, seeking another prize.

Jansen, on Nancy's other side, quickly grabbed the woman and thrust her forward, pushing her in front of himself, trying to get behind everyone else.

"What the fuck?" Jim, Steph and Tril yelled in unison.

The giant took Nancy in his big hand, though his eyes didn't seem to leave the group as a whole. Then he reached over and set her on the shelf away from the others. His mouth opened wide as he bellowed angrily, icy cold spit and blood spraying onto them. The sound would have hurt one's ears if they were outside. In the confines of this echoic cave, it was positively deafening.

Brandon froze, the gigantic roar crashing into him like a massive wave taking him off his feet at the beach. He switched his light off and knelt there, afraid to move, wondering what the hell had just happened. What was he crawling toward? He thought he was going to find a secret haven of people living in the security of the mountain where the giant couldn't find them.

That clearly wasn't the case.

But he was sure he'd heard a man's scream, followed by voices again, just before the huge wail of rage. As a matter of fact, he kind of thought he heard the f-bomb. Definitely people. But now what was happening? Shit.

He felt secure in this little tunnel. The giant hadn't been able to get to him in his cave and this tunnel wasn't any bigger than that. Whatever was going on, he had to find out, see it for himself. Maybe the giant was mad he couldn't get to those people either. That made sense. Though it definitely sounded like he got *someone.*

Brandon flipped on his light, saw what was in front of him and turned it off again. Then he crawled as far as he had been able to see before repeating the process.

The giant reached up, his big fingers pushing Steph, Jim, Tril and the others aside. Jansen scrambled to get out of reach but then, with alarming quickness, the giant's hand snatched out and grabbed the desperately fleeing man. Jansen screamed out in alarm.

"Help me! Help me," he cried. But no one moved from their frozen stances, staring at the guy who'd just tried to push a widow into the monster's grip.

He was lifted and brought in front of the giant's face, the big orbs that were its eyes boring holes through the wretched creature it held. Jansen quit wiggling and stared back at his doom. Then the monster held him so he was directly in front of, and facing, Nancy.

To Steph, it looked like he was playing with his food. Taunting Jansen or Nancy or both. Geez, what a sick bastard. Nancy just looked at Jansen, pity and sorrow etched on her features. The monster held Jansen there for a full minute, at least. She didn't know if he expected, or wanted, Nancy to hit him or what. Whatever the giant's purpose, Nancy wasn't buying. She was shattered and nothing mattered to her at this point. She may have wanted to follow her husband in death, though not necessarily in the same manner.

"What's it doing?" one of the new arrivals asked. Steph didn't know him, though she wasn't from town so that wasn't unusual. She hadn't known Doug and Nancy until a couple of hours ago. Had it been that long?

"Dunno," Jim mumbled. "Quiet."

Suddenly the beast opened his mouth and tilted Jansen back until just his head and shoulders were within the shadow of his massive teeth. But it didn't bite down.

It chuckled. At least, that's the only way Steph could interpret the gravely sound that bounced out of his mouth. Then, slowly, so slowly, the teeth descended. Jansen cried and wailed, pleading for mercy, pleading for someone to save him. His screams intensified and rose to a glass-shattering pitch as the enormous incisors made contact with his body and started to crush down.

With a slow, squishing crunch, Jansen's voice was silenced.

Holy fucking shit! Brandon thought. *That sounded awful!* Someone else had just been killed.

The earth trembled beneath his hands and knees, slightly, but noticeably. He waited and then the tremors increased in severity before fading away. The giant had left.

He flicked on his flashlight and started to crawl forward quickly.

CHAPTER THIRTY

Bill raced home as fast as he could, given the darkness, the blinding flakes that raced at his face in the beam of his headlight, and the deep, fresh snow. He pulled up close to the door, had to shovel enough room so that it could open, and ran inside to grab his last pair of snowshoes. He'd have two pairs and only need one. Hopefully, Steph would get to wear this second pair. Better yet, Brandon, though he chased the thought away as fancy.

Back outside, he strapped the shoes to the back of his sled and headed off to Sam's house. He knew the door would be unlocked. Most of the homes around here were, unless the residents were out of town for a day or two. Again, he had to shovel to gain entrance to Sam's house, the snow piling up outside the door, preventing it from opening.

He stepped into the dark little house like he was entering sacred ground. Sam was gone, probably dead too. The room he was in felt small and cozy, the warmth seeping into him the way a swig of alcohol warmed its way out from the belly. He flipped the switch for the lights, forgetting the power was out. He pulled his flashlight out of one of the deep pockets of his heavy winter coat and used it to shine around the place, not wanting to act intrusive out of respect for the man who'd done his best to keep the community safe.

The snowshoes weren't in plain view, so he looked in the most likely spots; the closet near the front door, on the floor of the mud-room at the back. He finally found two more sets in the closet near the back door. Half-way to the front exit, he stopped and looked around at the empty house and breathed in its aroma.

"Thanks, Sam," he said. "I hope we find you soon."

Then he was outside adding two more pairs of snowshoes to the back of his machine. He sat down and was about to turn the ignition when the whole snowmobile vibrated. Then again and again in rapid succession.

With a curse, he dismounted and headed back into the house, just now remembering the rifle slung to his back. The useless rifle.

"Put more chicken in that pack," Ernest ordered.

Matti wrapped another couple of the cooked breasts in meat-packing paper and stuffed them into the backpack Ernest had pointed to. "This one is basically full."

"Does it have water in it?" Suzy asked.

"Yeah, they all do," Matti said, waving his hand over the five packs they had prepared. He hoped they could carry it all. Once they rescued the others, those folks could shoulder some of the burden themselves. "As soon as Bill and Mary get back, we can-" his words were interrupted by the tell-tale vibrations heralding the giant's approach.

"Kill the lights!" Ernest exclaimed.

Matti ran over and started flipping switches, dropping the tavern into darkness except for the glow of some 'Exit' signs and two lights above the stoves. He stood there watching the windows and his ears suddenly focused on the incessant droning of Ernest's generator outside. Shit. Talk about draw attention.

Rumble. The steps were getting much stronger and frequent. The thing must be coming this way.

Seeking the back door where he could run out and turn off the generator, he made his way into the kitchen where Ernest and Suzy were huddled together. Ernest held an axe in his gnarled hands, looking like some Viking from historic tales. As Matti slipped into the brewhouse section of the tavern, his right hand bumped up against the outlet valve of the hot-liquor tank and he let out a yelp. "Dammit," he said to himself. Before all this nonsense started, he had been about to brew a batch of beer and evidently left the tank on. The water within it was around 180 degrees and though the sides of the tank were insulated, the outlet was not. When he killed the generator, it'd turn off, so he kept moving.

The Biting Cold

A thundering crash, the sound of splintering wood and breaking glass burst from the front of the tavern. Cold air, filled with stinging flakes of snow rushed into the tavern like a medieval army flowing through the breach of a castle wall, spreading out in every direction. Matti peered through the little window of the brewery that looked out upon the dining room and saw two huge hands reach through a hole where the front wall met the roof. They gripped the ceiling and heaved upward, tearing an even larger hole in the tavern's roof. Through Jotnar's gaping wound, he could see the familiar shadow of the rampaging giant, a looming dark shape that was somehow darker even than the wintry, night sky.

Matti looked through the door to the kitchen, immediately concerned for Ernest and Suzy who, thankfully, remained in hiding, Ernest with his axe and Suzy now armed with a huge butcher's knife. He looked around the brewery for something he could use as a weapon, but unless he wanted to hit the giant with a long wooden stirring paddle or a stainless-steel bucket, he was out of luck.

A huge leg stomped into the tavern and more ceiling was ripped away, enough that now the monster would most likely see Ernest and Suzy hunkering behind the counter in the kitchen.

Matti rubbed his burned right hand, the ache that follows all burns penetrating the intensity of the catastrophe that was happening. It gave him a thought.

Over the chugging of the generator, he heard the monster give a satisfied grunt. Then it reached down toward the elderly couple who scrambled to get out of the way. Too late. It grasped Suzy around her middle and lifted her to the side so he could concentrate on snatching Ernest. But Suzy raised her big knife in both hands and started furiously stabbing into the creature's big fingers with crazed abandon. The knife chinked uselessly against the stony flesh, but one stab must have found a nerve because the giant twitched and roared in anger. He glared at the woman who was poking away at his fingers and considered her for a moment.

"Let her go, you big asshole!" Ernest wailed. He jumped forward and his axe flashed through the air to bite into one big, meaty calf where it didn't even sink in. But again, the giant yelled in annoyance and raised Suzy up and bit off the top of her torso, sending a fountain of blood spraying through the frigid air.

Matti's rage flared, that sweet woman who'd been like a tough mom to so many people in this town, was no more. And Ernest was sure to be next. Matti wasn't going out without a fight. If he could cause that big mother-fucker pain, he would do his damnedest to make sure he did. With practiced precision, he grabbed the transfer hose and connected one end to the outlet of the hot liquor tank the other to the pump. Another section of hose he connected to the output of the pump, but he left the other end free, with just the ball valve on the end to open or close it. He turned on the pump.

"Gah!" Ernest cried. Matti looked up to see the old tavern-keeper, lore-master, bartender, town patriarch, in the monster's grasp, axe held high over his head. Suzy's remains were still clutched in its other hand, two limp legs dangling from below the fingers. Ernest brought the axe down on the beast's wrist with all the might he could summon from his aged shoulders.

With a speed that belied his great size, the giant bit off Ernest's head, and the axe clanged to the floor, falling from the old man's dead hands.

"You want some fresh meat?" Matti screamed. "Come on you big fuck!" He waved his arms and quickly got the giant's attention. With a body in each hand, the monster lifted one gargantuan foot and reached out to squash the big brewer like a bug.

Matti opened the ball valve and pointed the spray of scalding water at the giant's descending foot. The sound of boiling skin was immediately drowned out by the most horrible scream that Matti had ever heard, the foot crashing down wide of the big man. Smiling, he sprayed the hot water at every gigantic body part he could reach.

CHAPTER THIRTY-ONE

The light bobbed and weaved with each crawling step forward. Brandon kept looking for the tunnel to open up into a big cavern where he'd find more people. But if that were the case, why didn't they climb through here? It sounded like some of them had just been killed. Then a thought occurred to him, what if the tunnel narrowed down too small for anyone to enter? Shit.

A frigid draft pushed at his face, moving down the tunnel from somewhere ahead. The farther he pushed on, the more he missed the gentle warmth of his fire. There had to be some sort of opening ahead. He was sure that's where he'd find whoever was in here. Ignoring the cold, he pressed forward. He had to find whoever was in here with him and do something to help. If he could. He may not have much time; the monster was sure to return.

Tril turned off the light just before the giant had killed Jansen. But that didn't mean she didn't see what happened in her mind's eye. She reached back and grabbed someone's hand, Steph's, she hoped.

When it was clear the giant was gone, she turned on the light and she and Steph rushed to Nancy's side, enveloping her with hugs and support. Jim was right behind them, his face a mix of sorrow and vengeful hate. Tril hadn't even thought to see who else had been brought in to wait with them in this miserable refrigerator, her main concern for Nancy.

Nancy was silent as tears slid down her cheeks. Her face was resolute with the knowledge that they would all be eaten eventually, each one of them a snack or a meal for the horrible creature that had devoured her husband. Her teary, brown eyes lacked hope, lacked rage, lacked emotion. They simply *were*.

Steph was talking quietly to Nancy, her words low and unintelligible. But Tril could guess at their content: condolence, encouragement, friendship, the promise of something better yet to come. She swallowed hard and stifled a sob. There was no room for grieving now, she had to be strong, strong until the very end. Crying wouldn't help anything.

Tril fought against the feeling of hopelessness that bore against her like a toppling stone slab. If she didn't survive this, her parents would never know what happened to her. They'd be distraught, perhaps ruined as some parents reasonably are when their child is taken from them. For a moment, she wanted them here with her, to hold her and tell her everything was going to be okay. But then she realized, if that were the case, she would probably have to see them die. She raised her eyes skyward and said a silent prayer for her parents, then for herself and the others. It was all she could think to do.

Something flashed high on the wall.

"Hey, what was that?" she said. She turned off the flashlight. "Above us."

She continued watching and saw a flickering light above them, about twelve feet up.

"A light!" Jim said.

"Hello?" she called, turning her light back on and shining it upward.

The light became brighter and then was shining down on the group. "Tril?" It was Brandon's voice. His face emerged from a tunnel that wasn't visible from the shelf and gazed down at them.

"Brandon?" Steph and Tril said.

"Yeah," came the response.

"What? How?" Tril asked.

"Your cave. Remember? This is where it leads," Brandon said.

"Jansen said the giant got you," Tril said.

"That fucker pushed me off his snowmobile so he could get away," Brandon said, anger heavily tainting his words.

"Well, he got his," Jim said. "Is that hole big enough to crawl through?"

Brandon swiveled his head around. "Yeah. Plenty of room."

"Got a rope?" Jim asked.

"Just a minute." Brandon disappeared and could be heard rummaging through a pack. Then a length of rope dropped from above and landed at Tril's feet with about four feet to spare.

The hair on Bill's arms and neck stood on end as the agonized wail of the giant reverberated throughout the light-less town. *What the hell just happened?* he thought. He'd heard the thing roar before, but this hadn't sounded like rage or a challenge. It had sounded like pain. What could have caused that big bastard enough pain that it would scream like that?

He opened the front door to Sam's house and cautiously stepped outside. The wailing continued and the ground trembled, the sound originating in the direction of Jotnar's Tavern. The beast was on the move and moving fast. The volume of the screams decreased as he waited, but they didn't cease. Just moved away, toward Brockway Mountain. Crap. Something had happened at the tavern.

Bill jumped back on the snowmobile and made his way back to Jotnar's as fast as he dared, carefully looking around, listening, and trying to sense any vibrations that weren't caused by the sled's engine. As he got near, he could see the lights were all off and there was wreckage strewn about the front parking lot. Huge logs that made up the walls were split apart like toothpicks, shards of broken glass were plunged into the snow, standing up like icicles that had fallen from the eaves of a roof and stabbed into the white banks. The parking lot had been roughly trampled down, the monster leaving his tracks everywhere in a haphazard pattern. A big, black hole was torn into the roof, the shattered lumber at its edges the teeth in some nightmarishly huge lamprey's mouth.

Somewhere in that wreckage were Ernest, Suzy and Matti. Or what was left of them, if the giant hadn't carried them off. He slumped on his seat, his arms losing their strength, his shoulders wanting to drag on the ground. The unbearable cold lost its sting, just as his life lost hope.

A sound made him raise his head. A snowmobile was coming fast from his left. He turned and saw Mary ride up, snowshoes strapped to the back of her machine. She pulled up next to him and killed the engine so Bill did the same. The only sound in the suddenly quiet winter night was the constant hum of Ernest's generator, somewhere behind the building. When Mary looked at the tavern, her face dropped.

"Oh, God. No," she said.

Together they walked to the destroyed front door of what had been their base of operations, what had been the most welcoming restaurant/tavern/brewery in the area. Bill pushed what was left of the front door aside and stepped into what had been the dining room.

"Hello," he said. He pulled out his flashlight and shone it around the mangled tables. Nothing stirred. Mary flipped on her light and together they scoured the wreckage, looking for any sign of the proprietors or their brewer. A splotch of bright, red blood splattered across the remains of the bar caught his eye. He walked over and found what must have been the lower portion of Suzy's body. Not far to his left was Ernest's headless corpse.

He turned to Mary and let out an audible sigh. She was glancing from one broken body to the next, silent tears running down her cheeks, but her face stoic, as if it were carved from granite. She too had seen too much of this.

"Ah! Fuck! Ow. What?" a voice said from beyond the kitchen.

Bill jumped up and staggered over the debris trying to get into the kitchen to see who it was, Mary right behind him. He could hear junk being tossed aside and more cursing.

"Matti?" he called.

"Yeah," the answer.

"You okay?" Bill found him with his light. The lumberjack-like brewer was bleeding from a gash on his head and struggling to get out from under a fallen table, a mixer and various pots and pans. He and Mary pulled the table upright and extended a hand to Matti as the brewer tossed the mixer off of his pelvis. "What the hell happened?"

Matti rubbed his head, grimacing at his own touch. "Did you happen to find my coat out there? Shit, it's cold."

Mary bounded back into the dining room and returned with Matti's coat, the hat and gloves stuffed neatly into one sleeve. The big man quickly threw on the gear, shivering as he did.

Dressed, he looked at Bill and Mary and fixed them with a cold, almost evil smile. "Did you hear that mother-fucker?" he asked. His eyes lit up with intense fire.

"It was hard not to," Mary said.

"What was that about?" Bill asked.

"Fricking hot water! That's what it was about." Matti looked back and forth between Mary and Bill. "It attacked us here. It got Suzy and Ernest, though they did their damnedest to fight it off." He paused, eyes fogging momentarily. "I didn't have any weapons, but my hot liquor tank was full and hot. I rigged it so I could spray the water at him." His eyebrows launched to his forehead and a crazed grin pulled his lips back, revealing perfect white teeth. "He did NOT like that. That bastard's skin bubbled and popped just like ours would."

"Really?" Bill said, thoughtfully. He looked at Mary who wore a wicked smile.

"I've got an idea. But let's go somewhere warm to work it out," Matti said.

"My place. Let's go."

As they got ready to start their snowmobiles, they heard an enraged roar in the direction of Brockway Mountain.

"Tril, you go first. You're the lightest and we'll need people up top to help us heavier folk," Jim said.

"Brandon! You all braced up there?" Tril called.

"I think so," his voice echoed down.

Tril grabbed the rope and suddenly Jim wrapped his arms around her legs, hoisting her up. As she went hand over hand, Jim let go and then put his hands below her feet, lifting her even higher. As a result, she didn't even have to climb on her own until the last four feet, easy for her. When her face cleared the edge, she saw Brandon sitting with his legs braced against the sides of a rough tunnel, rope gripped in his hands and wrapped around one wrist, a huge smile on his face. With his free hand, he reached forward and grabbed her behind one shoulder and pulled. She flopped onto the floor of the passage and scrambled to hug Brandon, tackling him in the process.

"We thought you were dead," she said, holding him tightly.

"So did I," he answered. "But I found your cave just in time. The giant can't get us in here."

"Hey! You ready for the next one?" Jim's voice rang.

"Just a sec," Brandon answered.

334

He squeezed against the wall so Tril could get behind him and grab hold of the three feet of rope that lay unused on the floor. Once they were both braced, Brandon called for the next climber.

Tril's heart was bursting with joy. They were safe, at least for now. And Brandon was still alive. There was hope.

The giant's wail of pain echoed into the cavern and through the tunnel, a distant sound, but clear and disconcerting.

"Hurry up," Jim yelled from below.

In seconds, Steph's head popped over the ledge and Brandon pulled her into the tunnel. She gave Brandon a quick hug then squeezed by to assist with the rope.

"We need more rope," Brandon yelled. They pulled up a couple more feet of rope for Steph and she anchored behind Tril. "Okay. Go."

Nancy was the next to arrive, her face pale and stoic, she was able to give Brandon a weak smile and a 'thank you' before sneaking to the back of the line. More rope was pulled up and Brandon gave the go-ahead.

The ground started to rumble, very quick successive jolts reverberating through the solid earth.

Tril saw Brandon jerk forward slightly as she felt the next climber begin the ascent. Whoever it was must have had to jump to reach the remaining rope. Then Gus Urten came over the lip of the tunnel. He was a big guy in his mid-fifties, 6'1" and well over two-hundred pounds. When he was safely up, he said, "I'll take point. Everyone shift back. Last in line let go of the rope. We don't have any to spare down there."

With that, the big man took up the principal bracing position, effectively blotting the next climbers from Tril's view. She didn't see who the next person was, just heard his voice as he made it to safety, then the whole process of shifting back began again, leaving her as the last person on the very end of the rope. Behind her, Steph and Nancy crawled backward a short distance, unable to see where the tunnel went as Brandon's flashlight was at the hole's entrance and the last climber was bringing up Jansen's light.

The inhuman wailing increased in volume like an approaching siren. The giant's footfalls were approaching fast, each tremor occurring in quick succession and with increasing strength. The volume of the beast's screams suddenly doubled, no, tripled. It had made it to the entrance of the cavern.

From this position on the rope, Tril hardly noticed when Jim began his climb. But as soon as he did, someone in front of her said, "Pull, pull, pull. Slide back!" She scrambled to slide in reverse on her butt, inadvertently bouncing down on one of Steph's feet momentarily. Together, the four rope tenders hoisted Jim up to the tunnel so fast he hit his head on the ceiling as he came through, drawing a vile curse.

"Move back. Kill the light."

They were enveloped in complete darkness and the seven collapsed against each other, struggling to quiet the sound of their heaving breath. The air around them pulsed as the whimpering giant made it into the chamber below.

The bellow that followed forced them all to bury their heads, covering their ears with their gloved hands.

CHAPTER THIRTY-TWO

"Brandon," Tril whispered. "Are we going to need flashlights to crawl out of here?"

"Not really," he answered. "It's pretty straight. Just watch your heads. It's low."

As far as they could tell, the giant was still in his cavern. They hadn't felt him leaving, but he had gone quiet now.

"Let me go first," Tril said, pushing her way past Steph and Nancy in the pitch black. "I kind of know these caves."

The little band of giant-treats quietly started to crawl deeper into the mountain. Occasionally there was a suppressed grunt of pain when someone banged their head into a low spot on the ceiling.

After they'd gone no less than sixty feet, Jim said, "Okay. Turn the lights on. But only shine them forward." Brandon flipped on his light and passed it forward to Tril. A warm glow came from behind him, casting wiggling shadows along the walls of the dark, stone tunnel, like giant spiders working their legs around the young man's body. He shivered reflexively, momentarily getting the willies.

It seemed like two hours before the line stopped and Brandon heard Tril's voice again. "Oh, thank God," she said. "You built a fire." Orange light danced as the girl added some of the wood he'd gathered to the glowing embers, blowing lightly on it to bring it back to life.

"Are you shitting me?" the big guy behind Brandon said. "There's nowhere to stand up?"

"Oh, shut up, Gus," Jim said. "We're safe and warmer than we were."

The man dropped onto his stomach, then rolled onto his back. Brandon looked at the guy laying there, Jim's light throwing too many shadows to see him well, but not so much he couldn't see the man's weak, but sincere, smile. He looked to be in his late fifties, big but not fat, with tufts of thick gray hair hanging out from below his wool cap. One hand extended up towards Brandon.

"Thank you. We were all good as dead until you showed up." Brandon shook the man's hand awkwardly. "Gus Urten. What's your name?"

"Brandon. Brandon Hitze."

"Ah, right. Bill's boy. We thought you were dead. Good to see you're not. Heard a lot of good things from your old man."

Brandon twitched his head to one side. *A lot of good things?* He couldn't imagine his dad saying anything good about him. Not that he expected him to say anything bad either. It simply surprised him that his dad talked about him at all. He suddenly felt guilty about griping about his dad to Jansen and Tril. Especially to Jansen, that shit-head. His father had tried to warn him to stay away from the guy, but he'd sought him out anyway. Part of it was just to spite his dad. Dammit.

"Is my dad okay?" he asked.

"He's not here, so that bodes well," Gus said.

"I don't know about that," Brandon said. "Sam isn't here either, because he's dead."

The reclined man took two deep breaths before saying, "The last I saw, he was alive. Hang in there."

"Brandon, climb up here," Steph said. She slid to one side of the tunnel to give him just enough room to sidle next to her. As soon as he was close, she wrapped him in a bear-hug. "I'm so glad you aren't dead. Your dad was wrecked when Jansen told him the giant got you. How did you get away?"

Then he told everyone the whole tale, starting with when they fled the scene of the fire-ambush, Jansen pushing him off the back of the snowmobile, and then Sam sacrificing himself to save him.

"Now I'm really glad that asshole went slow," Tril said. "Poor Sam."

"What do you mean, went slow?" Brandon asked.

Tril described in vivid detail the manner of Jansen's death. Brandon cringed. What an awful way to go. As glad as he was that Jansen had gotten what he deserved, he couldn't help but feel bad about it having been torturous.

"Hey," Tril said. "You have any arrows for this bow?" She'd found Jansen's bow stashed near the entrance of the little cave.

"I dropped them when I fell in the snow."

"What good would they do, anyway?" Steph asked.

"I could kill a rabbit or deer or something. We might be here a while."

"Tomorrow we'll pan out and look for them," Jim said. "How we set on wood?"

"We can get through the night easy enough," Tril answered.

"Then we should all get some sleep. We'll need our strength tomorrow."

Satisfied that the giant was well away from them, Bill, Matti and Mary rode over to Bill's house, careful not to rev the engines up too much, trying to keep the noise as low as possible. They pulled in front of the little house and shut down the machines and went inside before turning on their flashlights. Though the fire had gone out, the house was still comfortable enough to shed hats and gloves.

They gathered around Bill's table, looking expectantly at each other, but unsure of where to start. Finally, Bill said, "So hot water hurts it?"

"Obviously," Matti said.

"Then why didn't fire hurt it?" Mary asked.

"I've been thinking about that," Matti said. "Maybe his skin is kind of like ice. By that, I mean, what happens when you drop a match in the snow?"

"It goes out," Bill stated.

"Right. But what happens when you dump boiling water on snow?"

"It melts right through it," Mary said, her face lightening.

Matti nodded, smiling. "Yeah. It'll melt all the way through to the ground if you have enough of it. Maybe on this big bastard, it'll melt through to the bone."

Bill rubbed his chin. This was good news. Matti's logic certainly made sense. If that was the case, they could kill it.

"So, let's say we can kill it with boiling water. How do we get it to climb into a huge pot of boiling water? Not literally, of course, but effectively," Bill asked.

The trio sat pondering the question.

"How much water did you spray it with?" Mary asked.

Matti shook his head. "Boy, I don't know. A couple of gallons at most. It didn't hang around long once I started in on him."

"Do you think it might be dead already?" Bill asked.

Matti pursed his lips. "He was able to throw shit all over the place before taking off. I doubt it."

"Seems to me we need to 'melt all the way through to the ground'. Or in this case, all the way to a critical organ," Mary said.

"How do we lure it back to Jotnar's?" Matti asked.

Bill shook his head. "I don't think that's going to work. If he's smart enough to break the ice all along the shore so we can't escape, he isn't going back there."

Mary's face suddenly paled. "Is it just me or did he seem a lot stronger and faster when we attacked him with the fire than he did when we shot at him?"

Bill nodded. "It's not just you. What about it?"

"What if he was basically reverse hibernating? Coming out when it's cold and having to eat. Then, as he eats, he gains strength. What if eating helps him heal?"

Bill's eyes sagged as a sick realization burned at his stomach. Matti looked at him like he'd just thrown up and was trying to clear the vile taste from his mouth.

Mary nodded grimly. "If we want to save them, we're going to have to act fast."

"I wish we could fill up a firetruck with boiling water and use that to spray him," Bill said. "We can't carry the hot liquor tank. And if we can't get him to come here, we're shit out of luck."

"Too bad they don't make big, insulated squirt-guns," Mary said.

Matti's head snapped to look at Mary. "Insulated squirt-guns? Hmmm."

"What?" Bill asked.

Matti jumped up and stared at them. "I have an idea. We have some empty Corny-kegs at Jotnar's. They're the five-gallon kegs soda comes in. And I have two, maybe three small CO_2 tanks."

"And?"

"If we fill the Corny-kegs with hot water, then pressurize them with the CO_2 tanks, they'd be like five-gallon super-soakers!" Matti looked like a mischievous child as he finished talking. Bill wondered how anyone could still be optimistic in light of everything that had happened.

"Fifteen gallons going to be enough?" he asked.

"We can bring more kegs with us."

"How will we carry them?" Mary asked. She wore a not-so-well disguised frown.

"Yeah. Each keg will be a bit more than forty pounds. Each CO_2 tank is about ten. We'll have to strap it all on our backs," Matti said with a grimace.

"Fifty pounds," Bill said. Then he looked at Mary. She was in her mid-forties, slightly overweight, and not an Amazon by any approximation. "Can you carry that?"

Her eyelids drooped and she looked around at nothing in particular. Then she met Bill's gaze. "I'm going to."

"Everything's at the tavern?" Bill asked.

Matti nodded. "Should be."

"Then, let's go."

At Jotnar's, the generator was still humming away, the electricity maintaining the temperature of the hot liquor tank. As soon as they arrived at the tavern, Matti cranked up the portable gas burner under the tank to get the water even hotter.

It took them a full hour to gather all the parts they needed; Corny-kegs, CO_2 tanks, tubing for the outlet and CO_2, something to use as nozzles and on/off valves. The snow had penetrated the tavern through the wrecked roof, covering much of what they sought, and they had to look through the billowing clouds of their own breath in the flashlight beams. Bill didn't think the monster would be dumb enough to approach them there, where the hot liquor tank was, but they kept a wary eye anyway. They spent another fifteen minutes figuring out how to carry the tanks on their backs, using some of Ernest and Suzy's spare winter coats for tank insulation and some rope to make shoulder straps.

Bill slipped an empty tank on to try out their contraption. He held the hose out in front of him like a guy applying fertilizer to a yard and tested the range of motion. He nodded.

"Seems like it'll work," he said.

"I'll fill up the kegs," Matti said.

They'd had a total of five Corney-kegs and would bring them all. The spare two were wrapped in their own coats and Matti showed Bill and Mary how to hook up the spray hose and CO_2 hose to the kegs. When one of them ran out, they'd grab a spare tank and hand it to one of the others to replace on their back while the third person kept up the attack. At least that was the plan. They would keep the snowmobiles close for when the plan, inevitably, went to shit. Hopefully, the giant would be in no condition to pursue them.

Once all the kegs were full of the boiling water, they each slipped one of the "monster-soaker 200's", as Matti called them, onto their backs.

"Holy crap," Mary said. "Glad we aren't walking. Where the hell are we going, anyway?"

"Gonna follow his tracks 'til we find him. Or he finds us," Bill said.

"We should be ready to fight from the sleds," Matti said. "Let me open your CO_2 tanks so you'll be good to go." Once he'd done that, Bill returned the favor for the big brewer.

"Let's go," Bill said.

They started toward their snowmobiles and Bill suddenly stopped. "I'm not sure we'll make it through this. So if we don't, I'm glad to have gone down fighting with you."

"What the fuck, dude?" Matti said. "We're going to have giant-soup in a couple of hours!" He climbed on his snowmobile, gave a thumbs-up, and lead the way.

Bill wasn't nearly as optimistic.

CHAPTER THIRTY-THREE

Brandon and Tril lay mashed together, nearest the fire, staring at the darkness outside the cave. Behind them, the adults had huddled together, creeping as close to the fire as they could, but all of them insisting that the kids be next to it. Jim added the caveat that they needed to keep the fire going, which they promised wouldn't be a problem.

Brandon had finally met the other guy he'd pulled to safety. It was Jerry Torgensen. He was thirty-years-old and had been in Copper Harbor for the winter to take care of his parents' house before trying to sell it come spring. His father, a widower, had died last fall, leaving the house to Jerry. Jerry had been on one of the snowmobiles that planned on racing down the ice. He and Gus were the last additions to the giant's food stores, just before Brandon rescued them.

"Do you think we're going to make it?" Tril asked. Her voice was distant, quiet, not out of courtesy, but rather from an unwillingness to speak the words. She immediately regretted asking the question.

"I hope so," Brandon said. Not really the answer she'd been looking for, but honest. He rolled onto his side so he could face her. "Mr. Kearse said that when the town disappeared back in the eighteen-hundreds, it had looked like some of the houses had been smashed into."

"Like the giant is doing," Tril said.

"Yeah. If this is the same giant, maybe we'll make it out of here."

"How do you figure?" Tril asked.

"He said that after about a month of not hearing from anyone up here, they came up and everyone was gone."

Tril stared at him, wondering where he was going with this. It wasn't altogether encouraging to be reminded that the whole town had vanished because they'd probably been eaten. Then she thought for a moment, except for the people Brandon's dad and Steph had found out in the lake. "What's your point?" she asked.

"They came up here, like after a month, when it had warmed up a little, and everything was fine. They weren't attacked."

She understood then. "So, we just have to last until it warms up?"

"Yeah," Brandon said. "And we're safe in here." Then his face dropped as he gazed outside again. "But my dad, if he's still alive, is still out there."

"And my parents will try to be back soon. The plows will break through eventually, and then what'll happen?"

"Maybe they'll send in the Army," Brandon said.

Thoughts started racing through Tril's head and for a minute she was standing in the middle of a charging herd of horses, each horse a thought that sped by, veering before it crashed into her. Finally, she recognized one and seized it by its neck as it passed, spinning up to ride it into consciousness.

"He's going to have to replenish his supply," she said.

"What?"

"We escaped. He's going to need more people. And where do you think he'll bring them?"

Brandon's face lit with hope. "If he gets my dad, maybe he'll bring him here."

"And we can be waiting to rescue him, too." She smiled at him, very proud of her plan and extremely pleased to be finding hope of survival, not just for herself, but for Brandon's dad. She couldn't imagine losing her parents, and he'd just lost his mom a couple of months ago.

"That's brilliant, Tril," Brandon said. "You are so fricking smart. Tell the others." Then he reached out and hugged her. In the hug, she felt his sincere gratitude and hope. When the hug lingered, she felt the appreciation and friendship. Then it lingered just long enough that she felt a bit of something more and he pulled away. "I'm glad we met."

"Me too."

It was a little past midnight when Bill, Matti and Mary left Jotnar's. Matti out in front, taking a slow but steady pace, following the hard-to-miss tracks that had already been partially filled in with snow. They suspected the giant was stationary, not having felt his earthquake-like footfalls since he fled from Matti's attack earlier. Bill silently hoped that they'd come across the big monster's corpse lying half-buried in the snow, but he didn't expect it. Knowing otherwise, they all had their heads on swivels, personal lighthouses panning a strong LED beam around them from their headlamps as they searched for the huge bastard who may lay in ambush.

The tracks headed west of town and toward the north side of Brockway Mountain. Bill's muscles tightened the farther they got from Jotnar's. He wondered then if they should just try making a break for it, but remembered what Mary had said about the roads being blocked. And if there was any chance his son, or anyone else, was still alive, they had to try and save them. His breath came in tight gasps, the feeling of being watched building. Yet he saw nothing, felt no tremors. All was dark with only the sound of the snowmobile engines to pierce the silence.

The snowflakes lilted by as they drove, and as cold as it still was, Bill didn't notice it. His hands had been icy for so long, it felt like a part of who he was. The five-gallon keg of steaming water on his back radiated some heat through to his body, helping to make the ride more bearable. But it did nothing for his aching hands and feet. Those were minor irritations at this point, ones he pushed from his mind.

A vibration shivered up through Bill's machine and he saw Matti stop and jump off, holding his sprayer in front of himself defensively. Bill and Mary pulled to either side of Matti, leaving their sleds running, headlights shining forward into the snowy darkness. Quickly, they jumped off their snowmobiles, feet only sinking a few inches in the monster-packed snow. Bill could feel the acid rise in the back of his throat and he fought to control his breathing. The air suddenly smelled crisp and clean, and the darkness changed somehow, shadows of trees now discernible in the blackness. Adrenaline was surging through his veins and now even his hearing filtered out the hum of the snowmobiles' idling engines to find the sound of the giant's feet slamming down through the deep snow, his shoulders and arms brushing through the tree branches. He thought he even heard the sound of tree boughs dropping their burdens of snow to the ground as the monster drew closer. Without so much as a gentle forewarning, Bill felt the need to urinate. It passed as quickly as it had come, one of a hundred sensations Bill experienced.

Somewhere to his right, Matti and Mary stood waiting, their spray guns ready. He gave a glance to his sprayer, making sure he knew how to open the valve and let loose with boiling water. When he looked up again, a huge shadow loomed in the trees, getting closer with every earth-shaking step the giant took. The wall of light from the snowmobile headlights was filled with one big foot, followed by a second. Bill had to pee again.

Then the giant was there, a feral snarl on his lips, red, boiled skin sloughing off his left arm and spots of his belly. A gruesome stench hit Bill, the smell of rot, infection, death. From some twenty-five or thirty feet above them, the huge whitish-blue eyes glared down on the three. And like striking serpents, his arms shot downward, reaching for Matti and Mary.

Huge clouds of steam filled the air as the trio unleashed their secret weapons. The monster screamed in pain, his big arms retracting faster than they'd lunged forward. He kicked out defensively, his left foot firing at Mary. The woman leaped backward, landing on her back in the snow and the foot swished by, crashing into her snowmobile and sending it spiraling through the air and crashing into the trunk of a monumental white pine, taking one of the spare kegs with it.

Matti and Bill lunged forward, pressing the attack, sending streams of scalding water into the giant's abdomen and chest. The beast crossed his arms in front of his torso, hands splayed, to defend himself, taking the acid-like water on his palms. He made one more feeble kick before spinning and running into the darkness.

"Mary," Bill heard Matti yell. Then they were stomping through the snow to get to the downed woman who wiggled on her back like an overturned turtle.

"He missed me," she said as they pulled her to her feet.

"Climb on with me," Bill said. Matti's machine had the other keg strapped to it.

They ran to the two remaining snowmobiles and took off in pursuit of the wounded giant. Matti did his best to avoid the indentations the big feet left in the snow, but with the giant's approach, and then its crazed departure, it was nearly impossible to avoid the haphazard prints and they proceeded with painful slowness, the machines dropping and climbing through the pitfall-like tracks.

When Matti finally stopped, Bill pulled up next to him and immediately saw why the lumberjack-sized man's jaw was hanging open as he stared forward. Before him, the steep slope of Brockway Mountain angled upward in the night, covered in a deep blanket of snow, the pristine white everywhere, except for where a gaping black wound in the mountainside, at least fifteen feet high and twelve feet wide, stared back at them. The cave entrance was something none of them had ever seen before, clearly because the massive rock that had covered it had been pushed aside by the monster that now waited within, groaning in pain.

Matti turned off his engine, Bill following suit.

"That doesn't give me a warm fuzzy," Bill said.

Matti looked at him as though he couldn't understand a word that Bill had uttered. "This is perfect. We have the son-of-a-bitch cornered."

"A cornered squirrel is fucking mean," Mary said. "That thing is going to be hell."

Steph, Jim and the others were on-board with Tril's idea of waiting to rescue anyone else that was brought into the giant's cave. They all agreed that it would be best if Jim and Jerry work the rope as they were the two strongest and could anchor anyone who'd have to climb up to freedom without unnecessarily limiting the length of rope that could reach down to the stranded. Also, if they had to hoist the climber, they were the best suited to do that.

Gus would stay back and tend the fire with Steph and Nancy so they didn't clog the tunnel for whoever had to escape from the cavern. Brandon and Tril would man the flashlights, Tril snuggling up close behind the anchors to provide light for the climber, and Brandon to escort the newly saved back to the fire.

Half-way through their crawling trek back through the tunnel, they felt the shallow trembling they'd come to recognize as the giant's footfalls as he left or entered the cavern through the relatively cramped confines of its entrance hall.

Jim, in the lead, shined the light back at Jerry, Tril and Brandon. "Shouldn't be long now." With a devious smile, he turned and continued on.

They were almost back to the rescue perch when the giant's wailing penetrated the little tunnel, growing louder as it returned, paired with the shuddering of the stone mountain all around them. Again, Jim turned around with the light, this time the unspoken question clear upon his face. *What the hell is going on?* He put a finger to his lips, extinguished the light and waited.

Down the echoic channel came deep, grumbling sounds, whimpering exhalations, and what might have passed as gigantic sobs. The four lay there in the dark, each trying to puzzle out what had caused such anguish in a monster that, as far as they knew, couldn't be hurt, much less killed. It was clear the sounds weren't human, they were desperately listening for any sign of more captives and heard none. They wouldn't know for sure until they shined the light down on the shelf the giant used to store people. And they couldn't do that until the cur left the cave.

So, the four lay down to wait, growing colder and colder.

CHAPTER THIRTY-FOUR

Bill stared in awe at the huge, black hole only a few feet in front of him, his sprayer in hand. Mary flanked him on his left, Matti on his right.

"Oh, this is not good," Mary said, barely loud enough to be heard.

"What are you talking about," Matti replied. "This is perfect. We'll sneak in and melt that sorry son-of-a-bitch right here."

"Keep an eye out for survivors in there," Bill said. "Don't want to spray them or cause them to get stepped on or something." The other two shut up, remembering that both Brandon and Steph might be captive in the giant's lair. "Let's go," Bill said. He checked his head-mounted light and started into the cave.

The walls were of the characteristic black or gray stone, the whole chamber apparently natural as Bill didn't see any tool marks where the rock had been chiseled or drilled and blown up. He was amazed that this cave was here this whole time and no one knew about it. Then he did some mental calculations and realized that the hole Brandon had almost fallen into could possibly lead down into this chamber. A breath caught in his throat when he remembered that Brandon and Tril had tried an expedition down that hole. What would have happened if they'd dropped right in on the giant? He shook the thought away. It hadn't happened.

But the kids were both gone anyway.

The floor was rough but relatively free of debris. Good. He didn't want to kick a rock and prematurely announce their arrival when their lights would already put them at a disadvantage. The tunnel curved gently to the right, preventing him from seeing as far as he'd like, but it might help them to close the distance on the beast before he realized they were there.

A fetid reek assailed his nostrils, somehow made worse in the cold, dry air. It was as though he could detect every tiny particle of the stink that he inhaled, yet couldn't escape it. He was glad it wasn't hot and humid or he would probably throw up.

The giant's groaning had quieted, either because the pain had subsided or... or because he'd already heard them and was setting an ambush.

The cave started to feel steadily warmer and Bill pulled his hood back. When the frigid air met the moisture on his brow, he quickly realized that the warmth was solely due to his rapidly pounding heart and heavy breathing. Shit. He even felt a trickle of sweat roll down his back. He was quietly glad he was wearing gloves because he'd no doubt drop the spray hose with his sweaty palms. And for all the moisture on his skin, there was none in his mouth. It was like he'd tried to drink a glass of corn starch and the powdery gunk now coated his lips and gums.

Bill glanced to his left and it seemed as though Mary's eyes had tripled in size, darting this way and that, searching for their prey or their doom. She licked her lips incessantly and he could see that her chest heaved with every breath.

To his right, Matti stalked like a cat entering a rat-hole, eyes fixed straight ahead, his teeth gleaming through his half-smile. The man looked like he believed he could kill the giant simply by placing a well-aimed kick into its groin. Bill was glad Matti was on his side, even if he didn't share his confidence.

Then the tunnel straightened and opened into a large chamber. Bill stopped in mid-stride when he saw the form of the giant sitting against the far wall, eyes closed, arms held tight across its chest. The skin on its arms and chest was oozing and pink, deep pits melted into the thick, stony surfaces of its body. Quickly, he looked at Mary, then at Matti who mouthed the words, "get that fucker."

Without hesitation, Matti scampered to close the distance, leaving Bill and Mary scrambling to back him up.

And just that quick, the giant's eyes opened and it let out a deafening war-cry and leaped to its feet.

What the hell is this? Jim wondered, watching as lights flickered and bobbed in the tunnel that served as the giant's chamber entrance. He nudged Jerry and guided him forward enough so he could see too.

Why wasn't the giant attacking them? Who was dumb enough to just wander in here? Oh, God. They were going to see someone else die. He hoped then that maybe the giant would just lift them right up to the ledge and leave so they could rescue the idiots.

But he knew that wasn't going to happen. That was the best-case scenario, and they were all out of 'best-case'.

Finally, three distinct lights came into view and stopped. He looked down and realized that the ledge blocked his view of the giant. Odd. Then, in the oncoming lights, he saw the monstrous legs extended toward the exit tunnel and realized the thing was sitting. And for some reason, not attacking.

Then, without warning, first one, and then all three lights were racing forward and the giant was instantly on his feet, issuing forth his terrible yell.

Bill saw the stream from Matti's sprayer arc up and splash all over the giant's left hand and arm. He directed his straight up at the monster's chest and abdomen, both water streams eliciting a booming scream of pain. Mary finally unleashed her attack, apparently having had some difficulty with her hardware or her courage. But now she pressed in and the monster recoiled.

Bill hardly noticed the steam that filled the icy air of the chamber as the hot water scalded giant flesh. His attention was on the horrible beast that he'd come here to kill.

The huge body spun and whirled, like a child under squirt-gun attack, eyes closed, blindly trying to avoid the drenching hot liquid. It kicked out randomly, the massive feet like one-ton battering rams, looking to destroy the hated raiders, but each kick was easily avoided by the adrenaline-cranked team. An occasional sweep of the giant's hand passed overhead by only a foot, but it was enough to make all three of them drop down defensively, losing their aim. They quickly recovered and drove the beast into a corner where it huddled, standing on one leg, pulling its other leg and arms tight to cover its vital organs.

Then a light shone down from somewhere above, but only for a moment, and Bill heard someone utter, "Get that bastard!" He looked up, but all he saw was the rock extending upward to where it looked like it may extend back onto a shelf.

Jim held his breath and watched as the giant started screaming in pain and the entire chamber began to fill with smoke. No, not smoke. Steam! He saw flashes as the intruders' head-lamps reflected off long streams of steaming water, shot from hoses they held in their hands.

"What's happening?" Tril hissed, trying to jam into a position to see.

"They're attacking it with hot water."

He shined the light down, the giant too distracted to take notice. In the beam, Jim could see the injuries the water was causing; the giant's skin melting wherever the boiling liquid hit it, leaving open sores.

Then he had a thought and flipped off the light. "Tril! You and Brandon go see if you can find those arrows. And bring some burning wood. We might have a chance here to get that bastard!"

Tril turned and hurriedly pushed Brandon back toward the fire. Mission accepted.

The giant continued to kick and swat at the diminutive warriors who stood before him, dousing him with as much of the scalding water as possible. Though ineffective, if even one of those flailing limbs were to connect, it would probably be the death of whoever was the unfortunate target.

It seemed the monster's strength was starting to flag. Bill thought the thing was leaning more heavily against the wall than before, and it looked to be sliding downward as its legs grew weak. They were going to do it!

Then, Matti's spray trailed off, his keg running dry. Almost as quickly, Bill's and Mary's hoses were spitting air instead of water.

And the giant was still on its feet.

"Get out of here," he yelled, then grabbed Mary, thrusting her toward the exit and falling in behind her, Matti tight on his heels. It didn't sound or feel like the monster was pursuing, but it wouldn't take long for him to catch them once he realized what had happened.

Bursting into the open air, he said, "Back to Jotnar's. Refill fast!"

He and Mary jumped on his snowmobile and he had it fired up and zipping back toward the tavern and the still-hot tank of boiling water. He glanced back and saw Matti following, his machine's headlight bobbing along as he kept pace.

He didn't see the massive shape emerge from the cavern or feel the tremors of its unsteady feet.

Jim watched the three press their attack, the giant now up against the wall of the shelf below. They had it on the ropes! Just when he thought the thing must fall down and die, three head-lamps sprinted for the exit of the cave.

Dammit!

In the darkness he heard the sound of the monster's body scraping against the stone wall of the cavern as it slid to the ground, making a heavy 'thud' and sending a jolt through the ground. Was it dead?

After a few tense breaths, it sounded like the giant was getting to its feet. Shit. This was confirmed when the ground shook with each slow footstep as it left the cave.

Jim felt the blood abandon his limbs when he realized that Brandon and Tril were going out, may already be outside, to search for those arrows.

Brandon scrambled to get back to the fire as fast as his hands and knees would allow. The flashlight in one hand provided momentary glimpses of their surroundings as it rode that hand like a cowboy on an enraged bull, shining up, then down, then sideways, then repeating. Stone bit into his kneecaps without mercy, the battered snow-pants far too inadequate a cushion.

Someone was attacking the giant in its cave, using hot water as their only weapon. Evidently, it was proving very effective and Jim thought they should take the opportunity to hit the beast with some fire-arrows. Brandon was pretty sure, from his science classes in kindergarten, that fire and water made poor bed-fellows, but at this point, he was willing to do anything to try and kill that fucking thing.

"Move, move, move," he hissed at Steph and Nancy, pushing past them as fast as he could. Tril was right behind him. He leaped to his feet as soon as he was out of the cave entrance.

"Where are they?" Tril asked.

"Follow me. They're over here somewhere." He began plodding through the deep snow as fast as he could, ignoring the single path Sam's beat-up snowmobile had cut when he brought it over, knowing he'd just break through at odd and unpredictable moments, slowing his pace. Tril, smaller and lighter than he, carefully heel-toed it along the packed path, quickly passing him.

"They should be over there," Brandon said, waving the flashlight in a small circle, farther ahead. "Kind of where the snow is all trampled."

Tril scampered over to where Brandon was shining the light and started kicking around in the snow. Brandon had found some of his own tracks from when he'd walked over to get Sam's snowmobile running and was making better time, though it was still slow going.

"Dammit. This is going to be impossible," Tril cursed.

"They were rubber-banded together. I can't imagine they're that buried yet."

"Unless asshole stepped on them."

He hadn't considered that. The whole bundle might be broken to bits. They still had to look.

Finally, he arrived where Tril was furiously kicking at the snow, contributing her own array of flakes to those falling naturally. He scrunched his brow as he looked around, the light casting shadows on the wildly rolling surface of the snow. "No. This isn't right." Tril looked at him, exasperated.

"That looks like the trail asshole, mother-fucker Jansen left after pushing me off," he said, illuminating the snowy indentation where Jansen's snowmobile track was covered with several inches of new snow. With the light, he traced the track back to where they stood. "Okay. This is where Sam attacked the giant." He paused for a moment, involuntarily remembering the heroic action of a guy he hardly knew. He turned and looked at the incoming snowmobile tracks, then illuminated the tree-trunks. "Yeah, back that way," he said pointing in the direction of town. "That's where I fell in the snow."

They struggled to wade through the uneven snow, over to where Brandon believed he'd been when he got knocked off the back of Jansen's sled. They'd hardly started searching through the snow when they realized the giant was out of his cave.

"Hurry up," Bill said, leading the three water-warriors back to the hot liquor tank.

"It didn't die," Mary groaned.

"Not yet," Matti agreed. "But we've almost got him. This next bunch should finish him." Matti set his keg down and started filling it with the hot water. "Don't let me forget to bring in that fourth keg this time. Maybe, if I'd had it, it would have been just enough to do the job."

"Yeah," Bill agreed. "I'll grab it. Probably should put new water in it. It's probably getting cold."

Matti and Mary continued filling the other two kegs while Bill ran back to Matti's snowmobile and unstrapped the fourth keg. He paused for a second when he felt the ground shudder. Then it trembled again and again, but didn't feel like it was getting any stronger. He ran back to the team.

"It's out walking around," he said through tight lips.

"We felt," Mary said.

"Almost done here," Matti said. Then he turned off the water. "There. Give me that one." He filled the last keg like the fueler on a NASCAR pit crew. He smiled up at Bill and Mary. "Mary, take Ernie's machine. Keys are already in it. Now, let's go finish him."

"They have to be here somewhere," Brandon said, digging frantically. The tremors were increasing in severity, if not frequency. It was coming their way.

"We should get back in the cave," Tril whispered as loud as she dared. She glanced in the direction where she thought the giant was, then back to Brandon. "Come on!"

With one hand, Brandon swept snow away, sweeping back and forth, the light grasped in his other hand. "Dammit!" He shone the light straight up at the bare branches of the tree canopies, then he looked over his left shoulder. "Here." He dove at the snow like an arctic-fox and emerged more triumphantly than the furry predators, the bundle of arrows clasped in his fist.

He jumped to his feet, but Tril was already moving, skittering along the snowmobile path like some weightless elf, her feet only sinking a couple of inches into the fresh snow that had fallen on the trail. Brandon's legs churned once again. Luckily, he'd established a half-beaten trail back to the cave when they came out to search, but it wasn't as passable as a groomed trail. As a result, he foundered well behind Tril, holding the light in one hand, arrows in the other.

The vibrations shaking up through his legs inspired him to ignore all pain and fatigue. He remembered all too well, how it felt when the giant nearly had him here, so many hours ago.

He could barely make out Tril in the weak, leading edge of the flashlight beam, just a figure fleeing through the woods. The sound of branches breaking, high in the trees to his right sparked terror through his already taxed body. He tried to run faster, but there was nothing extra to give. Fire lanced its way through his limbs, sucking the strength away, seeming to add ten pounds of weight to every fatigued step.

"Hurry," a female voice hissed from the cave somewhere ahead.

Then, like each foot had suddenly been caught in immovable bear-traps, Brandon's legs abruptly quit moving and he fell face first in the snow, still clutching the bundle of arrows. He felt the pounding of the giant's footfalls and knew he was about to be on the underside of one of them, getting squished to some macabre jelly-like goo. His heart was pounding harder than it ever had, even during the most strenuous hockey practices. He had to get up, keep moving. It wasn't that much farther to the cave.

He pushed down with both arms, willing himself to rise, to stand. As soon as he was on his knees, hands grabbed each of his arms, not even bothering to set him on his feet, just pulled him through the snow toward the safety of the cave. He looked up to see the sturdy Gus Urten latched onto his arms. He was still struggling to get his legs underneath him when Gus launched him into the cave, diving in behind him and pushing him past Steph and Tril.

Steph and Tril sidled deeper into the cave too, the huge beast approaching. In a flurry of white, cold snow, the hand of the giant swept down, just barely hitting Tril's legs, but enough to slam her left foot hard against the unforgiving stone wall. Globs of snow fell onto the fire, dousing half of it, and the massive hand reached for anything he could grab. Steph yanked on the girl, dragging her away from danger, even as the monster's blistered arm passed over the flames and he let out a scream of agony.

Steph made a quick mental note as she watched the giant jerk back and throw himself into the snow, rolling around like a dog scratching its spine in the light of Brandon's flashlight.

With an idea formulating in her mind, she quietly prayed the damned behemoth didn't crush Sam's already damaged snowmobile.

She watched as the giant stood up, somehow looking healed from his roll in the snow. Though he was still obviously wounded, skin that had been open and red was once again whitish and stony. The monstrous humanoid stood up and grabbed a medium-sized tree, bending it over until the trunk splintered at its base. Then it snapped off the spindly top of the tree, held it in one hand like a weapon and jogged off.

The booming sound of the giant's pain echoed through the darkness, blasting apart the silent white flakes that dropped peacefully to the ground. Matti stopped immediately, turning his head around to ascertain the direction from which the scream had come. Then he pointed to the left and took off in that direction without a word.

Bill followed, his body numb, his mind locked into a state where fear no longer survived. It was only resolve; either they would live and the giant would die, or vice versa. This is where everything would end. It had to. If it continued much longer this way, fighting then running and fighting again, he and Matti and Mary, would all be forever damaged, shells of who they really were. But one thing he knew for certain; they had to do whatever they could to make sure this thing died here tonight. He'd seen the light in the cavern, heard a voice. Someone was alive in there and needed saving. And now that they'd discovered a way they might facilitate that, he was going to commit to that effort with every thought, every breath, and every twitch of every muscle. Or he would die trying.

Just before they made it to the trees at the edge of town, Matti suddenly stood up on his machine and dove into the snow to his right. Out of the black of the forest, a huge tree trunk swung horizontally like a baseball bat, hitting Matti's sled broadside and sending it tumbling onto the fallen brewer. Matti was trapped.

The giant was wielding a broken tree like a club, giving him a dangerously long reach. A reach that would be difficult to equal with their sprayers.

"Spread out," Bill yelled, turning right to go to Matti's aid. He waved Mary away from them. She pulled left, sped to the side and stopped, mechanically pulling out her sprayer. Bill turned tightly to his right and raced to Matti. He jumped off and with one heave, threw the wrecked snowmobile off of the big man.

"Damn! You are one strong son-of-a-bitch," Matti exclaimed. He climbed to his feet, not injured enough to slow him down.

They both jumped back onto Bill's snowmobile and he accelerated away from the raging giant just as the tree-club slammed into the snow, blasting a deep hole where Bill's machine had been just a split second earlier.

"You have your sprayer?" Bill shouted over his shoulder.

"Yeah. Get into the woods so he can't use that club like a bat."

Bill headed for the confines of the trees, looking for Mary. It seemed that he was the only one of the three who hadn't instantly realized the safety of the forest, as she was deep within the protection offered by the towering pines, oaks and maples.

"Zoom in, close," Matti said. Bill could feel him readying his sprayer. He turned to his left and realized they were going to be close to the monster whether he drove them there or not. The huge dark shape was rushing directly at them through the woods, slowed somewhat by his wounds, but still unavoidably fast. He couldn't let that damned thing land a blow with that tree-trunk or they'd be finished.

"Turn right. Rightrightright!" Matti said in a panic.

Bill pulled on the handlebars, leaning to his right, praying they wouldn't hit the tree that was in their path or get hit by the-

A thunderous 'whoomp' interrupted his worry as the tree-club hammered into the snow two feet from Bill's left knee, followed by an angry howl that morphed into a scream of pain.

"Come around," Matti shouted.

Bill responded, steering the snowmobile in a tight arc to head back towards the monster. He already knew that Mary had gotten in close on the creature's back-side and had laid into it with boiling water. She needed backup, and she needed it now. The snowmobile's headlight illuminated the giant as it spun around giving his back to Bill and Matti. Mary's lights set the steam glowing as it rose from behind the massive, screaming body, Mary now focused on dousing its chest and abdomen.

He stopped the sled within shooting distance and Matti was off like a soldier deploying from an armored personnel carrier into the heat of battle, his spray nozzle aimed at the giant's sizzling back, his headlamp swinging wildly with every movement. Bill got his nozzle caught up in his coat, struggling to get off the snowmobile, and gave himself a dose of scalding water down his right leg. Even through the heavy snow pants and undergarments, the pain bit into the limb. But not enough to keep him from joining the fight.

The air filled with white clouds of steam as he and Matti attacked. With horror, he saw the club raise above the mist and descend with furious speed, concluding with a victorious snarl from the beast. But its pained voice rose again as Matti and he closed on it, hot water melting into its back and buttocks.

Then it was on the move, running with a wavering, staggering gait, right over the mangled red pulp that had been Mary.

"Let's go," Matti said, stumbling through the wildly strewn snow to Mary's still idling machine. Bill saw him take a quick sorrowful glance at their dead friend before the big man was off in pursuit of the giant.

Bill threw up what little was in his stomach and then was on his sled as fast as he could move and was racing after Matti. They knew the giant was heading for the cave again, its safe haven.

Steph heard snowmobiles in the distance. With the giant obviously in pursuit, this was her chance.

She ran as fast as the uneven snow would allow and climbed on Sam's snowmobile. She had it started and was moving in an instant.

The cold air clawed at her face and limbs as she struggled to keep the beat-up snowmobile moving in a straight line. She was making her way back to town, but giving the monster wide berth, hoping that whoever was coming had distracted it, but praying that they would be safe.

Brandon and Tril were well down the tunnel by the time Steph took off on her self-conceived mission. Tril had two flaming sticks in one hand and several fresh ones in the other so she could establish a little fire at the 'overlook' as they'd come to call it. Behind her, Brandon carried the arrows they'd retrieved and the bow he'd managed to bring to the cave initially.

"You're okay," Jerry said as the two kids approached. "Oh, thank God. The damned thing left not long after you did. We thought he might find you out there."

"He found us," Tril said. She went about getting a little fire going, tight to the side of the tunnel. "But we got away." She said this as if she'd won a game of tag. Brandon couldn't decide if this girl was that brave or that ignorant. He decided it didn't matter, she was extremely cool.

"Got the arrows?" Jim asked. Brandon handed them and the bow forward.

"Jim, I thought the fire arrows didn't work," Brandon said.

"They didn't. But it looked like that hot water melted the skin off in places. I'm hoping without the skin, the arrows will do some damage."

"What's the plan?" Tril asked.

"When it comes back, Jerry will light it up with a flashlight, I'll shoot it."

Jerry sighed. "You think it'll work?"

"Got any better ideas?"

Bill could see Matti flying through the trees in the beam of the snowmobile's headlight, fighting to stay on the machine that dipped and tipped through the monster's tracks. Then Matti cut sharply to one side, getting off the giant's trail, and increased speed. Bill followed, happy to be off the bucking path, but concerned that Matti was going so fast through the forest.

His concern evaporated when he felt the entire earth start to shudder and vibrate. It was as it felt when he and Steph had been up on the mountain, overlooking the town. Ahead, in the light of Matti's snowmobile, Bill saw the opening of the monster's cave.

It was closing.

From within, the giant was rolling the massive stone that had covered the entrance back in place. Matti obviously saw it too, steering his snowmobile directly at the diminishing gap in the mountainside. The big man stood up on his sled, spray nozzle in his left hand and drove into the opening, water and steam pouring forth from his makeshift weapon. The stone passage proved too tight for the machine and it crashed to a halt, sending Matti somersaulting over the windshield, hot water spraying around randomly like an unattended fire-hose. He disappeared inside the cavern entrance.

Bill stopped within three feet of the crashed sled and was clambering over it in a heartbeat, his sprayer held forward, ready to defend Matti from the monster within. But Matti was already on his feet, the giant's screams of pain, evidence that the stream of hot water the brewer shot before him was hitting its target. Bill tapped Matti on the shoulder to let him know he was there, then spread to the left as they chased the humongous terror deeper into the cavern, their steaming attack peeling skin from wherever it landed.

The beast fled before them, the lights of their headlamps showing the red burns on the back of its legs and huge, bare feet. They knew it had nowhere to go in here, only a cavern where it would make its last stand. If either of them was hit by one of its mountainous fists, or stomped on, the fight would be over. At this point, Bill didn't care. He'd lost everyone, his ex-wife, Brandon, Steph. He'd even failed poor Tril. If he died in this endeavor, so be it. But he'd be damned if this big, man-eating, evil, son-of-a-bitch thought he would go down without a fight. He glanced at Matti, who seemed too hopped up on energy-drinks to care about danger. So be it.

Into the cavern they charged, boiling water flying before them. The giant had turned to face them and Bill could see the rage on its visage in the fading light that struggled to reach the titan's full height. Bill turned his spray on the creature's abdomen while Matti shot higher, onto its chest. The roars of pain were deafening in the dank chamber and the meaty arms flailed, trying vainly to hit the attackers.

An orange flash of light zipped through the air from somewhere above and behind the monster and its body snapped upright and back, both arms reaching for its shoulder-blades. It spun with a hideous howl and Bill saw an arrow sticking from one shoulder, flames licking the seared flesh that had been melted away by the boiling water. Another orange flash shot down from somewhere high against the ceiling, this one taking purchase in the giant's chest.

Bill and Matti pressed the attack, now focusing both of their streams on one unified point on the thing's back, trying to sear a hole through to vital organs.

The brute swept at the arrows flying down at it, snapping them off as soon as they hit, but Bill could see the flames and smell the burning flesh, despite its best efforts.

This time, they would kill it.

Jim sent one arrow after another down upon the massive man-eater, each one sending up a tendril of smoke from the sizzling meat. A fetid stench rose to the little overlook, a smell that would be forever seared into the memories of the four people huddled there. Jim's next shot struck an exposed wound high on the behemoth's cheek, the flames flaring up into the creature's eye. With speed born of agony, the giant grabbed a boulder and hurled it at the man who tormented it from above.

The boulder crashed into Jim, smashing his head to a bloody pulp against the wall of the tunnel.

Brandon felt the bile rise in his throat as he and Jerry stared at the wrecked body of their comrade. He snapped out of his revulsion when Tril dove forward, catching the bow that had dropped from the dead man's hands and was teetering dangerously on the edge of their overlook.

In an instant, she had knocked another arrow and was taking aim. "Light!" she demanded. Then she kicked Jerry with her knee. "Light!" she repeated louder. This time, Jerry shone the light down at the giant, focusing on the seeping wounds on its back. It was engaging the two fighters on the ground again, believing the threat from behind had been eliminated.

"Shit," Bill exclaimed when he saw the boulder crash into the ceiling. No arrows followed and the giant turned and started swinging rock-like fists wildly. Matti suddenly spun and went down, suffering a grazing blow. He lay dazed on the floor, blinking his eyes. Bill jumped forward to drive the giant back, hoping Matti would regain his feet, but he sat there still.

Another flash of orange streaked down from above like a meteor, clearly hitting the titanic back once again. The arrows came faster now, with a rapidity that made Bill think there must be two archers sending down the fiery missiles. The gigantic being turned once again to address this new threat and Bill saw that its back was engulfed in flames.

He jumped over to Matti, who had seemed to recover his senses, if not his feet.

"I think my leg is broken," he said. His lips pursed tightly as he tried to roll up to a sitting position. "Ah, fuck," he said. "Here." He handed his spray nozzle to Bill and slipped the tank off of his back. "Hit him with both barrels." Then he started dragging himself toward the cavern wall.

Bill walked forward, both nozzles sending the scalding water at the monster. He aimed both of them at the back of one of the monster's knees, not wanting to extinguish the flames that danced along its back. The great monster moved toward the far wall and slumped, dropping below the angle of attack of the archers. Then it turned to face Bill as it slid to the floor.

Its massive white eyes found Bill's, flames dancing up from the creature's chest. Bill decided to go for the heart and risk putting out some of the flames. He focused the streams of water where, in a normal man, the heart would reside. As soon as the hot water hit the area, the giant pulled his arms in to protect himself, making it impossible for Bill to spray his chosen target.

Then the strength of the water streams died, arcing down slowly until both nozzles produced no more than drips.

"Dammit!" Bill shouted. He strode forward, making to strike the brute with one of the empty kegs, when the giant shot one foot outward, catching Bill square in the chest. The kick sent him flying backward where he landed in a heap, pain shooting through his body from a dozen places. He lay there staring into the cold eyes of the giant, the cold rocky floor stinging his cheek. The flames on the monster's chest were starting to dwindle and he could see the steady rhythm of the giant's breathing expand and contract the blackened muscles.

"Why won't you die?" Bill said.

"You motherfucker!" Matti screamed at it. "Bill. You have to go get more water and finish him!"

Bill shook his head, the beam of his headlamp dancing across the brewer who was crumpled against the black, stone wall. "My arms are tingling. I can't move them."

Matti let out a long breath. "Shit." He glanced at the giant, then back at Bill. "We almost got him."

Matti faded from Bill's view, his eyes focusing on a surface that didn't exist, focusing on a screen in his mind. On it he saw himself and Brandon, laughing like a normal father and son as he roughed the boy's hair. Then he saw himself jumping to his feet in the stands as Brandon scored the winning goal in the state hockey tournament. He saw Brandon graduating from high school, then college. He saw himself and Steph at Brandon's wedding, the two of them already married and sharing a moment of joy with their son. Then he saw Brandon as a five-year-old, unable to ride a bike because his father wasn't there to teach him and his mother was too busy with her new boyfriend. He saw a young Brandon watching other boys throw the football with their fathers while he stood alone.

He saw all the things he should have done differently and all the things he would have done better in the future. And he saw them all turn to white, frozen, dust.

A sound brought him back into the present. It had come from the cavern entrance. But no one was out there, Mary was dead. What had he heard? He strained his ringing ears, desperate to decipher the noise, praying silently that it was the National Guard or any sort of help. It became clearer now, the sound of feet creeping through the rocky debris of the cavern entrance tunnel. At least, that's what it sounded like.

The giant still sat against the far wall, the flames all but gone now. Only two or three small areas still burned. Though the flesh was horribly marred and the skin had been boiled away, the titan continued to draw breath, eyes filled with hatred locked on Bill. To his right, Matti was fighting to get to his feet, his right leg bent awkwardly and in no shape to bear weight. The man just wouldn't quit. "Sisu" is what those of Finnish descent, the "Finlanders", up here called it; the spirit of never giving up, of persevering through all adversity. And Matti evidently was loaded with it.

The brewer managed to get upright, all of his weight on his left leg, mouth snarling in either pain or determination. He hopped once and groaned in agony as the motion jarred his broken limb. Then, in the light of Bill's headlamp, he could see Matti's eyes start to swim and flutter and the big man crashed to the ground like a towering pine being felled.

"Ah!" A voice squeaked from the entrance tunnel.

Bill turned and saw Steph take off at a run, a big red jug in her hand. With her other hand, she flung the can's cap onto the floor as she rushed the smoldering giant. She skidded to a halt ten feet from one of the huge, extended legs, and launched the gas can through the air. It hit the monster full in the chest, fuel splashing out all over the miserable beast who had no idea what was about to happen.

Somewhere on the terrible, giant being, a trickle of gasoline found an open flame and five gallons of petroleum exploded in a blinding, fiery ball.

CHAPTER THIRTY-FIVE

Sometime during the early morning hours, the snow had finally slowed to flurries. The Keweenaw highway department was attacking the toppled cell tower before the sun had broken over the horizon, which wasn't usually until 9:00 AM in the middle of winter. Two men cut through a couple of the girders with torches and then they dragged a piece away with a massive tow-truck, enough so the plow could get around it and head up to Copper Harbor.

No one had heard from anyone in the little town for several days due to the closed roads and disrupted communications. The Sheriff wanted to get up there and make sure no one had a medical emergency, though everyone agreed that they would probably get up there to find the whole town hunkered down eating s'mores cooked in their fireplaces, playing cards.

With the cell tower off the road, Larry James fired up his plow, affixed with one of the snow-thrower attachments and headed up to Copper Harbor. Sheriff James Miller in his four-wheel-drive was right behind him. Larry looked with awe at the massive amounts of snow he had to cut through like a three-year-old witnessing their first snowfall. He was amazed at the nearly five-feet of snow that covered the road.

It took him almost an hour to cut through the ten miles up to the harbor town. When he got there, he went straight up the main drag where he could turn around at Jotnar's Tavern. He pulled into the parking lot and thought the snow had collapsed a portion of the roof. But it was obvious something more destructive had happened. He climbed out of his cab as the Sheriff came walking up, surveying the scene and pulling his collar up against the still frigid air.

"What happened here?" Larry asked.

The lawman shook his head and turned a complete circle, taking in everything he could see; the parking lot looked like five professional football teams had been holding practice there, debris from the tavern scattered about, surrounding buildings covered with snow, smokeless chimneys poking up from the drifts. "I dunno, Larry. I haven't seen hide nor hair of anyone." He pointed toward the destroyed section of the tavern. "Clear this out as close as you can get so we can take a look."

Larry was able to get within four feet of the building, with the Sheriff's guidance. He pulled the truck back and together the two men pushed through the remaining snowbank until they were standing in the ruins of the popular establishment. Fresh snow blanketed all of the dining room, the bar and extended back into the kitchen. No one was anywhere to be seen.

"Start clearing the streets. I'll pound on some doors," Sheriff Miller said.

Larry set about his job and the Sheriff went to the first homes he could reach. He had to don snowshoes to reach the doors as no one had cleared their walks, a fact he found odd given that 'Yoopers', as folks from the upper peninsula of Michigan or 'U.P.' called themselves, wouldn't let this much snow pile up because it was too hard to move it. You attacked it frequently before it became an overwhelming chore.

At each of the first three houses he checked, there was no response, though he thought maybe two of the houses were summer homes. The roof and side wall of the fourth house was smashed in, similar to the tavern. Again, with no evidence that anyone was there.

The old legend clawed its way into his mind, the stories of the entire town gone missing during a winter, not unlike this one. "What the hell?" he murmured. There is no way the whole town disappeared again, not in this day and age.

A deep, reverberating tone assailed him. Larry was blaring on the plow's horn. "Now what?" He made his way through the snow to his truck, shucked off the snowshoes and tossed them in the bed and drove off looking for Larry.

Larry had cleared two of the streets that ran east to west just off of the main road and he hadn't seen a soul. Though smoke trailed from the chimneys of some of the houses he had passed, none of them had driveways or front walks that appeared to have been cleared any time in the last two days. Even the front doors had snow piled right up against them, making it next to impossible to open them. Several of the houses looked like they'd been smashed with a giant hammer, similar to the tavern. But it was evident that snowmobiles had been all over the roads.

Something was far from right.

Then he saw something coming towards him through the woods from the direction of Brockway Mountain. He stopped his truck and wiped at the frosty windshield with his bare hand, trying to get a clearer view. What he saw filled him with a sick dread.

He did the only thing he could think of and laid on his horn.

Sheriff Miller saw Larry's truck at the end of the street, still facing Brockway Mountain. He tripped the siren twice as he came to a stop behind the big, orange vehicle. The driver's side door flew open and Larry jumped down.

Miller climbed out of his truck and started forward.

"Sheriff, I don't know what's going on but you should get some help up here."

"What kind of help?"

"Medical. Come look."

The two men walked to the front of the plow and saw a group of people struggling through the snow, a snowmobile slowly leading the way. A big, gray-haired man drove the machine and a figure rode behind, seated facing the rear. The second person's coat was black and frayed, as though they'd escaped a house fire. A group of people was at least thirty feet behind, trying desperately to stay suspended on the snowmobile's track, but breaking through more often than not. A string of two sleds was being pulled by the snowmobile, each bearing a body.

"Clear the road up to them as far as you can. I'll get EMS." The sheriff ran to his car and placed an urgent call on his radio, then pulled up to where Larry had driven his plow. Larry was already busting through the snow to offer assistance when Miller arrived to do the same.

"You have injured?" Miller asked the man driving the snowmobile.

Gus Urten nodded. "One with a broken leg, one... I dunno. He lost feeling in his arms and legs and couldn't move them. He's moving a little now. Some sort of neck or spine injury I'd guess."

"What in hell happened here?" Larry asked.

Dr. Stephanie Crowe slogged forward, her face pink and black from the inferno she'd delivered upon the giant. "We found out what happened to the missing villagers from Copper Harbor back in 1842. We found out the hard way."

Sheriff Miller and Larry listened to the extraordinary tale the singed woman told them, growing more mentally distant with every word. He watched others in the group, those who didn't look like they'd rolled in a campfire and saw confirming nods. He looked at the injured men lying in the sleds. Had this group suffered some form of mass hysteria and caused this harm to themselves? It was more likely than a 'giant' ravaging the town. The only 'giant' Miller could see was the big bastard on one of the sleds, his broken leg dragging through the snow behind him, looking over his shoulder, scowling at the sheriff.

"Well, I don't see any giant now. All I see is a group of people who need medical care. Let's get you all safe and warm, or to the hospital," Miller said.

"We're telling you the truth!" spat a young woman who was clenching a bow. "It's dead, up in the cave, like Professor Crowe said." Her eyes were frighteningly hard. Something Miller usually only saw in hardened adults.

Miller just nodded weakly and said, "The ambulance will be here soon."

The big man on the sled spoke up. "Get on a snowmobile and drive your dumb-ass up to the cave! The remains are probably still smoking." This was met with grunts of approval and enthusiastic nodding from the others.

"Okay. After you are all taken care of," Miller said. "If something is up there dead, it isn't going anywhere." *Most likely, it's a cave filled with carbon dioxide, or other toxic fumes,* Miller thought. *But I'd better find out what the hell happened and put this nonsense to rest.*

Matthew Hellman

CHAPTER THIRTY-SIX

At the hospital, Brandon, Tril and Steph were crowded into Matti's room, each sitting in a chair around the big man's bed. Matti had been lucky; he wouldn't need surgery but he was in a cast for several weeks which would be followed by physical therapy. No one spoke, lending a foreboding air to the room. Even Matti was silent, not having had an energy drink in over eight hours and being medicated for the pain put him in an uncharacteristic stupor. Everyone waited for word on Bill's status.

When the paramedics had arrived on the scene, they immediately secured Bill to an immobilization backboard, fearing he'd suffered a spinal injury. Though he'd already regained limited movement in his limbs, they weren't taking chances.

Brandon worried about his father, whether he'd be able to walk and use his arms normally again. He found that the thought of not being able to go outside and do things with his dad upset him more than he would have guessed. It had cut the boy deeply when he first saw his father lying there, unable to move anything other than his eyes. And when his eyes landed on Brandon, he'd started to cry. Brandon had moved to hug him then, but

Steph held him back, concerned for Bill's spine. Brandon was angry at the time, but was very grateful to her now, realizing that she was looking out for Bill's best interest.

A doctor walked into the room, his face stoic. He looked at Brandon. "Your dad is going to be okay, but it's going to take some time. Athletes refer to what happened to your dad as a 'stinger', though his was significantly worse than what a football player would get. He'll be in the hospital for a couple of days for observation while we treat the swelling in his neck. When he leaves, he's going to have to wear a collar for a while. But he should walk and regain full function of all his limbs, though it'll take some therapy."

There was a collective sigh of relief in the little hospital room and Brandon felt his shoulders relax, dropping from the hunched-up heights they'd reached in his tense anticipation. Steph reached over and rubbed his back gently, wiping a tear from her eye. Tril grabbed one of his hands and said, "I told you he'd be all right."

"That's good news," Matti said. Then, "Hey doc, could you send in some Red Bull or Monster Energy or something?"

The doctor huffed out a laugh. "No, you should rest for a day or two. We don't want you trucking down the hallway in your cast." He looked at Brandon and said, "They're bringing your dad back to his room from the MRI now. You can go see him, just don't jostle him."

Brandon nodded. "Thanks."

"Tell him I said, 'hi'," Matti said as the trio left his room to find Bill.

Bill's vision started to blur as soon as he saw Brandon, Steph and Tril. He blinked away the tears that were fighting to fall and took a deep breath. "I thought I'd lost all of you. Jansen told me the giant got you," he said to Brandon. He reached a shaky hand up toward his son who took it in his own and gave a slight squeeze.

"I got away," Brandon said. He didn't want to upset his dad just yet, so he let the truth about what had happened wait until some other day.

Steph stepped around to the other side of his bed and took his other hand. He looked at her and raised his eyebrows. "Thank you, so much," he said. "You finished him off. If you hadn't come in, he would have recovered and killed the rest of us."

"You, Matti and Tril got him to a point where I could finish him," she said. "And Mary."

At the mention of Mary's name, Bill tightened his mouth and closed his eyes, wishing she could have made it too. Then he thought about Ernest and Suzy Kearse, and Rangers Sam and Greg, of good ole Paavo, Jim, and all the others that had died at the hands of the giant.

Maybe they could have prevented all their deaths. If Trillium had been able to look through the hole at the bottom of the shaft that had opened up, she might have seen the giant slumbering in its chamber. If they'd done a proper exploration after she'd passed out in the sinkhole, instead of just fencing it off to be examined later, they may have discovered the lair. If, if, if...

"How are you feeling?" Steph asked.

"Sore. But nothing's tingling."

"Doctor says you gotta stay here a couple of days," Brandon said.

"You going to be okay at home, alone?"

Brandon's face tightened, but he nodded. Poor kid was probably going to have nightmares for years. Bill really didn't want him staying there by himself.

"I can stay at your house with him if you want," Steph said, "and it's okay with Brandon."

Brandon nodded quickly. "Yeah. That sounds good. Dad?"

"Thank you. That'd really help." Bill's brow furrowed and he locked eyes with Steph. "What the hell? A giant? Where did that thing come from? How..." He closed his eyes and let out a long breath.

"I don't know," Steph replied.

"Maybe that stone says something about where it came from," Tril said. "The one with the carving on it."

Steph looked at the girl. "Maybe. But don't you two go down there again trying to get better pictures. We'll worry about that later."

Sheriff Miller sat astride his snowmobile, staring up the trail shrouded in shadows cast by the setting sun as it broke through gaps in the clouds. That trail supposedly led to the 'giant's lair'. He turned and looked at Deputy Stance waiting behind him on a second machine.

"You got the air quality monitor?" he asked. The deputy gave a thumbs up. "Let's get this done," he said and started his sled.

They rode at a moderate pace, an unusual sense of dread filling him as they progressed. He was sure they'd find a cave full of toxic levels of gases that contributed to the group of survivors hallucinating. In such a foggy state, they could easily have fallen and hurt themselves.

But images of the tavern and several of the houses, destroyed as though smashed by a wrecking-ball, lent far too much credence to Dr. Crowe's explanation, as crazy as it sounded.

Then a chilling thought surfaced; what if the giant was real and what if it wasn't dead? He checked to make sure he had his side-arm and suddenly wished he'd thought to bring his shotgun.

Just ahead, he saw a gaping black hole in the side of the hill, the snowmobile tracks leading directly to it, machine smashed into the opening. He stopped several feet away and turned off his machine as Stance pulled up next to him, looking at the cavern entrance with wide eyes.

"Huh," Miller said, eyeing the cave.

Stance pulled the air quality monitor out of a pack and stepped into the thigh-deep snow. "Shit," he said, struggling to get to the hard-packed trail.

Miller climbed down and blasted through to the packed down area around the entrance, huffing at the effort. He drew his pistol and with his other hand brought out his big flashlight. Stance walked next to the Sheriff, gun in one hand and monitor in the other. Together they strode into the 'lair'.

The stench was immediately evident; death, burnt flesh, rotting meat, mold, smoke, a virulent mix of fetid odors. Miller glanced over at the monitor and saw nothing alarming. Slowly, they walked deeper. As they rounded a curve, Miller's light fell across a disturbing sight at the rear of the cave.

"Are you fucking kidding me?" Stance asked.

The blackened bones were huge, charred flesh clinging to most of them and holding the form together in a shape eerily similar to human. But it was monstrous. The remains of a giant. Miller looked from the giant to Stance and said, "Huh."

When Steph drove Bill home, several days later, he was welcomed into his house by a sign reading 'Welcome home Dad!' that hung above the door. Inside waited Brandon, Matti in an easy chair with his leg propped up on the footrest, Tril and her parents, Ken and Diane. Ken and Diane Post fell upon him, thanking him profusely for taking care of their daughter in such a dangerous time while they were stranded in Detroit. He felt like an idiot, given that she'd been taken by the damned monster and could have died, but they insisted that he and the others had saved her. He wondered then if Tril had told her parents about her role, sending burning arrow after arrow into the open wounds of the giant, providing the flame that Steph needed to ignite the gasoline can. He hoped she had because she was every bit as heroic as they thought he was. Hell, Jim had just been smashed like a grape, right in front of her, and she stepped in and picked up where he had left off. He doubted he could have done as well.

Still seated in the easy chair, Matti held a beer aloft, "Steph, Bill, Tril, Brandon, cheers! We finally killed that big fucker." Then, realizing no one else had a drink yet, he said, "Beer's on me. It's in the fridge. You'll have to grab one yourself though." He pointed at the long cast on his elevated leg.

Steph motioned for Bill to sit and stepped quickly to the refrigerator and grabbed beers for everyone who wanted one, and some soda for the kids.

"What are your plans for the tavern?" Bill asked. Matti had learned just the day before, that Ernie and Suzy had left him the establishment in their wills. They had no other family and said that they wanted it to go to the only other person who seemed to love it as much as they did, Matti.

"Fix it up and get it open as soon as I can. Ernie had insurance on it, so hopefully, I can get rolling on it, have it open by Spring." He looked at Brandon and Tril. "I'll probably need some help next summer, if either of you is looking for work." The kids both smiled, nodding their heads.

"You going to keep it as Jotnar's Tavern?" Bill asked.

"Oh, hell no. I'm going to call it 'Giant Slayer's' or 'Jack's Axe'. Something like that. It's going to have a whole theme around what happened. Going to have to get pictures of you all for the walls." Then his face grew somber. "I'll have a wall dedicated to the fallen too. Pictures of Mary, Sam, Greg, Jim, Paavo... everyone. Well, except for Jansen, that bag of turds. I'll just have his name scratched onto a hunk of wood." He smiled wickedly. "Maybe I'll hang it on the inside of the door to the men's stall."

At her suggestion, Steph did not leave when Bill got home. She stayed on to 'help out' as Bill regained his strength. Neither Bill nor Brandon seemed to mind. It was good that she did, because, over the next several weeks, scientists of every make and model descended on the little town, requesting lengthy interviews with the survivors. They were especially interested in those who'd finally been able to kill the beast.

The bones and flesh of the giant were studied and sampled. Other small human bone fragments discovered were dated back approximately 1000 years. DNA analysis of the monster's bones showed it was a new, unknown species. The revelation that it had reproductive organs was the most chilling of their findings. Where were the others?

The petroglyph was excavated and studied. Dr. Crowe was involved with everything being done and all the discoveries made. Additional runes on the stone revealed that Vikings had discovered the giant and done battle with it before it disappeared into the cave and closed the entrance behind it. When they discovered the vertical shaft leading down into the beast's lair, they marked it with a warning. Some members of the team thought the way the warning was written indicated the Vikings had more than a chance knowledge of the giants, but the point was debated without resolution.

Steph and the research team theorized that the giant went into hibernation after feeding, waking approximately every 275 years and when it was cold enough to function. But without an intact corpse, they couldn't determine why it thrived only in the extreme cold.

For the remainder of her career, Steph would try to find more answers, including; what happened to the other giants?

The Biting Cold

Early that summer, Tril and her parents came by to announce that plans were underway to establish the cave as a tourist attraction. The remains of the giant were to be completely removed, then reproductions of the bones would be placed in as original position as was possible. No doubt, it would be a huge boon for the town.

It was a pleasant coincidence that the new tavern would have its grand opening on the same day that Bill's charter service started operating again. Bill saved the first outing to take Steph out so he could teach her to fish. And to show her the diamond ring he bought for her, if she would have him. She said yes.

The grand opening of 'The Beanstalk' turned into a celebration of Bill and Steph's engagement. Brandon seemed very pleased and hugged both his dad and Steph. Then he and Tril dragged Bill and Steph outside into the new beer garden where a live band was playing. Though it was standing room only, a table was quickly abandoned to the honor of the newly engaged giant-slayers.

When the band took a break, Matti Tervonen took the microphone and raised his hand for silence. Then he said, "I ask that you all raise your mugs in honor of the giant-killers. Hey, I'm one of those. But in particular, to the newly engaged Bill and Stephanie!" After a hearty cheer, Matti raised his hand for silence again. "And now, a moment of silence for those we lost, and a blessing. My friends, may none of your winters ever be so biting cold."

And none of them ever were.

Acknowledgements

I'd like to thank my beta-readers/pseudo-editors, Melany Kaiser and Todd Loehr. Your opinions and corrections were really bizarre and I didn't quite understand them, but they helped to craft a better, cleaner story. So, you can all see that the "acknowledgments" section is where my non-creepy personality comes out... Thank you to my advanced readers, authors John Smolens and Craig A. Brockman. Your advice was very welcome and your comment very helpful. Thank you also to Beacon Publishing Group for giving the green-light to my third project.

To the hearty people of Copper Harbor; I apologize for some creative liberties with the geography such as moving the petroglyph to up on Brockway Mountain and some town layout differences. It just made the story easier to tell. Hopefully you all enjoyed the tale!

Other titles available by Matthew Hellman include "Solomon's Seal" and "The Hawthorne Blow".

CPSIA information can be obtained
at www.ICGtesting.com
Printed in the USA
LVHW011250190222
711485LV00013B/870